The Vicious Deep

ZORAIDA CÓRDOVA

sourcebooks
fire

Copyright © 2012 by Zoraida Córdova
Cover and internal design © 2012 by Sourcebooks, Inc.
Cover design by Peny Pkwy
Cover digital illustration © 2012 by Tony Sahara

Sourcebooks and the colophon are registered trademarks of Sourcebooks, Inc.

Published by Sourcebooks Fire, an imprint of Sourcebooks, Inc.
P.O. Box 4410, Naperville, Illinois 60567-4410
(630) 961-3900
Fax: (630) 961-2168
teenfire.sourcebooks.com

Library of Congress Cataloging-in-Publication data is on file with the publisher.

Printed and bound in the United States of America.
BG 10 9 8 7 6 5 4 3 2 1

This novel is dedicated to Marcos Medina:
Caco, brother, uncle, and father all in one.
For your patience and love and for being
everything that is Good in this world.

Oh, and for styling my bangs
like Ariel when I was little.

Part I

Some things you learn best in calm, and some in storm.

—WILLA CATHER

Part 1

chapter
ONE

I hear the first wave before I see it—

Hear the rumble of the sky that reaches down to the belly of the sea, hear the clouds that appear out of nowhere. They churn and curl inside themselves in big gray mouths across the sky. The sky that up to a few seconds ago was perfect and blue.

I'm standing at the bottom of the lifeguard tower. The whitewashed wood is warm where I lean my arm. It's supposed to be mine and Layla's shift, but I've given up my seat so she can sit with Maddy. Together they sit up top in that way girls do when they're joined in a single purpose—and that's *loathing* me with all their evil-eyed, purse-lipped, cross-armed attitude. And I take it like a man, because after what I did to Maddy, that's the least I can do to make things right.

I can't shake the feeling of water stuck in my ear. But that could also be because I'm hungover, which means I shouldn't be swimming or actually trying to save anyone's life. I hate not showing up for work or a meet. I may be a lot of things, but flaky isn't one of them.

Behind me is a stretch of the Coney Island boardwalk, and behind that are Luna Park, Nathan's Hot Dogs, and the Cyclone. There's Sideshows by the Seashore and the unused parachute tower, which is the best place to take a girl on a cheap date after all the rides are shut down. I've come here every day since I can remember. There's just something in the air that makes you want to be here. It's in the screams and thrills of the rickety rides that have been running longer than most people's grandparents have been alive. In the food courts that sell you questionable but delicious meat. It is beauty and grime all mixed in one, and I love being in the middle of it. Plus, chicks love lifeguards.

Chicks who aren't Layla and Maddy—at least, not anymore. I can hear Maddy whisper to Layla, and both of them scoff. A group of girls walks past me. They're the same bunch of girls who have been pacing back and forth in bikinis too small for their goods, and on any other day, I wouldn't be complaining. They hold paddling boards with Hawaiian flower patterns on them, even though their hair is ironed perfectly straight and their fake eyelashes haven't been touched by the water.

I know what Maddy and Layla are thinking—that I'm enjoying the way these girls tiptoe around shells, winking in my direction. Sure, they're regular-hot, but they're doing the Lifeguard Catwalk from one end of the beach to the other. It's when girls are on the prowl to pick us up, and honestly, I'm not the only one they're checking out. No matter what a lifeguard looks like, the girls just go nuts. They're past our station now and halfway down to Jerry, who isn't exactly a girl magnet, but, hey, lifeguards are the more naked version of firemen—the girls just love the uniforms. In my case, the orange Speedo.

Suddenly, Layla's laugh cuts through the noise around us—girls giggling on beach towels taking turns pouring baby oil on their already browned shoulders, cops in a 4x4 giving some kids hell because they're drinking, two little girls fighting over a pink plastic shovel. Layla's laugh has a certain effect on me. It always comes from her gut when she thinks something is really funny. When we were little, we'd have contests to see who had the best evil-villain laugh. She'd always win. I glance up at her, and my hungover stomach does a flip. She smirks with her heart-shaped lips, listening to Maddy, who wears a T-shirt over her bathing suit. I can practically feel their eyes rolling into the back of their heads. Probably about me.

Something catches Layla's attention on the shore. She lowers the aviators she "borrowed" from her dad right to the tip of her nose. I follow her stare toward some guy wearing only ripped pants and looking like he just washed up on shore from a sinking ship. The water bounces off his shoulders like light on glass. I really hate kids who wear clothes to the beach. It's *the beach*. If you don't want to tan, stay at home. That must be the reason she's staring. He stands with one hand blocking the sun from his eyes, scanning the crowd. What he needs to look for is a pair of trunks and a towel.

I blow my whistle lightly, even though no one is doing anything wrong. The little girls still fighting over the shovel think it's at them, and they stop, so at least that's something.

That's when my ears start feeling clogged and my head a little fuzzy, like when I sit too long on the lifeguard tower without a cap. That's when people start standing up and looking out at the water. That's when people start screaming.

chapter
TWO

Behind me is the world I've known since forever. The sliver of sun that is still out is shining down on us, like the big guy in the sky is pointing a finger, going, *There, down there, get 'em!*

Around me are the first screams, the kind that start off at the top of a coaster before you take the deep plunge because you're actually enjoying the pull in the pit of your stomach. Like the whole world is pulled right out from under your feet, and even though, technically, you're safe in the harness, you're still scared of falling.

That was the first wave

The second screams come from their guts—fearful, shrill, run-for-your-lives screaming. It's the biggest wave I've seen in person. Not tsunami big, not in the way they teach us in earth science. But for this beach, in the middle of June, in the middle of the most perfect day up to one minute ago, it sure feels tsunami big.

Someone knocks into me as he's running away from the water, red towel in one hand and shoes in the other. The smarter ones abandon their towels, their smuggled beer bottles, their half-built sand castles, their sandy cheese fries, and their garbage, which they would've left behind anyway, really.

They follow their instincts and they run away.

I catch on to the signal of whistles and blow my own. A little girl with white-blond hair and a red face from screaming runs to me. She's cold and shaking, and I pick her up because I don't know what else to do. I look around, but it's no use trying to find who she belongs to. The lifeguard whistles mingle with the screaming crowd. The sun that was burning my shoulders in that good kind of way is completely swallowed by mammoth clouds.

A haze on the horizon separates the gunmetal gray of the sky and the darkening sea. It's raining miles away. Pinpricks of lightning flash against the sky. The storm is racing to our shore. The little girl hits my chest with her cold fists and points at the crowds wading in against the pulling of the tide, like the sea has hands and wants to drag them back in.

Between the undulating water and the stampede splashing off the beach, I see a set of pale arms struggling against the current. She's close enough. I can make it.

Maddy climbs down the tower first.

"Take her." I shove the little girl at her.

"What the—"

I grab the buoy and sling it around my neck as I run toward the water. A whistle blows hard and clean through the noise. It's Layla. She climbs down the tower in the orange-and-white bathing suit she hates to wear, her long, rich brown hair swishing in its ponytail.

I don't know if it's the chaos of the storm or the adrenaline rushing through my body, but I kiss her. Not on the mouth. Not the way I want to. I put my hand on the back of her neck and kiss the top of her head. Her hand closes around my wrist, panicked. She says something like, *Nothing we can do. Let's go*, and pulls me away from the shore.

But I don't listen. I can't listen. I only see the flailing arms, the face that comes up for air too quickly before getting sucked back down. I brace against the ice coldness of the water and dive. It takes me seconds to wait for the shock of cold to leave my lungs, breathe, and dive back in. I paddle with strength and speed I didn't even know I was capable of. The water pushes against me hard, harder than any water I've ever been in. I squint against the sting of salt water and sand in my eyes. I can hear my heart in the silence of the even strokes of my arms. For all the commotion on the surface, down here it's just a rustle.

When I surface for air I'm a little more than halfway to her. The tide has risen severely in seconds, and it isn't stopping. I turn to look back at the shore. I can make out a cluster of orange and blue where lifeguards and cops crowd the beach. And then there's Layla screaming my name. It could be anyone, really, but it isn't. It's Layla, screaming my name.

Coach Bellini always says, "*Know your finish line. It isn't getting to one end of the pool first. It's making it back first. Swim to it. Swim back.*" That's not what I've done. When I turn around to dive again, I can't see the set of arms waving at me in the distance anymore. I'm farther away from shore than I had thought. There is the second huge wave. Green, dark, and cold.

It swallows me whole before I can catch my breath.

chapter
THREE

I was born at sea.

Or so my mother said. They were in my dad's rented summer rowboat having one of their seaside picnics way out on the peninsular nook of Manhattan Beach and the rest of Brooklyn. That's when she went into labor. I've always pictured her in the middle of biting her sandwich, then dropping it and putting her arms around her stomach with me inside. And my dad all flustered with his glasses practically falling of his nose, not knowing if they'd make it to the dock in time. Mom said she grabbed at the sides of the boat, and he tried to row at the rhythm of her breaths until they reached the dock and she could start pushing. But they didn't make it to the dock, and I was born right there in the water.

When I was little, my mom would tell me this story every night before I went to bed, after all the other fairy-tale books had been exhausted. It's funny—I haven't thought about that in a long time.

The morning sun lashes my eyes like a whip.

I roll over and cough up sand and water. I pick at something stuck in my teeth. It comes off on the tip of my finger. It looks like a contact lens. I start to think of what I must have swallowed in that water, but it's really best not to.

My body feels like I've been pressed together by a set of boulders and then shaken—and then stirred.

I want to stand, but I can't figure out what hurts more—the dryness scratching its way down my throat, the salt burning at my tear ducts, or my legs aching all the way down to the bone. I want to burrow in the sand until the itch along my skin goes away. The back of my skull is heavy. I can only lift it for a moment to see where I am. The sky—overcast but still white-hot where the sun is hiding—spins. I catch a glimpse of the boardwalk and the Wonder Wheel, and I'm a little relieved that heaven looks a lot like home.

My ears pop, and there is a warm emptiness where the water was clogged. My heart pounds, and it feels like someone is playing a bass drum right beside my head. I can hear sirens and four-wheelers far, far away. I can hear crabs making their way up the beach, the surf racing to suck them back into the water. My eyelids are heavy but I fight to keep them open. For a moment, just a moment, I fear I'm not really alive, because I must have drowned. I must have.

I try to stand again, and everything hurts too much for me to be dead.

"Down there!" someone shouts. A dude's voice.

"Where?" A girl's voice.

"By the pile of garbage."

"Which pile?"

"Where all the wood is." He sounds exasperated, like he's too hot and too tired to be out here.

"Ohmigod." I know her voice. "Ohmigod. Ohmigod. Ohmigod."

"Layla, stay in the car!" he says. "You're not even supposed to be on patrol with me!"

Feet hit the sand and run.

Engine turns off.

Guy grunts.

Second set of feet on sand.

Hands on my chest. "Tristan?" *Her* hands on my chest.

I keep my eyes shut, which isn't hard to do, because I've never wanted to go back to sleep so bad before, not even during homeroom with Mr. Adlemare. My heart skips, because I know she's going to do it. She doesn't even press her ear on my chest or check the pulse at my wrist, which is the first thing we are certified to do. Good thing too, because the bass drum has moved from my head to inside my chest. Her fingers slide into my mouth and push my jaw open. Now, I can't say I haven't dreamt about this moment before, because when your best friend suddenly transforms into the girl every guy notices walking along the beach, believe me, it's the only thing *to* think about.

I press the back of my tongue to the roof of my mouth so her CPR doesn't choke me. I've had enough of nearly drowning for the day. Her lips are warm, like leaning your face up at the sky and wishing the sun would kiss you, and it does. It really does.

I can't help it. I fight the ache in my arms and press her down against me. I touch my tongue against hers and taste the salt on her bottom lip.

Now, I should remember that the last time I tried to kiss her was on my seventh birthday during pin-the-tail-on-the-donkey. She pinned the sticker on my cheek, so I kissed her, because when you're seven, a kiss from a boy is the worst kind of punishment. That time she slugged me on the chest and ran to my mom. She's gotten stronger since then. Her fist comes down on my chest like a hammer.

"Damn," I go, "you hit like a dude."

Her lips are open, all shocked like whatever she was going to yell at me is lodged in her throat. I don't know if I'll ever be able to look at her without thinking of this moment. Her entire face is red, and her cheeks puff up in that way they do when she's so angry she can't stand it.

"On the bright side, you saved me," I go. I can't stop from grinning. "Right?"

"Looks like he didn't need CPR after all," says a strange guy's voice. I notice him for the first time, a guy so orange that his white hoodie radiates against his skin. He's got muscles that put boulders to shame, even though his face doesn't look older than mine by much. He brings his radio to his lips and mumbles something into it. The feedback pinches my eardrums.

"Hey, man," I say. I try to nod my chin up in the universal guy-salute, but my neck's too stiff and I must look like a spaz.

"Don't act like anything hurts all of a sudden," Layla says. Why's she so mad anyway? It was just a kiss.

"Look, I'm sorry. I didn't know it was you," I lie. "I thought it was some hot EMT coming to my rescue."

Orange guy chuckles and talks into his radio some more. "The actual EMTs are on their way if you want to play dead some more."

"Don't mind if I do." I avoid looking at her. I have to. I prop myself up on my elbows, though my muscles contract in protest. I don't need this guy telling other lifeguards that I'm a wimp. Though I guess I have that almost-being-mangled-by-the-ocean thing as an excuse. "Good to see you, though. That was some sick wave. Wish I'd had a surfboard. Oh, yeah, thanks for finding me."

"I'm calling your *mother*."

"Aw, come on, Layla. I was just playing."

She stomps up the sandy hill until the only thing I can see is her ponytail swinging in place, taunting me and moving steadily out of my reach.

chapter
FOUR

My favorite memory of Layla is when she told off a cop.

She was nine and change, because I was already ten and she still had some weeks to go. She hated that I was born on June 24, right smack in the best part of our Coney Island summers, and her birthday was all the way in August, when the water started getting cold and the trash piled up as tall as we were.

The cop, three times our heights and with a gleaming gun at his side, stepped right in front of me. I was pulling our raft toward the water by some moldy rope I'd found under the pier. We'd just read *Huckleberry Finn* and wanted to sail off onto the Mississippi, but all we had was the Coney Island Beach. The raft was my greatest accomplishment, wood planks supported by our boogie boards held together with Krazy Glue taken from the baby-sitter's desk drawer. The tips of my fingers were raw from having stuck them to each other and then pulling them apart.

"What do you think you're doing?" the cop said. He was too tall for me to read his badge, but I remember his face, fat and red with caterpillar eyebrows.

"Why?" Layla asked.

"Answer the question."

"We're not supposed to talk to strangers," she said, her hands on her hips, the same way she did when her dad told her she wasn't allowed to play with me so often. That she also needed friends who were girls.

The cop pulled out his badge. "See this? I'm not a stranger." And then the cop reached for me. Just to grab my shoulder, just to take us back to the boardwalk. But I struggled and Layla kicked him on his shin, and we left the raft that we'd worked on for a whole week.

Sure, another cop found us on the boardwalk and called our parents. I lied and said *I* was the one who had kicked the cop, and he didn't say different. Layla was pissed at me for trying to cover for her, but I always have and I always will. Just like I know she'd do the same for me. She's my best friend. She's my Layla. She's my girl.

⁓

In the ambulance they give me extra-strength hospital-approved painkillers that numb my muscles until they feel like putty and the stretcher feels like down feathers.

For a moment, I'm falling. It's one of those dreams where your mind zooms out and you're falling, falling, until you think it's actually happening, so you jump in real life, and that jolts you out of the dream.

But the nervous jolt lingers throughout my body like the world just dropped from under my feet and I still haven't hit the ground. I can barely keep my eyes open. What if I don't wake up? Why can't I remember anything? But my body is numb and sleepy and warm, and when I do push myself to open my eyes, I'm in the hospital. I'm hooked up to a bunch of beeping machines with screens that look like last week's algebra test I got a C on.

A nurse comes in. She's tiny, with a round face and eyes like the anime posters in the boys locker room. Except *those* anime girls are blowup dolls in Catholic school uniforms, and this nurse is just sweet. She comes up close, and I can see she doesn't have any makeup on, except for the pink on her cheeks. No one's cheeks can be that pink.

"Hello, nurse." When I hear my voice, it sounds raspy, the voice I always think Rip Van Winkle would've had after he woke up in the wrong century. That's how I feel—like I've slept for too long. I look around the white room, but there isn't even a clock.

She fumbles with her clipboard, flips through some pages. Her lips open, but it's like she doesn't know what to say, because she just stands like that.

"You're awake?" she says. It's supposed to be a statement, but it sounds like a question. Or maybe the other way around. You never know with girls.

"Yeah. Couldn't sleep with all this beeping."

She gives me a look that certifies me as the biggest douche bag this side of Brooklyn, and that says a lot. "Oh, that's a joke."

She looks down at the floor. She's wearing white sneakers with pink socks.

"Not a very good one, I guess."

"No, really. It's funny!" She gives me a truly pretty smile. She walks up to my bed and fixes the pillow. She smells like chemicals trying to smell like apples and vanilla, but it's still nice.

"What's your name?" I ask.

She points at her name tag. "Christine. You sure are popular. We had to put some of the flowers out at the nurses' station, because they don't fit in here."

For the first time, I look around the room. I've never been in a hospital before. I don't even remember having to go to the doctor before. This hospital looks just like the ones in the soap operas Layla's mom watches, all white with a TV running a basketball game in one corner and a little table full of yellow and white flowers. Except mine has bouquets on both windowsills, on the table beside my bed, and all along the wall on the floor. I can't even imagine who they'd be from. My mom wouldn't send flowers. She would be here. "I'm Tristan."

She laughs and fiddles with the wires taped to my pulse. "I know." She nods over to where my file is at the foot of the bed.

Duh, again. "So, Nurse Christine"—I take a deep breath and put on my best grave face—"am I terminal?"

It takes a second for her to register that I'm still just kidding. When she gets it, she looks at her white sneakers again, shaking her head. "You shouldn't joke about those things."

Stupid me. She sees death and sickness all day long.

"I'm sorry," I go. "You don't have any pills to cure me of being a jerk, do you? 'Cause that would help me out *a lot*. Maybe even some sedatives?"

This time she laughs for real. "I think the sedatives we already gave you give you nightmares. You were talking in your sleep."

"You were watching me sleep?" I think I say it because I like the way her cheeks flood fuchsia when she looks away from me, all shy.

"I should j-just go get someone, I think." She leaves the clipboard in the metal slot at the foot of my bed and is out the door. Man, as much as I can get girls to like me, I sure make them run away as fast as they came.

Two seconds later the door opens and in walks my mom. She takes three huge steps and pulls me into an iron grip.

"I think you just realigned my spine."

"Oh, honey, I'm sorry." She holds my face in her hands and says, "Let me look at you." Her voice is smooth and deep, like she should be singing everything she says.

Her eyes—a turquoise so sharp I would say they were freakish if mine weren't the same color—are all watery, and I can't stop myself from burying my face in her embrace, because when I ran out into the storm, I remember her face flashing in my mind.

She wipes her eyes with her index fingers and tries to laugh it off. "I could kill you for worrying me like this."

For the first time, I notice Layla and Maddy standing to the left of my bed like they're afraid to come too close.

"Do you remember what happened?" Mom asks.

I shake my head and regret it, because the room spins with it. I remember sand and a whole lot more pain than I'll ever admit to willingly.

"It was so strange," Layla says. "We were just talking—" She pauses, like she's not sure if she's remembering right either. She bites her lips before continuing, and I fidget because every part of me is happy to see her. *Every* part. I remember the CPR on the beach like a flash. Her angry face walking away from me. I rub the spot on my chest where she punched me.

Now, sitting in the visitor's chair, she plucks a daisy from the bouquet on the table beside her. She twirls the yellow flower in her hand and squeezes a petal between her fingers, like she's trying to get the sticky sweetness out of the flower before she plucks it. *She loves me.*

"We were talking," Maddy interrupts. She takes a seat at the very corner of my bed. She stares at my feet sticking out from the blankets. "Then we saw those storm clouds, and people just started screaming and freaking out and running out of the water all at once. You were holding this little girl who wouldn't stop *crying.* Then you gave her to *me.*" Her voice reaches a high pitch before she stops and takes a deep breath.

Layla plucks another petal. It falls onto her lap. She's wearing white shorts and a blue T-shirt that says "LOLA STAR" in big yellow letters. *She loves me not.*

"We were getting evacuated, and they couldn't go after you,

because they had to get everyone else off the beach. And then we made it to the boardwalk just as the wave crashed. It reached all the way up to the boardwalk."

"Yeah, Ruby's roof came down a bit, but nothing major."

"I remember spinning," I say, with sudden unease in my gut.

"They said there was a whirlpool a few miles out. Some schooners hit the bottom. They've been washing up for a few days."

"Do you remember anything else?" my mom asks, brushing my hair back. The gray overcast light makes the red of her hair look so much brighter. Actually, everything looks brighter. The golden tan on Layla's skin, even the dull blond of Maddy's pigtail braids shines. My hearing isn't as good as when I woke up on the shore, and I don't know if I was just imagining that stuff, but I swear I can hear the way my mom's heartbeat quickens and skips. "What's wrong?"

She shakes her head. "I hate hospitals." She hums something, which is what she does when she's distracted.

"You're such a fast swimmer," Layla says. *She loves me.* "You got out so far before the first wave even hit. I've never seen you swim like that." She says the last bit like she's really trying to remember the last time she saw me swim, like she's been missing something. I'm missing a lot of somethings, and it's making the back of my head pulse. *She loves me not.*

"Th-then the next day there was no sign of a storm. I mean, it's been overcast, but the water is super still. Beach patrol's been searching the shore for days."

"Whoa, wait. How many days has it been?" I ask.

"Three," they say in unison.

Three days? I can't even say it out loud.

"Alex and I found you this morning." *She loves me. She loves me not.*

I sit up and feel stronger right away, like lying down is the problem.

They're so quiet that I can't stand it. "Guys, what? What's wrong? I'm alive. Happy news. What's with the morbid?"

"It's just that…you're the only one we've found," Layla says. Then adds, "Alive."

"Shit."

She loves me. She loves me not. She loves me.

I jump when Mom goes, "Madison Shea! What *are* you doing?"

Maddy lets drop the corner of the covers she's holding up. "Sorry, I j-just…There's stuff on your feet, Tristan."

And there on the inside of my ankle is a thin residue of sand that looks like it's been mixed with glitter. That's Coney Island sand for you.

My mom forces a chuckle, the kind she reserves for PTA meetings and community brunches. "The sooner we're home, the faster you can have a real good bath."

"Mom, if I'm the only survivor so far, they're not just going to let me walk out of here. That nurse just went to get the doctor." Not that I want to stay here any longer. This is just like my mom, hating hospitals so much that even when she sprained her ankle

23

last December, she just sat on the couch for two weeks rather than see a doctor. Two *amazing* weeks for her, since Dad and I were her menservants.

The cute Asian nurse comes back in. "Hey," I say instantly.

She loves me not.

She gives me that shy smile, then looks directly at my mother. "Doctor Burke is taking off a cast, ma'am."

"Maddy, will you tell my husband that we'll only be a minute? Oh, and will you take one of these bouquets? They're just lovely. Pity we can't take them all." She plucks a card off one and reads it out loud. "'Get well soon, XOXO. Luv, Amanda.' Who's Amanda?"

"I don't remember," I say. Sometimes my mom acts like she's not part of this universe, living always in her head. Maddy is still in the room, and even though she looks away quickly, I don't miss the hurt on her face. She picks up the bouquet of daisies beside Layla and walks out of the room like she can't put enough distance between me and her.

"What a strange girl," Mom says before turning to me. "Your clothes are in the bathroom."

I don't know what to say. *This is insane?* Can you get arrested for leaving a hospital without a doctor's approval? Is it like walking out on a restaurant check? I hold up my wrists with all the tabs hooked to them. "Um, hello?"

"Oh." Nurse Christine grabs my wrist with her gentle fingers and then pulls at the white tabs with one swift movement. It doesn't exactly hurt, but it's like peeling off tape all at once.

"Tristan," Mom says in her *Did-you-hear-me-or-what?* tone. "Bathroom. Clothes. Now. Please."

I stand too quickly before realizing there is no back to my hospital gown. Not that my mother didn't give birth to me, and not that Layla hasn't seen me in nothing but a banana hammock from the swim team's uniform, and one time the team decided it'd be a good idea to skinny-dip for Valentine's Day. But this is a *tad* invasive.

Layla and my mother giggle behind their hands while I try to hold the back of my gown together and walk backward into the bathroom.

"You wouldn't think it's so funny after you've just escaped the hands of *death*," I shout at them once I've closed the door. I sit on the toilet to inspect my body for any more grime they missed. The sand is mostly gone, but I wish I had a life-sized scratch post to rub my entire body against until the itch goes away. I scratch at my chest and wince at the burn. In the mirror I notice thin red scratches that are still scabbing. *What happened to me?*

I put on my navy-blue canvas shorts and a white V-neck that's almost worn thin from salt water and detergent. I run the faucet and splash cold water on my face. I could have died. I could have drowned. I've been missing for three days, and I don't remember any of it. I want to throw up, but all I do is dry heave into the sink.

I rinse out my mouth, examine myself in the mirror. The skin on my cheekbones and over my nose is slightly red and peeling. My lips are dry and flaky. I have some bruises on my forearms and bumps on either side of my neck like a rash. But all in all, nothing that'll scar my face and put me on active duty in the school's bell tower.

When I walk back into the room, Nurse Christine stops at the door when she sees me. She smiles again, really smiles. Her teeth are a little big for her tiny round face, but it's still a pretty effect. She ducks out of room without saying anything else but, "It was nice to meet you."

Layla rolls her eyes and takes a manila folder my mom hands her. She's stuck the mangled daisy behind her ear. She stuffs the folder in a canvas bag so old that one of the straps has ripped and been replaced with a red leather belt I got as a white-elephant gift a few grades ago from a person who forgot to buy a unisex gift. I remember Layla's gift being a Han Solo action figure, and we traded.

"Are those my records?"

Mom and Layla shrug.

I shake my head. "So you're in on this too?"

Layla looks at me with her honey hazel eyes and nods. The flower is already drooping, missing its water bed. It isn't staying in place, so she takes it and throws it in the wastebasket by the door. "The doctor was talking about keeping you here for 'extended observation.' There is no way you should've survived, but you did. So just shut up and listen." She pokes her finger on my chest where the scratches are.

"Stop hitting me. *Mom*."

"You two stop that," Mom says, holding on to a huge bouquet

of orchids and some strange wildflowers I've never seen before. She loves orchids. "How do you feel?"

I know when I'm being overruled. "I feel good. Sore, obviously. Nothing some Tylenol won't fix." Oh, and the giant black spot where a memory of the last three days ought to be, but surely nothing to worry about.

"Now, you listen to me. I don't want you ending up in a government lab experiment, because that's what's going to happen." She looks through the little glass window on the door and sticks her head out. I'm used to my mom being—*eccentric* is what the other mothers call her—but this is different. It's like she's actually scared for me. She has to stop watching those conspiracy shows.

Layla leans in close to whisper, "Your mom's been acting a little crazy, but don't argue. You don't know what it's been like for her."

I pull a yellow petal from her hair. "Just for her?"

But she doesn't answer me, because Mom goes, "Okay, just follow me." And she's out the door, leaving us to follow her trail of red hair.

chapter
FIVE

The hospital is a mess of white and blue coats and stethoscopes. Everyone walks like a windup toy, forward and side to side, but never backward. Nurses push trays; doctors walk in and out of rooms. I wonder if Nurse Christine will get in any trouble because of me.

My train of thought is broken when an old lady in a wheelchair *harrumphs* loudly as she gets in the elevator with us, as if our closeness offends her. She's got a pink pamphlet in her hand, folded like a little accordion. She's fanning herself lightly with it. She's humming a melody that I've heard somewhere but can't remember where. When she looks up at me, she purses her lips and lifts her fan higher to cover everything except her eyes.

I lean back against the elevator wall between my mom and Layla, who hold their flower pots as they stare at the descending numbers lighting up. A phone rings, and Layla reaches into her pocket. I wonder who it is.

The old woman looks back up at me, but this time the face isn't her own. Her eyes are the color of pearl with dilated irises. Her skin is translucent, like it's pulled too tightly over bone.

I feel my heart jump in my throat. I stumble backward and hit the wall. I close my eyes hard, the way I used to when I thought something was hiding in my room behind the window curtains. I count to three, just like I did back then, and when I open them, the old woman is the old woman again. My mom and Layla stare at me as if to say, *Have you lost your mind?*

The doors open and the woman rolls out onto the second floor.

I swallow hard. "Thought I saw a spider by her feet." And the medal for the manliest man in the hospital goes to…*Tristan Hart!*

When the doors close, Layla slaps my shoulder. "What is wrong with you? She's like one hundred."

"Me? She was just kind of scary-looking—"

"You're so—"

"Tristan, that was unkind," my mom interjects, standing in front of the door. Before I can respond, the door opens and we're in the lobby. We get out and a group of women holding shiny blue balloons walks in. One of them stares at me so long that she trips on the girl in front of her and a balloons floats up to the hospital ceiling.

"Is it just me, or does it smell like puke?"

Layla rolls her eyes. I can't remember a time when she found me this irritating. Usually she laughs at my stupid jokes or contributes to them. "It's a *hospital*. You're being weirder than usual," she says.

How can I tell her that I'm going crazy without her freaking out? Maybe I can drop it into normal dinner conversation. *"Say, Mom and Dad and other people present? I think I'm seeing a monstrous woman's face on the head of an old lady and hearing this incessant humming every now and then. No, nothing to worry about. Just wanted to let you know in case my heart suddenly stops from being scared shitless."*

"Hell-*o?*" Layla snaps her fingers in front of my face. She adjusts the weight of the bouquet against her chest. One of the flowers keeps falling into her face.

"Sorry." I grab the vase from her and follow her out. Mom is already stepping through the revolving doors with her chin up like we're walking through the mall, and she's glancing at the people around us.

"What are you thinking about?" Layla asks when we step out into the warm, sticky air.

I squint against the bright white-gray sky. "The weather, of course."

"It's been like this since—you know. The *Brooklyn Star* is calling it the Perfect Storm. So original, ugh. I'm pretty sure they have all their reporters scavenging the beach, even though they've been told not to."

I struggle to laugh, but I can't. Either something really wrong is happening here, or I'm just imagining things. Either way, I've decided I'm crazy.

My dad is parked down the block in his 1969 surf-green Mustang. He bought it at the monthly Coney Island Community Auction. It's the only way to keep the buildings from being bought up by developers who want to make Coney Island like Atlantic

City. Dad got the car cheap because so much work needed to be done to it. At that point it was the color of rust, and the interior looked like it was a hostel for runaway possums. With the help of my six-year-old self, Dad restored it. He couldn't have put this baby together if I hadn't been his wrench and sandwich gofer. Now it smells like eleven years of worn leather and pine-tree air freshener.

I usually jump over the side of the car and hop into the backseat, but now I have zero energy. I think they notice, but no one says anything as they strap themselves into their seat belts. Maddy is already sitting with the bouquet of daisies on her lap. She's in the middle seat, even though her legs are too long and she'd be better at either window. I suspect she wants to sit next to me, even though I don't see how she can stand being in the same room as me. Why do some girls put themselves in such painful situations?

She gives me a tiny smile, and for a second I feel even more miserable because she's here. It's kind of pathetic. She means well, she does, but she's like a stray that won't take a hint.

"Gave me quite a scare, Finn." Dad looks at me in the rearview mirror. He hasn't called me that in a long time.

"I'm fine," I say, but I'm not starting to feel so fine anymore. Something I don't say often, if ever. My stomach hurts, and my head is throbbing. "Just starving. Oh, and Mom's going to get us arrested."

"Come now, honey. That's absurd."

Dad laughs. "I've already given them a check for the estimated bill. Good thing you were only there a day." He pulls into the

Brooklyn traffic. With his ash-blond hair and freckly Irish nose, he and I look nothing alike. My hair comes down just to the bottom of my neck in brown waves. It looks curlier when I just get out of water, though. He's five-foot-eight to my six-foot-two-and-still-growing. Dad wears round glasses under his blue-framed Ray-Bans when he drives in the summer. When he was my age, he was a Long Beach surfer who just happened to be a computer whiz in the early '80s. But I think I'm like him in the way that matters. We love the beach, old rock, fried food, and driving my mother crazy.

Mom turns in her seat and pulls down the sun visor. Her red hair blows all over her face. Viking red, she calls it, though we've never met any of her family, not even her parents, to compare.

"You should know that there are going to be a few people acting strangely around you," Dad adds.

I think of the old lady in the elevator, the white of her eyes, and try to shake it off by staring at other things. There's the Real Taj Mahal restaurant and the DVD store that never has any new releases. And the grocery store with all the expired canned food but with the best illegal fireworks China can make.

"I had to unplug the house phone, because somehow every reporter in New York City has our number."

"Yeah," I go. "Layla said the *Brooklyn Star* is all over it. Maybe we should charge them a dollar every time they call."

"It's not worth the invasion of privacy," Dad says.

"Or the government people who'll want to take you away," Mom says, which makes everyone laugh. Except I think she's really serious.

Maddy runs a hand over the length of her braid, something she does when she feels uncomfortable and awkward, which is pretty much all the time. She's painted her nails black, which is surprising since her mother doesn't even let her own makeup.

"You got lucky," she says to me, but keeps her eyes on the road ahead. "I don't know how you got so lucky, but someone out there is madly in love with you."

I want to shrink into my seat at that. That was the last thing she said to me the night before the storm. The night of the bonfire at the beach when she saw me kissing another girl right after she said the words, "Tristan, I am madly in love with you."

"How does pizza sound?" my dad asks.

"Good," the three of us say in unison.

The sky rumbles, and the staticky radio station has completely gone into white noise. Dad pulls over in front of Dominick's Pizza on the corner of our street. Lightning crashes in the distance. The streets are uncommonly empty. Layla and Maddy volunteer to get us a table and run inside, even though it doesn't look necessary. I walk a little slower behind them as they whisper hand in hand and turn only once to look at me over their shoulders. *Girls.*

There is only one man sitting in the pizzeria at the counter in front of the window. The man's skin is sunburn-leather brown, and he wears a blue cap with the words "Save the Whales" stitched in white. There's something funny about one of his eyes. It's coated with a yellow film. The other one is perfect. He rests his chin on his knuckles. I push the door and it jingles. The men behind the counter are already showering the girls with attention, getting the booth ready for five as if we're the only customers they've seen all day. With the exception of the "Save the Whales" guy.

When the man sees me, he sets his bad eye in my direction and points out the window.

"Can't be long now," he says.

"For what?" I'm born and raised in Brooklyn. I know better than to engage with the crazies. But his craziness makes me feel less so.

He shakes his head, picks up his paper plate, translucent with pizza grease, rolls it into the cylinder shape of a telescope, and puts his good eye to one opening. He points the other end toward the shore. "No, not too long. Must be quick. Vicious they is." He smacks his lips like he's still trying to taste the tomato sauce on them.

I'm about to say, "Quicker than who?" but Mom and Dad walk in with a jingle. They hold hands and look from me to the old man. I shrug and stand aside, kind of wanting to hear more of what he has to say but knowing I should really go and sit down.

The man crunches up his telescope into a little ball and throws it over his shoulder onto the floor, the way my mom does with salt. He makes for the exit. There's a heavy thud on the ground when his wooden leg struggles to hold his weight.

He leans in close to me and whispers, "Don't go trustin' them." He points at his face. "They'll take your eyes out, they will."

He looks at my mother as if he's surprised to see her standing there, like he knows her. He straightens out his cap and smooths his face where pizza crumbs cluster at the corners of his lips. He bows a little. "My Lady," he says, and then is down the street as fast as anyone with a wooden leg can hobble.

"Gotta love Brooklyn," Dad says with a smile. He tucks his Ray-Bans into his shirt, and Mom and I follow him to where Maddy and Layla sit.

After we decide on a meat-lover's pizza and a Hawaiian with extra cheese, Mom takes a sip of her ice water and looks right at me with her mirror turquoise eyes. "I hope you don't mind. We invited some of the other lifeguards and your coach for a little welcome-home celebration tomorrow."

I'm not really in the mood for people. I'm just glad I'm breathing. I scratch at my throat where I'm breaking out in a rash.

Layla looks over at me. "You need a real good shower, *Finn*."

"You're not allowed to call me that," I say. This is good. If I argue with Layla, I'll feel like something is still normal.

"Oh, you love it," she says.

"Can't you be nice to me for one more hour before you start hating me again? Pretty please?" I grab a garlic knot and put the whole thing into my mouth.

"I do not *hate* you" is her response. I can't see her face, because Maddy is sitting between us. "Maybe a little, but only because you didn't listen to me when I was screaming at you not to go into the water."

Maddy whispers, "I was screaming that too." But no one addresses that.

"He's fine," Mom goes. "That's what matters."

Two steaming pies are set in front of us. My stomach is making happy noises, and for three whole slices I sit there eating without saying anything.

When the waiter comes around again, he looks at me and claps his hands together. "Man, you're that guy!"

People acting weird around me, Take 1.

"Man, can I take a picture with you?" he asks, grabbing his cell phone from his pocket. "I want to show my girlfriend. She thinks you're like awesome, man."

"But I didn't *do* anything," I say. He doesn't hear it, because he shouts toward the kitchen, "'Ey, Dad, it's the Perfect Storm guy!"

A round man in an apron stained with tomato sauce, giving him the look of an all-too-happy butcher, comes out. His thick, smiling mustache reminds me of Super Mario. "Oh, my boy!" He comes around the table, leans over Maddy, and kisses me on both cheeks. "The pizza is on the house! Brave boy."

Dad slaps the waiter on the arm like they're buddies and says, "Mike, no more pictures. You understand."

"No problem, my man." Mike puts away his phone, and they return to the kitchen.

"I really hope that's the last time that happens," I say, laughing despite myself.

"At least you got kissed by an Italian guy," Layla says. "How many guys do you know who have that street cred?"

"What about that time you and Angelo—" Maddy starts, but I cut her off.

"Whoa, hey. So anything else I need to know? As in, I don't have to go to class for the rest of the month?"

"You really *must've* hit your head on something," Dad says.

"Great. Good, I'm glad we're laughing at my tragedy so soon." More garlic knots. It's not like I'll be kissing anyone later, I think.

"Listen, you kids can hang out at the house, stay up all night." Mom fidgets with her necklace. "Just don't touch my strawberry ice cream."

"Oh, actually, I have to go home, if that's okay," Maddy whispers. For a second I forgot she was there. "Do you care if I bring some friends to your party?" She looks at me with her big blue eyes and sort of reminds me of a lost kitten.

"What friends?"

She scoffs. "I have friends."

"I didn't mean it like that."

"Yes, you did. You just don't know it."

"How can I do something without knowing it?"

She stands up from the table, her chair sliding back and falling with a thud. "You do everything without *knowing*, don't you?" She looks at my mom, her lips trembling, and I know she's going to cry and everyone is going to blame it on me. "I'm sorry," she says, looking down at her feet because she can't seem to look at my parents. "Thank you for the pizza."

"*Maddy*," Layla and I call after her. But she's already out the jingling door.

Dad picks up the chair and sets it straight. "Am I to understand that you two are no longer *going out*?" He says *going out* in quotation marks.

"No, we're not *going out* anymore."

My parents trade sly glances.

"What?"

They shrug together, but they don't answer. They look at Layla, who makes a zipper motion over her lips.

"If we'd known, we wouldn't have invited her to the hospital. Poor girl." Mom folds a napkin into an accordion.

"By we, your mom means *she*," Dad says in a whisper that's meant to be heard.

"Yeah, well, I was kind of lost at sea." I sit back and leave the piece of crust I was nibbling on alone.

Outside, the thunder breaks through the darkening sky. It starts to rain. I really do hope Maddy gets home safely. She only lives a few blocks away. I picture her answering my mom's call telling her I was alive. Maybe she was wishing I'd stay gone. I slump lower against my seat, feeling a little bit like the pieces of crust on my greasy plate.

chapter
SIX

No matter what they say on the news and in the papers, I'm not a hero. I didn't save the person I meant to save. I'm not even sure anyone was out there.

From the moment that wave crashed over me, I've felt different. I smell things differently. I hear differently. I know that there's something I can't remember. It's taking shape in my head, but it's like looking at a picture that's out of focus.

I throw the covers off and go to the living room. My mother has owned our apartment since before she met my dad. It is technically two apartments now with a few walls broken down to make one huge place. Two bathrooms, my room, my parents' room, Dad's office, a dining room, and a living room with huge windows looking out to the Coney Island shore. The walls are gray blue with white trim, except for the kitchen, which is yellow.

I lie across the chocolate leather sofa, and when I can't find a soft spot, I lie on the giant, furry sheepskin rug. I remember being little when my mother bought this rug. I thought she'd gone out hunting and killed the abominable snowman. I used to stretch out reading a book, picking out tortilla chips and popcorn from the hairs before my mother noticed.

I push myself up and stand in front of our entertainment center, which my dad built from pieces of an ancient shipwreck. We call it the public library because books cover the whole wall, from floor to ceiling. I run a finger along their spines, leather-bound books older than this apartment building and slick new paperbacks.

I feel like I'm looking for something but I don't know what. I shut my eyes and stop at a black leather-bound book with a worn spine. *Fairy Tales and Other Stories* by Hans Christian Andersen. We have everything he ever wrote and everything everyone has written about him. Mom's always wanted me to read fairy tales. Sometimes I'd tell her she and Dad should've tried for a daughter, and then I realized I was telling my parents to keep having sex. That's why I think she loves Layla so much. She's like the daughter Mom probably wanted me to be. Even though I never want to think of Layla as my sister, I never want her to go away either.

I flip through the black leather-bound book and notice something I never have before. It's signed. It says, "Maia, ever drifting, drifting, drifting." Followed by a signature scrawl I can't quite make out.

I shut the book and put it back in place.

My head is throbbing. A steady dull pulse at my temples. I drink a cup of water and take it back into Dad's study, where electronic parts go to die. I step on a little silver rectangle with green wires sticking out and bite my tongue to keep from yelling out. Dad likes taking things apart to see how they work, and then he tries to put them back together. *Tries.*

The Apple desktop computer is on screen saver, a stream of pictures from our lives. Us on the Wonder Wheel, me eating a corn dog, Mom holding me on the beach, me and Layla at Six Flags, me holding my swimming trophies, my elementary-school graduation, Mom jumping in the air at the park.

It's like all these things happened to a different guy in a different life.

I wonder if something happened to me in the water. I trace the cuts on my neck, which are already scabbing over. *What happened to me?* I can keep asking myself that, but I might as well be asking the ocean itself. And maybe I have to snap out of it, because I might never know.

I give the mouse a little shake, and the pictures go away. I click on the Internet icon and type "near-death body changes" into Google. It's all a bunch of white lights and tunnels, angels and the voice of God, and waking up with the ability to get radio signals in your brain.

I don't have that. At least I *hope* I don't start getting radio signals in my head. Then again, that might make sitting through class more entertaining. But what if I only ever get one station?

My headache gets worse. The computer screen bothers my eyes. I finish my glass of water and go back to bed. My room spins around me like after riding roller coasters all day and then trying to lie down. I pull my covers tightly around me. I'm so tired, but I'm afraid to close my eyes.

The minute I do, I'm back in that water.

chapter
SEVEN

The first thing they tell you is not to panic.

Don't panic. Don't panic. Don't panic.

I wasn't panicking when my gut told me to ignore how the clouds turned from white to black, how the waves got higher with each crash, the fleeing screams around me. I didn't panic, and I dove into the middle of the water to save her.

But every time I surface she isn't there, and I keep getting farther from land. I'm pulled under with so much pressure I can barely move my arms and legs. The one gulp before I'm truly under escapes in tiny bubbles. The suction of the undulating waves tosses me like a bit of driftwood. I can't tell which way is up or down, but as the water stills, I swim to where it lightens. The moon makes a streak of weak light through the water, like my personal lighthouse beam leading me home.

Something ice-cold touches my spine. When I turn around, nothing is there. There's a trail of foam in its place, and I pray to every god that has ever or will ever exist that it's not a shark.

In the lighter water, blood clouds around me. I don't think anything bit me, but my throat and ribs burn like nothing I've ever felt before, like the skin there is burned to a crisp. My feet ache the way they do when I run barefoot on hot sand for too long. The still water churns faster and faster and faster, and I don't know what to worry about first—the cuts on my neck, the burning in my muscles, or the whirlpool that's starting with me at its center.

When I try to kick, I keep sinking. The whirlpool pulls me farther and farther away from the surface. I can't see the bottom, just pitch-black and more pitch-black. The pressure around me feels as though my bones will turn to foam. I scream because that's what my mind tells me to do. A muffled sound and some bubbles is all I get, even though I know if I were on land, all of New York would be able to hear me.

Then, as fast as the whirlpool started, it stops spinning. The current changes to a gentle bob, and I swear—I swear on every trophy I've ever won—that the water is taking me somewhere.

I float over a cluster of giant black rocks that seem to be the beginning of an even bigger precipice. Bits of light start blooming. They're pinpricks around the rock at first, then blooms of seaweed that glow like the buzzing neon sign of a bodega. Starfish with beads of glowing lights. Fish in colors that live in between other colors. A long red fish with the longest golden fins spins around my head. It presses its face against my cheek.

Somewhere in the distance there's a deep wail—an angry guttural sound that echoes on the rocks until it becomes the tail end of a sigh. The fish scatter, and everything stops glowing.

I'm alone again.

I fight the numbness in my legs and use all my strength to push myself up. I've spent every day of my life swimming, but doing laps around a pool is different from pushing yourself up to the surface when you're in the middle of the ocean. The pressure down here is like a vise grip around my limbs, but I swim, harder than I ever thought I could, until the water looks lighter and I can see my hand in front of my face again.

A white shape comes into focus in the distance. The echo is back. This time it's a song-cry, a lullaby that feels like it's slithering into my heart and finding pieces to break. I let it calm me, pull me back down. I stop fighting to get to the surface and think about my mom and her shining red hair, her sad turquoise eyes when they find me. She always told me I was born to swim, but I don't think this is what she meant. I think of my dad fixing computers alone in his office. I think of Layla, despite myself, and wish I'd chosen her every time.

The song-cry is closer still. My leg muscles get that familiar twinge when I'm in the water too long, like muscle bending the wrong way. My eyes are getting blurry. I keep stroking, but there isn't any strength behind it. I'm sinking, and there's a shark coming at me. Its nose points upward, like it's always smelling. The unmistakable rows of jagged teeth, the red gums that always look bloody.

This guy has chains, like he just busted out of shark prison and he's happy to see me. He speeds up, fin flicking whippet fast. I push myself backward, as if that's going to do any good. I hit something cold, a wall. Something grabs me. The singing is right at my ear. I try to pull myself out of the grip. They're hands. Cold, slender hands with nails like crushed glass.

It still sings, whatever it is. No words, just a sad wail, the low notes of a violin being plucked with a tire iron. It's the only thing I want to listen to. I want to wrap myself in those notes and sleep forever. A hand moves from my chest to my neck. I've stopped struggling. I want to close my eyes. The shark charges at me like a silver bullet.

I shut my eyes and wait for the bite that never comes.

The nails cut into my chest as the arms let go. The shark flips around, magnificent, and slaps the creature with his great white fin. It pushes back a few yards, but it doesn't stop. It wails, screeches into the expanse of sea, stretching out so I can finally see her true form. I can see *her*. From head to fins. A mass of silvery-white hair spreads out around her face, so pale she's almost see-through. Her eyes radiate in the water, white as lightning with needle pinpricks in the center.

Her cheekbones are sharp and slope down to full blue lips that smirk at me. She's long and slender, so skinny her bones look like they're trying to poke out of her skin. Her breasts are covered with slick silver scales that fade out at the slopes of her waist and bloom out to form her tail. There's an impression of legs, like they're under there right up to the kneecaps and disappear down to long silvery fins.

She swims in circles, a figure eight, her silver silhouette like a flash of light dancing in the water. Like she's dancing for me. She stops inches away from me with that smirk still on her lips, telling me she knows everything I don't. She grabs my wrists softly, like she's going to pull me to her and kiss me. And I want her to. I've never wanted anything this badly before.

The silver mermaid smiles, and when she smiles there is nothing more terrifying than the rows of her razor-sharp teeth.

chapter
EIGHT

She's holding my wrists when I wake up.

"You almost took my head off." Layla is staring at me with her giant hazel eyes. When we were little, I used to call her Bambi because her eyes were too big for her face and she was so skinny, almost frail-looking. It's just looks, though. Layla can swim almost as fast as I can. Almost.

Her hair is loose around her shoulders, thick and brown like fresh earth. She's wearing a purple dress that ties around her neck and reaches all the way down to cover her toes. I am suddenly aware of my morning erection.

"What are you doing here?"

"What kind of a 'good afternoon' is that?"

I look at the clock on my nightstand. It's 2:43 p.m. "How long have you been sitting there, creeper?" I take an extra pillow and use it as a buffer between my erection and the world.

"You wish."

"I'm just saying."

"I only just got here," Layla says. "I told your mom I'd pick up some chips and salsa on the way. My mom was still making her fancy Greek dip when I left, and my dad was sneaking a cigarette downstairs."

"Doesn't your dad know by now that he can't keep anything from your mom 'cause she's got that all-seeing third eye in the back of her head?" I ask.

"I actually think she gets a kick out of watching him squirm," she laughs, "when she finds the butts hidden around the backyard."

"Just like a woman."

She punches me on the shoulder.

"I'm going to start charging you every time you hit me." I tell her.

"That would negate your purpose as my personal punching bag. And speaking of people who'd like to use you as one. Maddy called me. She's not coming because she's at her *friend's* house."

"See! And she got all mad at me when I said *friends.*"

"Yeah, but you say *friends* in a mean way. I say *friends* because I don't like her new *friends*."

"Whatever. I don't need her crying all over the place, feeling guilty 'cause I'm not dead." I suck my teeth. I need a toothbrush ASAP.

We fall into silence. She tilts her head and combs her hair all to one side. She twirls a strand around her index finger and stares at my face. I wonder what she sees. If she sees something different from what everyone else does. I wonder if she's thinking I'm a piece-of-shit friend and an even worse boyfriend. I wonder if she's thought about our CPR kiss the way I have.

Instead she whispers, "What were you dreaming about?" She hesitates. "You were really tossing."

I shake my head. I know how this would make me sound. If there is anyone I let myself tell anything to, it's Layla. Well, *almost* anything. "Just some crazy stuff. You know, I still can't remember anything that happened to me out there. I see this blur. Then last night I was going through the apartment, reading, Googling, pacing, trying to make myself remember, like maybe it's memory loss. But nothing.

"I mean, I wasn't expecting an instant replay. But when I fell asleep, my dream was *so* impossible and it still felt *so* real. More real than this—" I pinch her and she squeals. "What if something happened to me down there? It would explain how I got this—" I pull my T-shirt at the collar so she can see the red scratches on my chest.

"Yes, Tristan, you have pecs of steel. The guys are outside. You really don't have to do that with me—"

"No, dumbass. I mean, I do, but look—" I really don't want to get up for fear of the pillow shifting. "Scratches."

"There's nothing there, Tristan." There's a sort of pity in her eyes.

She's right. I rub my hands on my chest and can't feel anything. Not even the impression of scabs.

"Is he awake yet?" My mom is standing at the door.

"Just now," I say, as Layla stands and pulls at where her dress clings to her thighs.

Mom lingers at the doorway. She stands half in and half out.

There's something about the way she's looking at me. It's not exactly wonder, but similar to it. I mean, I can't even imagine what it must've been like to think I was dead.

"Hurry up and get dressed, honey. People are on their way."

"Yeah, I'll be ready in just a minute." Though I don't feel ready for anything at all.

While my mom spared me a Welcome Home sign, my friends—if I'd even call them that after what they're holding up—have made a crude sign on white cardboard. It reads: "IT'S ALIVE!" With thunderbolts on the side.

Jerry, Angelo, Bertie, Ryan, and some other lifeguards and members of the swim team hang around the living room. They pat me on the back and tell me they've never seen anything like this. They can't believe it. I'm a miracle. I'm the coolest dude that ever lived on Planet Cool. They show me my mug on three newspapers, an awkward picture that I recognize from Mike's camera phone at the pizzeria, and one that looks like a girl was edited out of the left half. I'm halfway between a smile and a grimace, and my eyes don't really come out right in black-and-white. They almost look colorless.

Jerry polishes off his can of root beer and burps. From somewhere in the kitchen, Layla's mother scolds him, and he sinks into the chair, which makes him look like a grasshopper retracting his limbs. He's so tall that watching him swim reminds me of a log with branches flailing down a stream. "My mom was going to send flowers from her flower shop, you know? But half the girls in school were already buying them and sending them to your hospital room."

"Tell her thanks anyway."

Angelo sits up on the ottoman. "Bro, that nurse." He makes the symbol of the Father, the Son, and the Holy Ghost, then kisses his fingertips. I've seen his father do the exact same thing when they're sitting on their front porch drinking beer and a girl in short shorts walks in front of them. "You're the luckiest bastard who ever lived."

Now I'm a lucky-cool bastard. Hey, I've been called worse.

Layla walks over with a refilled bowl of tortilla chips, and the guys are all over her. I don't like the way Angelo's eyes linger on her. It's not like she's got giant boobs. I mean, they're a nice size for her height, but she's also not wearing a bra, just a bikini top under her dress. What's with these guys anyway? She's on our team. They see her in a suit all the time.

Layla takes a seat on the couch between Bertie and me. She's used to being one of the guys, so she doesn't notice how different they're acting, all shifty and nervous because she's sucked their breaths out just by being here. Maybe she doesn't realize how she's changed. How practically overnight her Bambi eyes and full lips have grown into a face that all you want to do is stare at it. How she's set the bar pretty damn high for every other girl.

Of course, none of the guys would try to get with her. She's still one of us.

I reach over the coffee table and eat chip after chip. My stomach lurches, and I can taste bile creeping up. I gulp down water, and I feel a little better.

"My mom actually wants me to quit my post," Angelo says. "She says the apocalypse is coming, so she's got these garlic wreaths all over the windows—"

"I knew I smelled something," Ryan goes, shrinking back from the threat of Angelo's fist.

"—and crosses all over the place. She asked Father Thomas to rebaptize me. He told her you're only supposed to do it once."

"Did you tell your mom that the apocalypse is coming, and not an army of vampires?" Layla jokes.

"Whatever. All I care is that she was so happy I woke up too late to go to work that day that she even let me sleep through school yesterday."

Angelo is a guy with no conscience and no worries. I almost envy him. He's the kind of guy who takes your lunch money at the beginning of the day and then asks to borrow another dollar after school so you can split a pizza. He smacks girls on their asses, and they actually turn around and giggle, because other than being macho and using more hair spray than the drama class, he's a pretty good-looking guy.

Mom walks in with a gallon of root beer. "I heard you boys were thirsty."

"And girls," Layla chimes in. Sandy, who's been looking through my mom's collection of books, looks up and smiles.

"Yes, please, Mrs. Hart," the boys say in unison, all smiles and politeness. She doesn't know them like I do.

The minute she walks out, Layla looks up at Ryan and says, "Ryan, you've got a little drool right here."

He wipes at his mouth with the sleeve of his hoodie. "It's kind of impossible not to. No offense."

"None taken." I shrug. I'm used to the guys all coming over just so they can be doted on by my mom. Even when we have school trips, the guys try to bribe me to get her to be the chaperone. Suddenly my living room, which has always seemed like a cave when I'm alone, feels too hot, too tight. The AC is on, and I'm still sweating. I want to tell everyone to get out so that I can jump in the shower, but that would be rude.

Ryan combs his fingers through his slick blond hair, a telltale sign that he's getting ready for a speech. Aside from being on the archery team, he writes for the *Thorne Hill High School Press* and is treasurer of the senior class. He has parents who are still married, don't hate each other, and work in the city. They live in the Sea Breeze gated community not a five-minute drive from here.

Sometimes it annoys me how perfect he is. It's like he can do no wrong. When we took a school-required test that's supposed to tell you what you should be when you grow up, he got "President of the United States." I got back an empty piece of paper, because they'd lost my results. And it bothers me even more because he always says he was born to be something great. He just knows it in his heart, and so does everyone who's ever met him.

Everyone who meets me likes me, sure, but I'll never be suave like Angelo, and I'll never be as smart as Ryan. I don't even know what I'm going to do tomorrow, didn't even know before my near-drowning. So I've got that going for me.

"So," Ryan starts. "I was thinking of getting a group together and heading down to the Wreck. They're having some end-of-the-world party all week long. Who's down?" He looks at me eagerly.

I'm not, but I say, "I'll think about it. They gave me this prescription that makes me want to sleep."

Layla gives me a sideways glance, because she knows we weren't at the hospital long enough for them to give me a prescription. "I just got a text from Maddy. She just invited me to the same thing."

"Dude, I'm surprised she's not here," Jerry says. "She was pacing in front of your hospital room for like days. I only went the one time. It was so crowded. But she was definitely there a while."

"Yeah, she was there when I went too," Ryan adds.

Layla's quiet, arms crossed over her chest. She looks small, like she's sinking into the couch. I get up from the floor and sit next to her. So does Jerry.

"Why'd you guys break up anyway?" Bertie asks. The whole room turns to look at me.

"When I broke up with Rebecca—" Ryan starts, but Bertie has his hand up. "Hold up. No, man. We've already heard the Rebecca story a bajillion times."

I asked Maddy out three months ago. I think the pigtail braids did it for me. Plus, we were already friends. I don't want to talk about me and Maddy. I don't want to talk about it ever. I want to jump in some cold water. But they're not going to let it drop until I at least say something.

"She's nice and all, don't get me wrong. But she wanted to be with me every single minute. She wanted to call me as soon as we got home from school and *watch TV* together over the *phone*. She waited by my locker. She waited in my lobby downstairs before school."

"Did she let you kiss her?" Bertie raises his thick black eyebrows and wiggles his head, giving him the effect of a cartoon bobblehead.

"I mean, yeah?"

"How far did you guys go?" Bertie leans over Layla to ask me this.

Layla's body feels hot next to mine. I glance at her. I can't say it. Not in front of her.

"Don't you dare say a word, Tristan Allen Hart," she says, evoking my whole name as if it's the ultimate command. Her eyes squint at me like she has lasers and they're about to slice right through me. *Oh god.* I want to bang my head against the wall. I want to jump out the window. She knows. Of course, Maddy told her.

The guys take it the wrong way. Even Wonder Ryan high-fives the other guys for me. I try to deny it, but they talk over me.

"Look, she'll get over it. It's not like you're going to be the only one."

"Plus, that friend of Samantha you made out with at the bonfire was ten times hotter than Maddy," Jerry blurts out, emitting a round of manly man cheers.

The bonfire. The night before the storm. The reason I was hungover the next day. I'm not a good drinker. I'll have a beer and a half and be plastered. That's why I don't usually drink. I just nurse the same bottle the entire night and pretend like it's always a new one. The Hot Mess that was with Samantha. She saw I was miserable. I was trying to avoid Maddy the whole day after she told me she was madly in love with me and then started undoing my belt buckle. I could've stopped her, but I wasn't exactly thinking with my brain.

Either way. The screwed-up part is that I don't even remember the girl I was kissing. I don't remember what she tasted like. I don't remember her eyes. Nothing. I just remember Maddy walking around the big boulder and gasping. Then crying. Then throwing her beer in my face and then the empty cup at the Hot Mess. She slapped me and I let her.

Maddy was the girl I wanted to take a chance with because I was tired of dating girls who couldn't put a whole sentence together but knew their father's credit card number by heart. It's just—she wasn't the right girl.

And now sitting here, with all my friends cheering me for being alive, for being their idol, I feel lower than low. Because Layla gets up, shaking her head at me. I try to grab her hand, but she pulls away, and I don't know what I can say right here, right now to make her want to stay.

chapter
NINE

My head is pulsing. I tell Ryan that I'll make it to the Wreck, but something doesn't feel right. I know I'll probably puke my guts out and go to bed. Layla and I take seats at the dining room table with our parents, who sip on red wine, and Coach Bellini, whose mustache is tipped in beer foam.

I vaguely understand now how it feels to be a wounded puppy that wants to be left alone to lick his wounds. A very manly, strong puppy, that is.

Mrs. Santos pops a cheddar cube into her mouth. Layla is a skinny version of her mother with her dad's hazel eyes. Mr. Santos is a tall and broad Ecuadorian dude with a mustache who always smells like his cigars. He extends his arm and pats my shoulder. I tighten my body against the pain that spreads down my entire back.

"Listen here, boy," says Coach, pointing a finger at me. Why do grown-ups seem to do that, like if they're not pointing in your direction, you're not going to know that they're serious. "What the hell happened out there? Don't you ever go doing anything so reckless again. Think of your momma right here. Your friends. Your team."

"He was trying save someone," Layla interrupts. She thinks Coach is right, but it's her nature to take the opposite side. Ms. Contrary. "He was being heroic."

"Firemen are heroic. Marines are heroic. You're just plain reckless." I've never seen Coach turn so many different colors so quickly. I think even his mustache is twitching. Everyone laughs at his expression, and for this moment, it's just a regular Saturday night with friends and family.

"I think what Arthur wants to say is that he's happy you're well," Mom chimes in, all smiles and bright eyes. She rubs my dad's back, and everything is calm again.

But then they all take a peek out the window, and we remember that something is changing and we don't know what it is.

I've started sweating. The rash at the side of my neck is getting worse. I want to crawl into my bed, but I know if I stand up I'll fall right back down.

My mom looks at me like she's snapping out of a nightmare. "I think Tristan needs to get some sleep."

"Do you need help cleaning up?" Layla offers.

"No, Layla, honey." Dad's voice is tight, the voice he uses when he's on the phone with his boss and trying to convince him he's working on a project but really hasn't started it.

"I don't feel so good," I groan. It's rude, but I wave at them and dash for the closest bathroom, which is my parents'. I shut the door and run cold water in the sink. I splash cold water on my face and all around my neck to calm the itching, which is spreading to my ribs. My mind flickers to a vision in my dream. The silver mermaid. The rows of teeth that don't fit with the rest of her beauty. I know it was just a dream, because I'm still here. I'm still here.

The faucet in the bathtub suddenly turns on by itself. The pipes squeak with the strong water pressure. I pull the sheer white curtain open and turn the water off.

I take off my T-shirt and soak it in the sink, then wrap it around my neck like a towel.

The knob jingles, but I've locked it. "I'm fine!"

"Tristan, let us in."

"I'm fine, Mom!"

"Everyone is gone, honey. Just let me in."

"Son." Now it's Dad. He pushes against the door with all his weight. "Don't make me break down the door."

"Something's happening." I want to say it, but I can't. I can hear the water in the bathtub making its way through the pipe. It smells like salt, even though it shouldn't. The tub faucet comes back on, and it's like a fire hydrant during the summer. I'm turning the knob, but the water doesn't stop coming.

In the sink, a tiny rainbow fish squeezes its way out of the faucet. I close the drain so that it doesn't get pulled back into the pipes. It jumps in the water until there's enough that it can swim in circles.

My stomach contracts. I can feel my insides shifting, moving apart, something inside of me breaking. My skin is on fire. My feet give out under me. I hold on to the edge of the sink on my knees, but I'm too heavy.

Dad has his drill out, undoing the doorknob. Two screws are out. He stops and jostles the knob, but he has to take them all out.

Pain. Pain like I've never felt, and that's now all I can think about. The water overflows from the sink, soaking the bath mat and spreading over the entire bathroom floor.

My mother is shouting my name. She's not asking me what's wrong. She's just repeating my name. *Tristan*, like a mantra, a prayer, a wish that I'll stay with them, so I say it too. *I am Tristan Hart. I am Tristan Hart. I am Tristan Hart.*

"Mom." I can hear myself whimper. Dad pulls the door open, dropping the doorknob and drill on the floor. The tiles crack where they fall.

The pain is going away, the fire subsiding. I don't want to try to move.

They stare, but not at me.

At my legs.

I know what's happened before I look down. My ripped shorts are in my mother's hands. I cannot read her face, but it isn't *surprise* like it should be. It's worry. The scent of bad lemon pie lingers around the both of them.

"What's happening to me?" I don't know if I've actually managed to say it aloud. I sit up on my elbows and look down. Even though I know what I'm going to see, I still shut my eyes for a little while. And when I open them, it's still there—

My great blue fishtail.

chapter
TEN

I have this memory of my first time in water.

It's insane, actually. There's no way I should be able to remember something like that, and I've convinced myself that it's a dream I made up.

Still, I remember. I remember my mom's face staring down at me in her arms. I remember being mesmerized, the way little kids are by such things, by the blue of her eyes. Her sitting me in the kiddie pool. I must have been a week old. And I remember swimming.

Sometimes during a meet, the memory would flash in my head. Then I'd push it away, because things like that just aren't real. But now I know they are, and some part of me has known it all along.

"Can you bring in the fan or something?" It might just be hotter than body building class at the end of summer. I'm slippery. Wet. Sweating.

When I try to sit up, my tail comes up and knocks my mom off her feet. She lands on her butt and grabs hold of my fins. I have fins.

"Let's put him in the tub." Dad's voice is calm. I know he's always Mr. Calm-and-Collected-and-Ready-to-Analyze, but all I want is a little bit of panic. I want him to scream, to run away from me, because I'm a freak. I'm beyond a freak. I'm unnatural. I want to bang my head against the tiles. I want to find a shrink who'll medicate me until I'm no longer a hazard to myself and others.

Mom grabs a towel and wraps it around my tail.

I. Have. A. Freaking. Tail.

Dad pushes his glasses up the bridge of his nose and hooks his arms under mine. They count to three and heave me into the tub with a splash. I'm suddenly nauseated, because I think of the times we've been fishing and we unhook the fish and throw them back in the water.

The water overflows with my weight. The tub is one of those grand claw-footed kind. It's big enough for two people, which by the way, since it's my parents' bathroom, is *gross*.

I let myself sink up to my shoulders and dangle my arms over the edge. My fins hang out over the brim, curling and uncurling. I wonder where my feet go? I wonder where my dick does! Holy crap. I'm about to start flailing around when my mother kneels at the side of the tub and dips her hand in. "Is the water okay?"

"Is the *water* okay? How about if *I'm* okay?"

"Don't you talk to your mother that way." Dad never uses that tone with me, because other than having shown up home at the ass-crack of dawn a couple of times, I don't do anything to give them heart attacks like my friends do to their parents.

Mom leaves the bathroom, and I'm afraid I've hurt her feelings. The water helps the dryness that's making my skin feel like I've been lying out in the sun all day. I submerge myself completely. I hold my breath, but it doesn't matter, because I'm still breathing. The shock of it makes me miss a beat of air when I sit upright.

Dad notices my surprise and finds Mom's mirror that magnifies pores three times. He hands it to me. I used to sit in this tub for hours playing with that thing. On my pores, I mean.

I hold it up to my neck. It's a hard angle, but there they are. The slits are shut now, lined by clusters of translucent metallic-blue scales. I throw the mirror to the side. It hits the wall and shatters.

"Bad luck, Finn," he says, trying to joke.

"Everything about that statement is unfunny."

My fins uncurl and knock the tray of bubble soaps into the tub. Under the water pressure, the bubbles fill the bath in seconds. I can smell the minuscule specks of metal in the water from the pipes it's traveling through. I can smell the chemicals in the soap more than the rose scent it's trying to mimic. I can smell Dad's amazement mingling with something like regret, like fireworks after they've all exploded.

"Say something," he tells me.

"Something." I chuckle.

He's quiet for what are probably seconds but feel like forever.

"Do you remember when I was ten," I start, "and Vicky Millanelli had that birthday pool party?"

"You kept wanting to leave," he says, "because you were the only boy who showed up."

"She only invited people she liked, and she didn't invite Layla. So all the girls started chasing me around, trying to kiss me. They were all wearing these matching pink-and-purple arm floats. So I jumped into the deep end of the pool, where they couldn't follow me. I just sat there at the bottom with my legs crossed, watching them scream and freak out. I don't remember wanting to come up for air. Vicky never invited me to her birthday parties again."

Dad pulls off his glasses and rubs the bridge of his nose. "Her dad called me to get you. You didn't even notice what you were doing."

"I never liked her much anyway."

Mom comes back with a Mason jar of sea salt. She runs her hand on my forearm, which is scattered with slick scales a few shades of blue lighter than the ones on my tail. She empties the Mason jar in the tub. We listen to the salt hiss when it meets water, the bubble bath deflating, and the careful intake of our breaths. Dad takes the jar from my mother and fills it. He picks up the little rainbow fish that's flopping on the wet floor with not enough water and drops him into the jar.

"Is he for dinner too?" I go.

We chuckle briefly. I want to fix the dark cloud that's hanging over all of us. Fix *this*. I can't remember us ever being this quiet, this careful of what we say. I know everyone says their family is different, happy. When it comes to my family, I really mean it.

Mom and I look at each other. Her cheeks are flushed red, but the rest of her is still the same porcelain pale she's always been. Her eyes are impossibly turquoise. The corners of her mouth tilt downward, and she's all trembles. Her lips, her chin, her hands. She wipes at her forehead with the back of her hand and breathes through her mouth. I can smell her regret, anxiety, fright. It's bitter, like dried lemons.

I don't know how, but I do. Now, I *may* be the fastest swimmer in Brooklyn, but that's about where my talents stop. Unless dating is counted as a talent, and recent events are proving me wrong.

"This wasn't supposed to happen," she says. She absently dips her hand in the water, like we're at Aunt Sylvia's pool and she's lying on the ledge. I've never seen her so sad, and my body flushes because I know this is somehow my fault.

"What was supposed to happen?" I don't mean to sound so bitter. I can't help it. "Why is this happening to me? Why now?" And before I can think to stop myself, "Who *are* you?"

She's Maia Hart, married to David Hart. Who was she before that? We've never met anyone from her side of the family. I've never asked, because I'm so used to it just being the three of us. New Year's we spend with friends; Christmas is the three of us; Thanksgiving, it's with Layla's family; and Independence Day is with the rest of Coney Island. Even if my grandparents were dead, there would be *someone*, wouldn't there? There would be pictures, no matter how old. People keep pictures of those they love, right?

"From the beginning." Dad says. He sits on the toilet with one hand under his chin, staring at my fins, like that statue of the thinking guy. "I met your mother when I had just graduated from Hunter and had moved back to my parents' apartment. I spent that entire summer on a little boat off Brighton, hating the world and wondering if I should take the job with Techsoft. That kind of post-college thing."

Mom lets herself chuckle. "It was on one of our visits to Coney Island. Every fifty or so years, we come back here. That's what we do. We spend most of our time visiting beaches all over the world. That's why it takes so long between visits."

I sat it slowly. "We?"

"The Sea People. The Beautiful Deadly Ones. The Fey of the Sea. Children of Poseidon. Dwellers of the Vicious Deep…" She pauses as if I don't already know I'm a moron. I just want her to *say* it. "Merfolk."

"Of course," I say. It's not enough that I'm in my parents' bathtub up to my gills in rose-scented bubble bath, that my entire world has quite literally slipped right out from under my feet, that I don't know anything about the changes in my body—if they're permanent, can I eat fish? Is that like semi-cannibalism? That my parents have been keeping this from me since I was little, which means they've been *lying* to me my entire life. I can forget all that. But of all the creatures in my mom's fairy-tale books, she had to go and be the girliest? *Come on!*

Dad's voice snaps me out of my thoughts. "I'd always wake up with a bottle of funny-shaped glass seashells or broken pieces of jewelry on my deck—"

Doesn't sound much different from the stuff she still collects in those trunks in their bedroom. "Let me guess. Mom would have her trusty but endearingly clumsy seagull friend deliver them to you? Am I right?"

Dad snorts, but Mom doesn't appreciate my humor. She folds her arms and sniffs. "Absolutely not. Seagulls are vile, nasty things. And back then I could control the water."

"You can't anymore?"

She shakes her head. "I showed myself to David. I didn't usually do that sort of thing—"

"—that's what *all* the mermaids say," he winks.

"—I didn't! My sisters were the ones always revealing themselves to humans. It was fine if they wanted to take humans as mates—for a short while—but they were careless. They always let them *drown*, and then Father would be furious at *me* because he always put me in charge to watch over them.

"On this last trip, when it was time to leave, I didn't want to go. I begged my father. He granted our wish to be together. He stripped my tail. Then I had you."

"That's the SparkNotes version, right?"

"Yes," she says, "it's a long story."

"What're you, like, a hundred? You've got plenty of time to tell it. Plus, it's not like I'm going anywhere, unless we toss me back into the Atlantic."

They're both about to protest, their fingers pointing up at my face, all *don't-you-talk-to-us-like-that*. But the faucet comes on by itself again. Water sloshes everywhere. There's a soft light coming from the faucet in the bathtub. Dad keeps twisting the handles to turn it off, but that doesn't work. There's a loud popping sound, followed by a tiny fish that flows right into the tub. "I hope this isn't a regular thing, because the downstairs neighbors are going to complain."

The water trembles. Something bumps and pushes against my tail. The water glows so brightly that I have to look away. There's a second splash, and the wind gets knocked out of me by a knee. My tail, with a mind of its own, knocks everything in its reach onto the floor. I try to pull myself as upright as I can. When I look again, he's taken full form. He's landed completely on top of me. He pushes himself up by holding the sides of the tub, as though he's afraid his legs will give out.

He takes in my mom, standing with the bottom of her dress soaking up the water, and Dad, looking more amused than should be allowed for someone sitting on the toilet. Naked guy notices he's *naked* and uses his hand to cover his junk. He tosses his hair back. The dark, wet curls stick to his neck and around a face that is familiar, but I just can't place it. Not that I want to. I want him to get out of my bathtub and put some clothes on. Instead the guy turns to me and *bows*—stands with his back straight in the world's best attempt to look poised, stoic even.

"Well," he says, clearing his throat, "this is awkward."

chapter
ELEVEN

S orry," the naked guy standing in the bathtub says, "so sorry."

There's a trace of not so much an accent but an over-enunciating of words. He looks down at the deflating bubble bath and thankfully sits immediately. He turns around and turns the faucet off. It stays off.

His hair is the same length as mine, right to the base of our ears and messy in curls like we spend too much time at the beach. There's this sculpture in the Greek section at the Met that Layla dragged me to a few weeks ago that looks just like him. He doesn't look fazed, but his violet eyes gape at me. He sort of bows.

"I have a fishtail, and that's not half as weird as this right here." I point at him and look to my mother for some sort of explanation. "Mom?"

"Priscilla—?" is what she says instead.

Naked guy bows at my mom too, then shakes his head. "She's dead. For quite a while, actually."

"Who the hell are you?" I say finally. "Am I going to be a mermaid magnet now or something?"

"Tristan!"

"My name is Kurtomathetis," he says with his head held high, "and I am not a *mermaid*, as I am clearly not a woman. I am a merman, as are you, but of course you've already figured that out."

"Fine—Kurtom—can I just call you Kurt?—we're mermen. Most importantly, how come you don't have a tail, and how do I get rid of mine?"

He sighs, and I can feel the exasperation in his voice as thick as wading in mud. "I am part of the Sea Court. I am to be your guide—your guardian, if you will. My purpose is to make sure you're safe at all times. It is the highest honor of the sea folk."

"Sea Court?" It's foreign in my mouth.

Kurt turns his attention to my mother. "He really knows nothing?"

"I know stuff!" I yell. "Not mermaid stuff but—"

Kurt and my mother move to talk over each other, but the sink faucet bursts on again. Dad stands back as a lime-green fish pops out. Like when Kurt appeared, the sink is flooded with a bright light. Dad has a bewildered smile on his face. "I hope the neighbors don't come up and complain," he says.

I sure hope it's not another naked mer-guarding guy. And it isn't. There's a girl no older than fourteen sitting in the sink. Her skin is pale, but it has a slight greenish tinge; her hair is long and wet and a shade of black with green. Her hair covers her breasts and pools in her lap. She reminds me of a green Rapunzel. Dad grabs

Mom's bathrobe off the hook behind the door and wraps her in it. She hops off the sink with the tiniest splash, ties the robe around her waist, and gathers her hair to one side.

"Thalia!" Kurt's proper nose is wrinkled with the kind of annoyance that I've only seen siblings have toward each other. He chokes on the beginning of every sentence he tries to speak and slaps his hands in the water, adding to the pool on the bathroom floor. "What—I can't believe—may I too have a cloth?—why—what are you doing here?"

Thalia's slender frame looks even more so in the big robe. Her lips are full and pink, and her eyes a cattish green-yellow, twinkling with mischief. She turns to me, gathers the hem of the bathrobe, tucks one foot behind the other, and curtseys. She turns to my mother and does the same. "Lady Sea."

She looks in the sink as Dad comes back with a red-and-black flannel robe for Kurt. She sticks her hand in the water and pulls out a long, skinny bottle full of iridescent black liquid that seems to be moving in a continuous swirl inside. "You forgot the ink," she says.

Kurt ties Dad's bathrobe around the middle and stumbles out of the tub like he's not used to his legs yet. He makes to grab for the vial between Thalia's fingers, but she takes one step back, smirking. "Only if I can stay."

"Very well." He makes fists at his sides.

She doesn't hesitate and hands it over.

He snatches it and puts it in the robe pocket. "Good. Great. Now leave!"

"But—you said I could stay! Your word is binding!"

"Right. Binding to the king, *not* my sister."

Mom brings her hand to her mouth, covering the chuckle that's escaping her lips. I laugh too, but only because I like seeing this guy get so huffy and puffy.

Thalia looks indignant but not defeated. She stomps one foot on the floor, and water splashes. "That's thanks for you. I'm not going anywhere."

"This is *my* duty, not yours. Now go before I tell the king."

Her yellow-green eyes are wide with a new realization. "You *can't*. We've no contact with Toliss until Arion's ship gets here." The silence that follows should be accompanied by a *So there. Na-na, na-na-na.*

"Hello? Remember me? One of you. Kurt, Kurt's little sister, Mom. Tell me how to turn back!" I say loudly.

Kurt pulls the vial out of his pocket. I don't have a good feeling about it.

"You were never given the rites of the newborn. Only court merfolk can shift. You are not an average merman, as you are, quite literally, half human. When you were born—"

"Kurt, one thing at a time, please," Mom says. And I thank her, because my headache is back and all I want is a warm, dry bed.

I dip myself into the bathwater, this time preparing for the gills to open and shut again when I surface.

"As part of the Sea Court, we get our legs whenever we visit shore. There was a time when all creatures coexisted on this plane. Humans, fey, shifters, and what humans started calling *monsters*.

Then suddenly it changed. Humans outnumbered all of us. They wanted us gone. Those who didn't want to start wars chose to move their courts to hidden islands. Ours is the only isle that is still in this realm, with the exception of two fairy islands. We cover them with mists so humans cannot detect them, and from a distance it looks like a storm at sea.

"Courts?" I find myself saying. "In the stories it's always just one mermaid."

"The Sea King took away our legs to keep us from straying. But that doesn't stop some from showing themselves to humans. The easiest thing in the world is to fall in love with one of us. Shakespeare and Donne were particularly obsessed, as were all the poets who'd caught a glimpse. Or thought they did. Besides, it's usually the mermaids who get caught on land."

"Because mermen don't like getting dry?"

Kurt takes on a face that Ryan made when he tried to explain to Angelo the difference between a microcosm and a macrocosm. "Mermaids are more likely to seek a human's affections than mermen. I suppose we lack the same amount of curiosity when it comes to human lovers. So there are fewer merman sightings recorded. Because of that, there's the misconception that mermen are unattractive. As you can see in the case of you and me, that is not so."

I mean, not to sound like an ass, but I was thinking the same thing.

My father snickers, and my mother purses her lips.

"But enough about us man-hungry *mermaids*," my mother says. "Are you *quite* sure you know how to do that, Kurt?"

He holds up the vial to the light and shrugs. "I've read all the texts, and I've seen it executed on a few lucky merfolk who've pleased the king enough and were granted land legs. And the less lucky, who've been banished to land for having displeased him as well."

Read. Seen. There is no *I've done* anywhere in there.

"What exactly are you going to do? What do you mean you've only seeing it done?" It's all making me so warm that I let the cold water run, adding another inch to the pool on the floor.

"Many pardons, Lord Sea—"

"Whoa." I hold up my hand. "Don't you ever call me that again."

But he continues over me. "—I forget you're half human and have a shorter attention span. It *is* incredibly rare that a human and our kind can actually conceive a fully human child that is also fully mer-kin. There have been creatures with the heads of fish and the bodies of humans. Sometimes they come out incredibly deformed and, usually, don't live past a few months.

"But I digress. This"—he holds the vial close to my face so that I can see that the ink is swirling on its own like a tiny black hole collapsing—"is an ink that allows us to shift whenever we want. It is the blood of the abyss, primordial and, of course, painfully difficult to extract. The king has one of the last known cephalopods that carry it. Once that's gone, we won't be able to go on land anymore. Not that it would be such a bad thing. Can't really miss what you never had, can you?"

"Cephalopod?" All those years of wandering through the Coney Island Aquarium, and I can't even remember that.

"Squid," Dad answers. His voice pulls me out of Kurt's explanation and grounds me. I'm glad he's here. Thalia is holding the rainbow fish in a jar. They both press their noses on the glass, like a double aquarium.

"Do I have to drink it?"

Kurt turns his back to me, and sure enough there's a tattoo on the center of his back level with his shoulder blades. It's a trident, the middle spear slightly longer than the outer two prongs. The stem of the trident ends in a sharp triangular point.

"Do you have one?" I ask my mother. The question leaves my mouth before I even know why it matters. It matters because she's my mother, and I would've noticed.

She pulls her hair over her shoulders, like opening a curtain. No, I would not have noticed it. The mark where the ink used to be is the color of pearl, maybe two shades lighter than the rest of her skin. "My father extracted the ink himself. I can never change again."

My fingers hover over the trident, stopping short of touching it. "What does it mean?"

"It is the symbol of the Sea Court." I'm glad she's not facing me, because now I can smell her sadness pouring over her, like pure sea.

"Okay, so a tattoo. I can deal with that. At least I don't have to get my lip pierced or have a stick driven though my nose." Kurt stares at me with confused violet eyes. I emphasize, "*Right?*"

"Oh, yes," he says. "I mean, *no*. No piercings. Though the trend has become popular among the younger ones."

"Darn that MTV," Dad says.

"I have your permission, right?" I ask him.

"If not, I think we're going to need a pretty big fish tank." Dad's smile betrays the smell of worry he's giving off like burnt rubber cement. "Or we could rent a room at the aquarium. Whatever is cheaper."

Kurt doesn't try to understand the joke and shrugs off the comment. He kneels beside me, and my mind races. What if he does it wrong and I get stuck like this forever? Can I still have sex with girls or only other mermaids? Where the hell does my dick go? What if Layla sees me this way?

I don't have much longer to think, because as soon as Kurt uncorks the vial with a surprising champagne-bottle pop, he tells me, "This is going to sting."

And sure enough, it does.

chapter
TWELVE

The ink is a shiny, black blur spilling out of the slim glass, and it knows just where to find me.

It coils in the air slowly, like a spinning Milky Way. I focus on the things that make it sparkle and wonder why I have to be a creature that's half glitter. Why can't my mom be half powerful genie or like a werewolf, anything that doesn't look like a ten-year-old girl bedazzled the bottom half of her Ken doll.

Kurt is whispering something in what I recognize as Latin, thanks to Mrs. Santos, who drags me and Layla to the Latin mass at the Greek church, even though Layla says she's an atheist and I'm not Greek.

The coil freezes, then blurs out of sight. I know where it's gone the instant I feel the burn in my skin. I let myself fall backward into the tub with a splash. I can feel my fins parting, and the burn is now everywhere. It's like being ripped in half over a fire pit and then being left there until the fire simmers and there's nothing left but ash.

The back of my head hits the bottom of the tub, and when I take a deep breath, I forget I don't have gills anymore. The rose-soap water snakes down my throat. The strangest feeling is not having water go down the wrong pipe but the fact that my leg muscles feel like they're reverberating right at the core. I push myself up and cough until my throat feels raw.

Mom holds a towel in front of me and I take it, drying my face first, then standing to wrap it around my waist. It hurts to stand, like the day after doing squats in Mr. Loughlin's fitness class.

"I'm sorry this is happening," Mom says. "It wasn't supposed to."

I'm shivering. I'm shivering, I'm naked, I'm wet, and in a handful of days I've nearly drowned, hallucinated, and turned into a mythical creature. Yeah, none of this was supposed to happen.

"I'm going to clean up," Dad says. He runs out and comes back with a mop and every towel we own to carpet the tiles and soak up the water.

"Get dressed, honey," Mom says. She rubs my face with her hand, and part of me wants to rest my head on her shoulder like when I was little and didn't want to start kindergarten without her. The other part of me, the part that's angry like I've never thought I could be, flinches from her touch.

"Let's get you kids some clothes," she tells Kurt and Thalia.

"I'm going to bed," I announce.

"But there's so much we have to discuss," Kurt protests. We stand in the living room. I can hear Mom rummaging through her closet and Dad wringing out the towels into the tub and then laying them out on the floor again.

"Yeah, well, unless the information is going to change in the next ten hours, I think it can wait."

Kurt goes to speak, but Thalia says his name hard. "*Kurtomathetis.* Remember our place."

Yeah, as in they're know-it-all mermaids and I'm just a human guy. Or I was.

Kurt's face changes from a tight-lipped expression to just plain pissed-off and then right back to full control in seconds. "Forgive me. This is a lot to gather."

"I'll see you guys in the morning."

The land-locked mer-siblings watch me sulk to my room and close the door. My navy blue sheets have never felt softer against my abused skin. I feel for traces of scales on my body, but this time there aren't any. Where my gills are shut against the air, I can feel raised keloids, like the scar on my mother's back.

I bury my face against my pillow and let my body sink into everything that's happening. I'd pinch myself if everything didn't already hurt. The sounds of my house slow down: the squeak of the metal in the pull-out couch as it's being unfolded, the rustle of Kurt and Thalia helping my parents making it up with sheets and blankets, and their low voices most likely discussing me, or maybe how much they wish they weren't here.

Duty was what Kurt had said. He has a duty, and it's me. What's my duty? Before the storm, before the shift, my only duty was being the best swimmer and saving a life if it needed saving. Can I still do those things without being this—thing?

I look at the clock on my nightstand before shutting my eyes. It isn't even midnight yet.

chapter

THIRTEEN

I dream of the whirlpool again, but all I see is the water. Clear bubbles. Stillness and the infinite black-blue ocean. This time I'm swimming with the Great White. Up close I can see he's got his own armor with a gleaming metal ring around his head. The ring has two grips at either side. I tighten my hold on them as he pulls me through the water.

When I wake up, I feel like I've been asleep for days. My legs ache when I push myself off my bed. For a moment, sitting in the middle of my blue comforter and surrounded by swim trophies, posters of vintage cars, calendar girls holding surfboards, and pictures of the past seventeen years of my life, I forget about the wave, the whirlpool, the silver mermaid, Kurt and Thalia, my mom's lack of worry at what's happening. Everything but the tattoo.

I reach over my back and trace the raised skin. In the mirror, I see myself as I have always been—the same wavy brown mess of hair, freaky turquoise eyes, lifeguard tan. The mirror doesn't show the other half—the gills and the scales, the giant blue fishtail. The magic hums in my veins, wanting to be released, craving water the way I also crave air, and I wonder if one of those needs is ever going to be greater than the other.

"Honey?" The knock on the door snaps my eyes away from my reflection. "Tristan, are you awake?"

Part of me, the part that wishes I were just a swim-team jock with nothing to worry about but girls and winning, wants to go back to sleep, to never change into a merman again. To know that I've just imagined this connection to the ocean. That I'm just a regular guy after all.

But I've never been that guy, not really. Kurt said that I'm rare, but being rare doesn't make you special. I feel like one of the freak-show acts on the boardwalk. Step right up and see the merboy, merguy, merman. Where does his ding-dong go? Nobody knows! How fast can he swim? Just step right up to the glass. Remember! He goes to school in your very neighborhood and doesn't do much else. Actually, come to think of it, he's not that interesting after all.

Yeah, I'm a crowd-pleaser.

———

The sky looks like a gray blanket that has been pulled tight at every corner. Not a spot of blue. It casts a bright white light in the kitchen. Angel light, Mom calls it.

When I show up, the laughter stops. There are biscuits and coffee and tea. The orange-juice jar has fresh pulp clinging to the sides. There is a mound of bacon and scrambled eggs, slices of cheddar, and a bowl of green grapes.

Thalia looks lovely in this light, tiny. Now that her hair is dry, it tumbles in soft black waves that look green when they're under the light. She's wearing one of my mom's sundresses that's two sizes too big. She's made a necklace out of the multicolored paper clips in Dad's office and a bracelet out of a fork. I wonder if she slept at all last night.

I take the empty seat next to Kurt, who bows his head slightly. That's going to get old quickly. Kurt spears a piece of bacon and examines the shades of burnt meat before bringing the tip to his mouth. His face is all concentration at first, then pleased, and settles on satisfied.

"Breakfast of champions," Dad says. He reaches over and ruffles my hair. Any other day, I'd pull away and whine. But today I welcome the gesture for what it is—familiar.

"I called the school," Mom says, pulling a handful of grapes from their stems, "and told them you'd be out just one more day."

"I feel fine." There's an argument I never thought I'd make.

She doesn't acknowledge it. "I also told them that we have family visiting and that they are curious about American schools. Since there are only two weeks left to the year, they agreed there wouldn't be any harm in letting Kurt and Thalia tag along with you."

I choke on orange pulp.

"I understand we will have to be appropriately dressed for this?" Kurt asks. He even *eats* like there's a stick up his merman ass. Where *is* a merman's ass? How am I supposed to be their tour guide at school? I might as well hold up a sign that reads: ←I'M WITH MERPEOPLE→.

85

I speak with my mouth full of eggs and bacon, "There are two and a half weeks left." I don't know why I'm so against this, other than everything that could go wrong. What if they say the wrong things? What if they lead someone off the pier like in the stories? My mother gives me the eye, and I keep eating in silence.

"They can't very well stay locked in the apartment," Dad chips in. *Traitor*.

"When was the last time you guys were around humans?" I ask.

Kurt raises an eyebrow at me. "We just left the Italian coast. Too soon, I must say. But duty calls."

And I go, "Feel free to hang up any time."

Dad clears his throat extra loudly, a signal for me to take it down a notch.

Thalia ignores the knives Kurt and I are throwing at each other and squeals, "Italy is *fantastic*. The beaches are mostly naked, so we never have to acquire many garments or go inland. We rarely go inland. I've never understood the concept of bikinis."

"That's my kind of girl," I say, before realizing that I'm with my parents and her brother, who shake their heads disapprovingly at me. "Okay, but you guys can't say things like *acquire* or *I do declare*. This is Brooklyn, not a Renaissance fair. Oh! Unless we say you guys are British. Then the uptight thing Kurt's got going won't seem so questionable."

"If you feel that would be beneficial, then we will align ourselves to a land nation, yes."

I let my face fall into my palms. This is going to be harder than I thought. "What are we doing today, then?"

"We have to get them clothes," Mom says, "and your father still has to go to work."

"Yep, we're going to need a lot of fish food around here."

Mom and Thalia giggle. Kurt and I don't.

Dad kisses my mom on her forehead and says, "You all be good and, you know, have fun." With that, he's out the door. We help clean up the kitchen after we've eaten all the food. I didn't realize how hungry I'd been until I looked down and saw that Kurt and I had finished the entire stack of bacon.

I lend Kurt a pair of shorts because my jeans are two inches too short, and my T-shirts are one size too small, making him look like a Eurotrash pop star.

He doesn't seem to mind, or maybe he does and he's trained not to care. He holds his head high, even though I can't keep from laughing as we file into the elevator. "We still have a lot to discuss," Kurt says.

"You know, I can tell you're going to be the life of the party."

chapter
FOURTEEN

W hat an interesting contraption," Thalia goes.

Before I can stop her, she runs her fingers all the way up and down the elevator numbers. B to 17.

"Thalia," Mom says in her best mom voice, "you must only push one button."

"Which one?"

"The level you wish to go to."

"Which level do we wish to go to?" Her eyes are less intense than yesterday, her lashes so long they look like they're reaching out for you.

My mother presses her finger to her mouth to suppress a giggle. Like I said, she's always wanted a daughter. "Level L to go out to the street. To go back home, Level 14."

I figure Kurt, in his own way, must be amazed by the elevator. That is, until he says, "We don't need metal boxes in Toliss. We can swim wherever we like. You remember, Lady Sea?"

Mom doesn't answer, but I can smell her longing—a petal being crushed between fingertips. Then I see Layla's face in the back of my mind. *She loves me not.*

"It's nice to rest your fins once in a while," Thalia says.

"Well, there's one reason merfolk are not as fat as humans," he says simply.

"The delicious kelp and algae diet?"

"Tristan, be nice."

"He called me fat! He called *us* fat!"

"I said, *humans*. Not ex-mermaids and their offspring"

I stuff my hands in my pockets and watch the numbers go down. My palms are sweating, and I don't think I've finished shedding my scales around some very sensitive areas. How the hell are the three of them so composed? I've turned into a merman, and now we're going to the mall. I feel like I'm about to erupt, as if the fish half of myself is trying to break through. Wasn't this tattoo supposed to help with that?

"I think your tattoo didn't work," I say.

Kurt observes me a moment. The doors open and we walk past the neighbors, who stare at Kurt and Thalia so long that the door starts to shut with them in the middle. The tall lovely boy whose clothes are too small for him and the young girl who makes you want to sigh when you glance at her.

"I believe it takes a bit to settle in. Magic is gradual, not instantaneous, contrary to whatever you've been exposed to."

"What's the point of that?"

"The point is that at least you're no longer in a bathtub too small to fit your fins."

"You mean you don't feel antsy at all?"

He thinks on it as we cross the street to the car. He looks like he's going to say something smart-ass-ish. Thalia suddenly stops. Her high-pitched voice comes out shapeless, just a mumble of hysterical sounds.

She stands in the middle of the street, reaching down to grab a Chihuahua the size of a football from the road, its puke-pink leash dangling as it wiggles in Thalia's grasp. She doesn't know not to stop in the middle of the street. Two cars honk and drive around her but don't slow down. I run and grab her around the waist. An SUV holds his horn down and hits the brakes, stopping right where she was standing two heartbeats ago. The driver rolls down his window to curse at us before running the red light.

"Oh my," Thalia says.

People on the street stop and stare. Others stand on their stoops and crane their necks to get a better look at us. I set Thalia on the ground. The puppy barks, and she holds him up so that he licks my face.

"Thank Lord Sea for saving us," she tells him. The ugly little thing barks at me with sharp teeth. She holds him like a baby doll while a girl runs across the street, struggling to hold on to five other leashes.

"Thank you! So much!" Her face is almost green with sickness. There's something that looks like gum stuck in her braces. "That's a five-thousand-dollar dog. Mrs. Hirschwitz would've killed me."

Thalia hands over the dog with a pout on her pretty lips. The dog walker waves at us as she gets pulled in six different directions by her borrowed hounds.

"What a horrific line of duty," Kurt says, opening the passenger door for Thalia and then letting himself into the back.

Mom reaches over and holds Thalia's chin gently. "I know this is a new world. It is different. It is dangerous. I can't have anything hurt you, okay? Please, stay close to us."

"Also, don't stand in front of moving metal," I say, slightly shaking from the rush of adrenaline.

Thalia nods. "I just missed my Atticus."

"Your catfish?"

"Her sea horse."

She lets my mom buckle her seat belt and slumps down, not unlike a girl her age who's been told she can't have a puppy. I picture her room as a giant cave with seaweed and tiny stolen trinkets.

Mom turns on the radio. The Beach Boys sing something about sunshine and girls in rainbow colors and surfing. We drive through the grayest day of the summer, passing girls in rain boots and short dresses and men with umbrellas tucked under their arms. I let all the images outside the car window drift through my mind so that I don't think of one concrete image. One I've dreamt every time I shut my eyes. The silver mermaid. Her beautiful, ghostly face. The sharp teeth. The nails long and dirty at the tips like they'd been dipped in blood.

And then the Beach Boys get completely drowned out by static.

Kurt turns to me and says, "I am indebted to you."

"I thought I'm already your duty," I say, in air quotes.

"I am here because the king wished it. But you have saved my sister. Now I also wish to be here."

He turns back to the window. I wonder if all merdudes are this stiff even when they're trying to be friendly. "To answer your question from before, I am antsy," he says. "I've just had more years to practice hiding it. Besides, at the end of it I always go back to the sea."

"So if you don't like being in human form, why even come on land?"

"Because I go where my family goes. Besides, it gets boring after a few years with the same people at court."

"When you guys get bored, you go island-hopping. When I get bored I watch a movie."

"We don't have those."

Thalia sits up in her seat. "The moving pictures! Oh, Lady Sea, may we *please* go see one? Though the last time we saw one on the Florida coast the automobile smelled like dead cow."

"The last movie you went to see was a drive-in, and you still look about fourteen?"

"We age slowly," Kurt says, "like the sea itself. I'm 103."

"God damn," I go. "How old are you, Mom?"

"Didn't your father tell you you're not supposed to ask a lady her age?"

We get on the expressway. I can't smell the sea anymore, but the smell of metal and burning rubber and oil makes me queasy.

"Is this normal?" I ask Kurt.

"It would depend on what is normal to you. What are you referring to?"

"The smells. I smell things a lot more than before I changed. When the storm was coming, I could smell it. Only I didn't know that I could. When people get too close to me, I can smell what they're *feeling*."

"It helps when you're swimming along to detect if there are any nasty things in the water with you. Or if you're looking for food."

In the rearview mirror I catch my mom looking at us and smirking. She flicks on the windshield wipers, and they squeak because it's only just begun to drizzle.

"What else should I expect?"

Kurt rolls down his window and lets the drizzle hit his face. "You already know how much the shift hurts. It *does* get easier, not because it hurts less but because you get used to the pain. Your sense of smell and hearing should be accelerated. Your libido will increase—"

"Whoa. Hey, not in front of my mom."

She goes, "How do you think you got here?"

Uncomfortable hot flash. "Please never say that again."

I lean in to Kurt and whisper. "Bro, where does *it* go?"

His brows are knit together, and he tilts his head to the side like he's never seen my species before. "Oh, you mean your phallus."

I elbow him.

He shakes his head at me, like he would hit me back if his *duty* weren't to keep me unharmed, or whatever it is he's supposed to do. He leans into my ear and whispers quickly, "Not to worry. There's a pocket."

We sit straight up again. Mom's taking the right into the mall parking lot. A pocket? Great, just when I thought I had it figured out the regular way.

chapter
FIFTEEN

We walk through the revolving doors.

Thalia keeps going, either because she doesn't know she's supposed to get out by herself, or because she's having too much fun spinning.

"You have the attention span of a goldfish," I tell her, wrapping my arm around her neck and giving her a noogie. For a moment, I imagine this is what having a bigger family feels like. A slightly pretentious older brother, a jumpy little sister, and a mom everyone stares at when we're walking around the mall.

"Actually, I've seen very well behaved goldfish," Kurt says.

"Of course you have," I grumble.

"I think I'll take Thalia to Glittering World, and you boys can go do your own thing," my mom says. They go to the escalator, and I stand a little longer and watch Thalia try to get on it. She reminds me of girls on the street playing double Dutch, waiting for just the right moment.

"You wouldn't think she's nearly half a century old," Kurt sighs. "I told her to stay, but I knew she wouldn't."

"What about your parents?"

"Our parents were killed during a battle with a rebel group of Hungarian dragons. There aren't many left, but they're ferocious, and they believe the whole of this plane and the others belong to them."

"Is there like a mermaid heaven or something?"

He doesn't laugh, which I'm thankful for. "We are of the sea," he says, "and to the sea we return. An ancient merman like the king, would become a great coral reef, no matter what the climate. Someone like me, like my parents, would turn to surf."

"Just like that."

"Precisely."

A burst of giggles erupts behind Kurt. A cluster of girls is pointing at us. I put my hand up when the flash of a camera hits my eye. What is their deal? Kurt glances behind me, and shock registers on his normally calm features.

When I turn around, every fish in the aquarium window of Exotic Pet Planet is gathered around my frame with their mouths pressed against the glass. I walk to the right and they follow.

Between that and the way Kurt's T-shirt keeps riding up his abs, we're drawing too much attention. Kurt clears his throat and picks up the pace beside me.

"I believe we should get me a change of wardrobe as soon as possible."

I pat him on the back and jump onto the escalator. "Don't worry. You'll blend in, in no time."

~

"For someone who is just now human and has free range to buy anything he wants, you sure are a bare-necessities kinda guy." I know if my mom gave me her credit card, I'd go nuts.

Kurt looks more comfortable in a pair of jeans and a long-sleeved white T-shirt that actually fit. "I learn to live without much. You leave fewer things behind that way."

We stand at the top floor of the mall against the railing and look down at the crowd. At people with worries like two-for-the-price-of-one sweaters, not strange cravings like wanting to jump into the fountain and splash around. But strangely, I'm having a good time, and the ink doesn't burn anymore.

Then the stench hits me hard. It smells like rotting fish. Kurt smells it too, because we both turn around. There's a woman on one knee. Her dress is big and gray around her slender frame. Dull and thinning brown hair frizzes around her head. Everything about her says homeless. Except for her face. Her skin is smooth like pale porcelain, and she has sapphire eyes that stare hungrily at me. "I pledge myself to you," she says. "I do."

I'm too stunned. Beside me, I see Kurt reach for something at his side, then realize nothing is there. He grabs the woman by her arm, hard.

"Whoa, what are you doing?"

"Stand back, Lord Sea." Kurt shakes her. "Who sent you?"

The woman's eyes are cold and laughing. She sniffs at the air.

"Don't trust them. Look what they did to me." She's about to pull down the neck of her dress when I stop her.

"Kurt, let her go." And he does, without questioning me.

She gives me one last bow, kisses the back of my hand, and pushes through the sea of shoppers.

"What am I, the mermaid flag? How come the fish aren't gathering around your head and following you where *you* walk? How come they don't pledge their allegiance to you?"

He rolls the sleeves of the white T-shirt up to his elbows. For the first time since he popped into my shower, his brow creases. Everything about him says that all he's missing is a sword and something to hit. "We need to find Lady—your mother. Now."

———

This is the first time we have ever found a parking spot so close to the boardwalk. I get out of the car first and run up the wooden incline, past Nathan's Hot Dogs. It's not much of a beach day: the sky is so gray and there's still police tape on the railings so that people will stay away from the water.

Ruby's is open, and we grab seats on the bench outside. The bartender cleans the countertop while watching the TV above him. There's a report of more bodies washing up along the strip, the bodies all mangled up.

I fill Mom in on what happened at the mall.

"So talk," I say to Kurt. "Who was that woman?"

"There's a faction of our people who rebelled against the king scores of years ago. They resented members of the court, who have the ability to shift into legs at will. Everyone else has to wait for the island to coast by a new shore. But it's the way it's always been."

"And you're one of the court people?" I ask.

"Of course," he says, with a hint of irritation. "If I may continue—the last rebellion wasn't the first one, but this time the king granted them what they wanted. He stripped them of their tails and let them swim to shore. Not many could have survived, but the few who did hate the throne. I believe that's why they see you as someone to relate to. You are one of us but you are also mostly human."

"Okay, what am I supposed to do for them? I'm only just a guy. A hot merman kind of guy, yeah, but still."

Thalia laughs, and I'm glad that at least I can do that to lighten the mood.

Kurt and my mom share a knowing look. The kind they've been giving each other since he showed up. It makes my stomach turn that they know something I don't.

"What aren't you guys saying?"

Kurt looks at his lap, and my mom saves him from whatever he wants to say.

"I can answer that," she says. She tucks loose red strands behind her ear and looks out at the horizon. I wish she'd look me in the eye at least. "When a mermaid conceives, she carries the child like a human woman. Because I was stripped of my tail, there was a chance you wouldn't be part merman at all. For your sake, I hoped you'd be human. But when I gave birth, I did it in water. My father visited that summer, and he brought our midwife. You were born with your fins, and he bound them so that you would not change ever again. He *promised* you would never change."

"So then why am I changing now? Why is this happening to me now?" I have to stop myself from yelling. I've never spoken like this to my mother. I feel ashamed and stupid and confused, and I just wish they would spit it out.

"Because the Sea King is getting old, and he needs an heir," Thalia says finally. "If there is not a new king by the summer solstice, that which binds us to the island, which allows us to live apart in secret, will disappear. And not all of our kind want to share a world with humans."

"I don't understand. What does this have to do with me? I've grown up human. I don't know your world."

"I'm supposed to teach you." Kurt says. He looks at me from the corner of his eye and clears his throat. "I was supposed to find you before the storm hit. I didn't take into account the beastly number of people who crowd that beach."

"That was you!" I smack the table. I remember Layla peering down at him from our post and Kurt looking lost on the shore. "The ripped pants? Not a good look for you."

Kurt shakes his head at me and says, "Besides, the king wants to keep the throne in the family."

And that's when it hits me. A giant *Duh* smacking me on the face. The Sea King. My mother.

"I'm guessing 'My Lady' isn't something you say just because you've got that polite British thing going, is it?"

Kurt looks pleased with himself. "The Sea King is your grandfather. Because Lady Maia, the king's eldest, has been stripped of her tail and the king has no sons, this makes you the rightful heir—"

Before he can finish, I run out to the boardwalk, jump the metal bars, and land on the sand. My gills itch with expectancy. If the tattoo weren't binding them, they'd open right now so that I could jump into the waves.

And just like that, everything inside me changes. Just like the mist rising, the tide pulling in and out, the easy shuffle of my bare feet on the sand. The hard surf crashes around my ankles— hugging, embracing, welcoming me back—and I swear it whispers my name.

Part II

Teach me to hear the mermaids singing,
Or to keep off envy's stinging.

—JOHN DONNE

chapter
SIXTEEN

So this is the famed Thorne Hill Academy," Kurt says

"It's a high school, bro, not an academy. We don't have any famous students. Unless you count the athletics department. Lots of Triborough champs. If we win the next swim meet, my team will be too."

Thorne Hill High School is not your average high school. They make you take a specialized test to get in if you don't live in the proper zoning. In the 1800s, the building was a church. The tall Gothic kind with gargoyles and sharp pillars that would make anyone think twice before going on the roof for a smoke break. The stones have faded over the years from what must've been white to a dirty gray.

The tall wooden doors that lead into the school are crowned by two angel statues. I'm not talking typical angels praying and glowing with light. These guys are tilted toward each other, like they were frozen in the middle of their fight. Their carved swords form the peak of the archway into the school.

"What I mean is I've heard of it," Kurt says. "And remember, you cannot tell anyone about us. At a time like this it would be extremely dangerous for anyone in our court to get caught. Your parents are safe. But anyone else could get killed."

I nod and lead the way up to the entrance. The steps themselves are too high for sea level. My first day here, I felt like a less glorious Rocky climbing the museum steps. Now it's not much different. It's only been a few days of not working out, and I'm already out of shape.

"Why couldn't Mom just let us stay home?" I grunt.

Kurt glances around, bored at the way girls trip on account of staring at him. "She wants you to resume something familiar. Once we're at Toliss, you'll never see things the same way."

"How many days did you say before we have to go to the island?"

"Two. Until the wall is completely down." Kurt stops halfway up the steps. First, I hope he doesn't get into another rant about how real mermaids don't wear shell bras. Second, I think he's just attracting too much attention. His skin is still too slick and tan, his eyes too violet. Third, he's staring at the angel archway like he doesn't know whether he's remembering something he forgot. Then I realize he's actually staring at Thalia, who reached the top steps before us.

She looks at the other kids with a kind of wonder I've only shown to the roller coasters at Cedar Point. The kids let themselves linger for too long, because they just can't help it. They've never seen someone like her. Full peach lips, sharp cheekbones, and eyes so bright green they teeter on yellow. Her hair falls long and dark over her shoulders. And there, finally, you notice her ears. Still a bit too pointy.

Shit, it's already started.

Wonder Ryan walks up to her. His hands are in his pockets. He lifts his chin at her in hello. I can practically hear this conversation. I've *taught* him this conversation. "I'm sorry. You've *got* to be a transfer. I would've remembered seeing your face."

Kurt and I look at each other, and as quick as a snap, we race up the second half of the steps.

"Tristan! Where the hell have you been, man?" Ryan says. "You missed yesterday's practice. Coach is scared we're not going to have you for the championship." We slap hands side to side, fists up and down, then knuckle to knuckle in a hello. "Who's your friend, man? Don't be rude."

"My cousins," I correct. "Thalia and Kurt."

Even Ryan stares at Kurt in a way that's uncool for dudes to look at other dudes. What if this is the worst idea in the history of mankind, including the time I entered the Nathan's hot-dog-eating contest and the time I let Layla give me highlights combined?

"Cousins from where?" Ryan goes. No one has ever heard me mention any family.

"Italy."

"Florida."

"Ireland."

Part of me is kicking myself for not having planned this out smoother. The other part is mentally kicking Kurt just because doing it for real would make me feel better.

"They travel a lot."

Ryan nods with this face that screams, *OMG! I'm so interested as long as I can talk to the new girl some more.* "Are you guys going to, like, *go* here?" If he had a tail, it'd be wagging right now.

"No, we're just visiting," Kurt says.

"Oh. Well, you should bring them to the after-school practices. I'm the best archer in this city," he says, tapping Kurt on the shoulder. "Could teach you a thing or two."

"Archery?" Kurt's voice softens to something similar to a sound Layla might make if she found a CD she'd been looking for on sale. "I'm pretty good with a bow and arrow."

"He's more than *good*!" Thalia chimes in. "He's the best on the gua—"

"Team," I say quickly. "He's the best on his team."

"Good. Great. Awesome-possum." I don't think even *he* believes he just said that. And there goes Wonder Ryan running into the building, because no matter how cool and interesting we are, he has never been late to class.

I stare at the ancient clock above the angels. The Roman numerals are rusty. The arms are getting closer to 8 a.m. when the bell will ring. Layla usually waits for me inside by my locker, even though hers is on the other end of the hall.

"Are we waiting for another one of your comrades?"

"Kurt, do me a favor," I go. "Chill. Relax. Take it easy. You're in Brooklyn, not at the bottom of the sea."

He shakes his head a bit, all *I don't know what you want me to do.*

"You're standing like you're ready to whip out your sword and go all Revenge of the Merman on them."

"Ryan is handsome," Thalia says with a smirk.

"And you, missy. Calm the siren allure. I don't want any of my teammates following you off the pier."

"Sirens aren't mermaids," Thalia laughs. "They're bird women."

"Whatever. I'm just saying."

"Come now, Tristan. Maybe you *and* Kurt should, how is it you said? *Chill.*" The bells chime long and hard. Pigeons fly. Kids run up the steps holding on to their pants and hats.

"Are we waiting for someone?" Kurt asks again.

I shake my head. She should be gone by now. "Follow me."

I turn around once and see the stark happiness on Thalia's face. Her big yellow-green eyes take in every part of the school. The linoleum floors, the crackling fluorescent lights, the archaic mahogany trim along the doors, and the random stained-glass windows that clash with the new water fountains and rows of lockers. The stickers on the lockers. The murals on the walls.

We stop in front of Room 311. Mr. Adlemare looks down on us through his glasses. He wears a light blue, short-sleeved button-down shirt with red suspenders that hold up brown trousers, and I wonder, out of everything that you could wear in public, why a purple polka-dot bow tie?

"Mr. Hart. Thank you for joining us. These must be your cousins from…?"

"Italy."

"Florida."

"Ireland."

"Ah, I see."

Kurt clears his throat. "We travel constantly."

"No one place is home! Lovely. Welcome, welcome."

"Thank you, sir," my cousins say in unison.

Some people snicker. The smells of everyone overwhelm me. Their interest smells of burning sugar.

We take the row in the back, where the Goth-punk-stoner kids sit. Homeroom gets less and less crowded toward the end of the year. I stare at the scratches on my desk and admire the announcements Mr. Adlemare has written on the board. Notice the way everyone gives us a long once-over. Anything not to look at Layla, sitting there and saving me a seat like always. I can feel her eyes on me, but I won't look.

Thalia takes out a notebook and pen, and I watch her draw Mr. Adlemare's face. She's quite good actually. I draw a mustache on her portrait of Mr. Adlemare, and she bursts into her bell-chime giggles. Kurt shakes his head, disapproving.

Someone sighs angrily, and I know it's Layla. But this is the only way I know she'll be safe. I can't drag her into this freakish sideshow. This past week has been the longest we've ever really been apart. It's just, what am I going to say? *Hey, guess what? I'm a merman now.* I just have to keep ignoring her, the best friend I've had my whole life. The only girl who gets it, gets me. Yeah, I'm a good guy. But right now, looking at her as she gives up trying to catch my attention, I wonder if I have enough strength to stay away from her, even though not doing that could kill her.

When I look at the clock again, it's already time to leave. She's the first one out the door, two seconds before the bell even rings.

chapter
SEVENTEEN

Yo, Hart!" Angelo's voice carries even from down the hall. "Ball drill!" He does this every time he thinks you're not looking. I'm the only one who ever catches the ball. It's in the air before he finishes his sentence. I can catch it; I know I can. I extend my hand up and to the left, but so does Kurt. The basketball is in his hands even before I hit the wall of lockers.

"I don't remember your name being *Hart*." I push myself up right away.

The guys walk over to us. I stretch out my shoulder. Kurt throws the ball back at him. Thalia watches them carefully. They really need to stop acting like the Mermaid Brigade.

"So these are your cousins. Where are you from again?"

Kurt looks to me and I answer, "Canada."

"Aren't Canadians more—?" Bertie looks like he's trying to do $x^2 + (a + b)x + ab = (x + a)(x + b)$.

"More what?" Kurt asks.

"Pale?" And he still hasn't solved it.

"We travel a lot," Thalia says, winking in their direction. I think she likes being a teenage girl more than Kurt likes being a teenage boy.

The effect is instant, though. The boys relax their posture and are all smiles. Angelo lets his basketball drop, and it bounces across the floor, causing three freshmen to trip over it.

Bertie can't seem to decide which foot he wants to shift his weight on. "Man, where have you been? You didn't show at the Wreck and you didn't show yesterday. The team is worried about you. They think you're seeing a shrink or something. And that guy? You know? The reporter? Nikky's dad? He's writing that you're going to be shipped into one of those psych facilities. Like in the movies?

"Oh. Check this." He turns around to show us the new design etched into his almost bald head. It's a series of zigzags that makes it look like his head is getting hit by lightning. "Pretty cool, huh?"

The bell rings, and I start to wonder if I'll ever get my "cousins" to class on time.

"We got *Español*," Angelo tells me but looks at Thalia. "*Adiós, amiga*. They speak Spanish in Canadia, right?"

"Yeah, see ya," Jerry and Bertie singsong.

Once they're down the hall, we're the only ones left except for the kids who aren't going to go to class at all.

"Is there a way you can fix that? Make yourselves look different so that you don't attract so much attention?"

"We do look different. We are glamoured," Kurt says indignantly.

"It's a light spell to tone down our natural colors. We are no longer achingly beautiful. Now we're just exceptionally beautiful."

English lit is just down the hall. I open the door for Thalia. This time Layla sits in the front row facing the window so that unless you're craning your neck, you can't really see her face. That smell of burnt sugar mixed with something else is back. Ms. Pippen sits at the edge of her teacher's desk, facing the door and waiting for the latecomers. Today she's wearing a skirt that ends tightly around her knees in a purple-and-green paisley pattern and a white button-down shirt that's one button shy of being inappropriate. She has the kind of waist that looks like it disappears under the cinched belt. I bet if I put my hands around it, my fingers would touch.

Her face is delicate and pointy, with shiny brown hair that is always perfectly waved to the side. If she said she was twenty-five or thirty-five, I wouldn't be surprised. She seems more like she should be teaching first grade in 1955 rather than a high-school English class in Brooklyn circa now.

"Old habits, Mr. Hart," she says. Ms. Pippen walks over to her desk. I can smell the springy wood cleaner she sprays on it between classes. There are two piles on her desk: homework coming IN, and homework going OUT. She uses a small Mason jar as a pencil holder and a red marble apple as a paperweight.

"Now, Mr. Hart, who are these lovely young people joining us today?"

"These are my cousins, Kurt and Thalia, visiting from Canada."

Kurt says, in his awkward splendor, "But we also travel a lot, which is why we aren't so pale."

Everyone laughs a little. Look at us: it's like we've been lying our whole lives.

As everyone giggles and fawns over Thalia and Kurt and how their favorite place to visit is Italy, I let myself look over at Layla, who stares out the window. The gray overcast sky is so bright that it floods everything on that side of the room, and she's cast in this kind of angel light, her golden-brown hair loose around her shoulders. She leans her face against one hand and doodles in her notebook with the other one.

On a normal day, before the storm, we'd have written each other letters throughout the day. Nothing specific, just our ramblings. She showed me how to fold the letters into four-pointed stars. I have a whole drawer full of them. I can't remember the last time we wrote each other one, and that's when I realize I can pick out her scent mingling in the expectant burnt-sugary sweetness of everyone else. The smell of disappointment that's coming from her—crushed flowers and dew and the fog before it rains. I lay my hands flat on my desk to give me something to do, because if I don't, I'm going to get up and go to her. What is wrong with me?

"Now, because there are still a few days left to our time together, we will continue with our *Greatest Poems by the Greatest Poets* anthology. Mr. Morehouse, flip so you land on a page randomly. Please read the poem on the page."

Wonder Ryan nods, sits up straight, and flips through the pages like a deck of cards. He lays the book out flat, open to a page somewhere in the beginning. He glances at Thalia before looking down at where his index finger is pointing, and his smile falters. It's incredible: Wonder Ryan's kryptonite is poetry. "Uh, it's 'Because I Could Not Stop for Death' by Emily Dickinson."

"Lovely," Ms. Pippen says.

Wonder Ryan clears his throat and gives a *well-I-guess-I-have-to* kind of smile and reads:

> Because I could not stop for Death—
> *Uh*, He kindly stopped for me—
> The carriage held but just Ourselves—
> And, *uh*, Immortality?
>
> We slowly drove—He knew no haste
> And I had put away
> My labor and my leisure too,
> For his civility—

Someone in the back shouts, "Go, Wonder Bread!" and the short burst of jeering stops. For a moment, Ms. Pippen frowns. I wonder if she's going to reprimand him for being such a shitty reader and the class for being jerks, but then I think it's something else. She smells of lament, of the sea before the storm. Her eyes trace Ryan's face and look away just as quickly. "Interesting, Mr. Morehouse," is all she says.

116

I start to feel light-headed with all these smells mixing together. How the hell can Kurt stand this all the time?

Ms. Pippen stands right in front of Kurt. Her peach mouth is pursed curiously, and a tiny part of me is annoyed that she never looks at me like that. When Wonder Ryan has finished, she says, "I wonder if our visiting Canadian gentleman would do us the honor?"

"Yes," Kurt says. He flips open to a page in the beginning and leans against the desk with his forearms. I try to picture him with his tutors, learning whatever merfolk learn—how to catch dinner, how to avoid human nets, how to fight a pirate? He'd have no one to pass notes to, no one to throw him a ball in between classes. But he reads like a pro, enunciating everything as though he's up on stage and this is his own soliloquy.

"'Ozymandias' by Percy Bysshe Shelley."

I met a traveller from an antique land
Who said: "Two vast and trunkless legs of stone
Stand in the desert...Near them, on the sand,
Half sunk a shattered visage lies, whose frown,
And wrinkled lip, and sneer of cold command,
Tell that its sculptor well those passions read
Which yet survive, stamped on these lifeless things,
The hand that mocked them, and the heart that fed;
And on the pedestal, these words appear:
'My name is Ozymandias, king of kings:
Look on my Works, ye Mighty, and despair!'

Nothing beside remains. Round the decay
Of that colossal Wreck, boundless and bare
The lone and level sands stretch far away."

There's a silence in the room that has a lot to do with everyone staring at him. The scent of burnt sugar is so strong that it makes my stomach turn. Whatever. He's just reading. It's not *that* impressive.

"That was wonderful," Ms. Pippen says. She looks out the window, like she's trying to remember. Or maybe there's something she wishes to forget. Either way, she gives a small sigh and crosses the span of the room to the window. She cracks it open to let in the cool fog. "I believe it's your turn, Mr. Hart."

I look down at the book. I hate reading in front of people. I always stumble over the words. I'm great at making my own stuff up, but have me read Romeo's lines aloud and I fumble.

Kurt hands me the anthology, and the pads of my fingers flip through the pages, hoping to land on something written at least in the twentieth century. Then the bell rings.

"You can start us off tomorrow," Ms. Pippen says, stepping around her desk and sitting on the edge like an owl as she watches us leave her classroom.

chapter
EIGHTEEN

I'm the first one out of the classroom and into the hall.

The lights flicker, poltergeist-style.

"That has nothing to do with you, does it?"

Kurt shakes his head. "Not unless I decided to play with electricity."

"This smell thing isn't getting much better."

"That's because we're not meant to live among humans for too long, especially in such close quarters. It's making me rather land-sick, to be honest." He leans in to whisper. "Like I told you. It's a predatory scent. It's different when you sense something underwater."

"Like a shark?"

"Oh! Like a typhon eel in the reefs," Thalia answers. "Oh! Or those nasty little Buccas near the British Isles. Or those giant electric jellyfish that are hard to see. But you can steer clear of them if you can sniff them out." She taps her little nose.

I hook him and Thalia with my arms. "I know we're in New York and all, but we're trying to keep this incognito." I change the subject. "Ms. Pippen was even weirder today than usual."

"I think she might be a seer," Kurt blurts out.

"A what?"

"A seer. She can see things that exist in other planes. There are all kinds of seers. Some can see the future, some only see the past, and some can only read your soul. In Ms. Pippen's case, I think she's a very rare kind that I've only heard about. She can see the future, but only when she's entranced in the words of others. For instance, when she had us read those poems, she was probably *seeing* at the same time. Either that or she gets extremely bored listening to you all butcher the poetic form."

"There's no way. She's, like, psychic? How—"

"Hey, guys! Wait up." Ryan jogs ahead of us and slows down to a backward trot. "You guys sure do walk fast."

I've got to give it to Ryan. As annoying as he is, he's persistent as hell.

Kurt nods. I push the cafeteria double doors and am thankful for the smell of sloppy joes and curly fries mixing with whatever my sixth sense is picking up.

"He has a good heart," Kurt says, nodding slightly toward where Ryan talks to Thalia. Ryan's eyes are lit up so that they're almost as blue as mine. He runs his hand through his hair with a kind of confidence I've only seen him give his science-fair projects and election videos for student council. I wonder if I should warn him he'll never be president if he has to keep his wife in a fish tank.

"Is that a mer-thing she's giving off?"

Kurt considers this for a moment. "No, I believe it is just his pure heart."

I grab a tray and hand it to him while we wait in line. "Pure heart?"

"As in all of his intentions are pure, and that radiates off him. In other times he would have been the queen's right-hand knight, a just leader, an honest politician."

Figures. "But she's definitely glamoured?"

Kurt nods once. "Our kind is naturally alluring to humans, since humans have weak minds. Her beauty, his pure heart—they're like magnets."

"Is that supposed to be like magic?"

"It's not magic, per se. It's a trace of it. Our father had true magic. Some have more. In the old days, we were more part of the sea than human. Our powers are rooted in the elements. My father could summon fires that melted sand into glass. He was one of the main architects who rebuilt Glass Castle after a battle with some nasty fey."

"So what do you do for fire now?"

"Barter with witches. Trade with dragons, the Chinese, not the Hungarian ones, of course—" He presses against the Styrofoam tray so hard that it cracks on either side and we have to get another one. "Sometimes pirates, but they're shifty."

Pirates! The eight-year-old boy in me is jumping for joy. Okay, the thirteen-year-old. "You and Thalia don't have any *powers?*"

"Thalia can speak to her sea horse, Atticus. Our father could do that too. Thalia and I can completely shift into fish form. We get it from our mother. It's temporary but useful when you need to get into tight spaces. I believe because of that, we are most valuable to the king—"

"Like in the bathtub?" I stick out my tray, and Lunch Lady Lourdes ladles a mess of chili onto my plate. "Which I'll never forgive you for, by the way."

Kurt smiles at me and then at the extra curly fries Lourdes gives him, along with her fake-eyelashed wink. I grab two apple juices from the cooler and a water bottle. He grabs an orange juice and two water bottles. Lourdes winks at him and gives him an extra ticket for dessert.

"You know," I tell him as we make our way to where Ryan and Thalia have found the rest of the swim team, "you're going to be bad for my image."

We walk into Jerry leaning too hard against Thalia. "I bet Italy was off the hook. Angelo went one time, and he came back with hickeys everywhere."

"I'm pretty sure you're confusing hickeys with bruises," Ryan corrects.

They laugh and it makes me feel easy again. Bertie leans closer to Thalia and goes, "You like it here best, though, right? I mean, it's Brooklyn, baby."

Thalia licks the sloppy joe off her wide smile. It has the same effect on all the boys, a deep sigh I don't think they're even aware of. "It's my favorite place," she tells him.

"Really?" Kurt says. His mouth is full of fries and chili sauce, and his violet eyes glint mischievously in the cafeteria light. "I always enjoyed the Galapagos Isles."

"What's in the Galapagos?"

Her voice sends a jolt right down my center. Layla pulls up a chair beside me. The suddenness of her voice makes me jump, and I squeeze the packet of ketchup outward. A big red blob lands on a girl at the next table.

"Ugh!" she squeals. And before I can apologize, she runs off in the direction of the bathroom.

Bertie pulls over her tray of fries. He shrugs. "What? It's not like she'll have time to eat them now."

I start mixing mayo into my mound of ketchup, until the swirls of red and white become a pale orange. I dip a fry and push the tray in the middle of the table so everyone can have some.

"So these are your cousins," Layla says. There's a tightness in her voice. It may be because she doesn't believe me, or because she hasn't been invited.

"Kurt, Thalia." I clear my throat. "This is Layla."

"Nice to meet you," Thalia says. "Would you like some of Tristan's special sauce?"

Layla shakes her head, ignoring the jeers from the guys. "No, thank you."

"Is there something else you would like?" Kurt goes.

She studies his face. I wonder if she remembers him from the beach. "No, I'm fine."

Bertie burps long and hard. "Ahh. Much better."

"How come you're flying solo, Layla?" Jerry takes a break from stuffing his face with curly fries and my special sauce. "Where's your other half?"

"Yeah, well, I've been without a lot of my friends lately." She isn't wearing any makeup, but her eyes look naturally bright and sparkly. She looks past me to where Kurt is sitting, eating curly fries and drinking water like he might just die of thirst. It's her way of avoiding my face. "So how long have you guys been here?"

Kurt instantly sits up straight and smooths out the front of his shirt. He tucks a loose strand of hair behind his ear. "A few days. We're visiting."

"Right. Canada. Ireland. Italy. I remember."

"Oh, you're so quiet in classes that I wasn't sure you were listening."

She looks up at the great clock against the wall. "Does this mean you're tagging along to art next period?"

Kurt looks to me and I nod at him. "Yep, art is next with Mrs. Elise. It's basically a free period."

Part of my ignore-Layla-for-her-own-well-being plan isn't going to work as long as we're in school together. We have the same friends, the same classes. I'm not going to outright diss her in public, but I can't let her in like I've always done. I can't say, "So guess what? I'm a merman. And I'm not just a regular merman. I'm a merman who can shift into human form, *and* my grandfather, whom I've never met, is the King of the Seas." And even though I can feel the words on the tip of my tongue now that she's sitting here, something in me falters. I know I shouldn't. But she's my best friend.

"So what did you do yesterday?" I ask her. But between Thalia talking about which beach has the most naked people, Kurt explaining why surfing is underrated, Bertie showing off his supreme burping skills, and the general cacophony of phones ringing and iPods blasting, she doesn't seem to hear me.

chapter
NINETEEN

This time I'm not in the middle of the sea waiting for the glint of silver that's going to attack me in the dark.

This time I'm not the one who's drowning.

I stand on a shore of white rock I don't have a name for. It isn't shiny like marble, but it still glistens, like sand that's been compacted together with tons of tiny crystal bits. There's a giant lake in the center, the edges blurry as dreams go. Just me on the white ground watching the water.

This time the same white arms aren't reaching for the surface as on the day of the storm. This time it's Layla. Her head breaks the surface, gasping for air before something pulls her back down. I feel everything at once—the sun on my back, fear in my veins, the pit of my stomach falling, because the ground feels like quicksand and I can't move. She opens her mouth to scream, but she gets sucked beneath the surface.

chapter
TWENTY

I take a moment and breathe in deeply, closing my eyes against the dark gray sky. I don't know what I was expecting. Maybe for the school to look different, because now I'm different. Like all of a sudden everyone else is going to change just to match me, a big, freaking under-the-sea world right in front of me. And I wonder how many other people are changing just like me, well minus the fins part, but keeping it to themselves.

My body aches from lack of sleep. There was no way I could fall asleep again after that dream about Layla. Drowning. And I didn't do anything to stop it.

Maybe it's because there are only a handful of days till the end of school. Maybe it's the weather. Whatever it is, the groups of students waiting for the first bell to ring are pretty thin. A group of girls walks past me. I don't know what they're doing with those bikini straps playing peekaboo from under their T-shirts, but I don't really mind. They walk a little slower past me and Kurt and smile their lip-glossed smiles. They smell like whatever perfume they doused themselves with this morning, and underneath that somewhere they smell like the freshness that comes with having zero to worry about.

"Is there a cut day that no one told me about?" Ryan climbs the steps in twos to get to us.

"I don't think so," I say, even though he's not paying any attention to me, because he walks past me and stands directly in front of Thalia. She's wearing a powder-pink ballerina tulle skirt and a white T-shirt with sequins on it. She has on these purple stockings on that got caught on something somewhere between leaving the house and standing here, because there's a tiny run on the knee. It doesn't look bad on her, though. I think she could wear a paper bag and still be able to pull it off. Her slightly green hair shines, even in the overcast light. She sure as hell spends enough time brushing it.

Ryan looks like he's standing in front of a goddess. I wouldn't be surprised if he fell to his knees right now and asked her to marry him. The two of them smile like lunatics. Part of me wants to warn him. Part of me is glad that he gets to feel this way, even if just for a little while. The rest of me is just jealous.

The bell rings, and when I breathe deeply, I know it's Layla. I don't need a sixth sense to describe the way she smells today, like sunshine on this terribly cloudy day. I hesitate in turning around, but when I do, I only catch the tip of her swaying ponytail.

⌒

I keep in mind what Kurt said about Ms. Pippen. Today she wears an electric-blue dress that fits every single curve. It comes down to the knee, and it has sleeves and all, but man, I can't stop looking at her. There is no way that Kurt is right about her being like a psychic. I think I start to get an erection when she says, "Tristan, you're supposed to start us off today, if my memory serves me right."

And I wave good-bye to Mr. Happy.

She makes the motion of opening a book. So I flip open the *Greatest Poems by the Greatest Poets* anthology to any page and sigh. "The Young Man's Song."

"Yeats," she says, giddy. There's surprise in her eyes, and she leans forward, legs crossed, showing off her smooth calves. Her heels are yellow like sunflowers.

> I whispered, "I am too young,"
> And then, "I am old enough";
> Wherefore I threw a penny—

Thankfully, a voice crackles through the speaker. The feedback pierces my eardrums like needles. A shy voice clears its throat. "Sorry about that—microphone—I mean—Will the members of the swim team—varsity, that is—please report to the pool? Oh, at Coach Bellini's behest. I mean, request. Bye now."

I catch Ms. Pippen watching me from the perch of her desk. For just a moment, I think something passes in her eyes. What if Kurt is right? Of course he's right, isn't he? Then I realize it's just light coming from the window, beaming down on her—a stray bit of sun that breaks through the cover of clouds and halos her.

"Curious," she says. "Very well, off goes the swim team—" and we do. I motion for Kurt and Thalia to follow me, but Ryan's already got hold of Thalia's hand. On the way down to the pool we meet up with the guys, who hoot and holler over being set free from their classes.

I keep my eyes on the back of Layla's head. She doesn't even turn around to look at me. There is nothing like the silent treatment from the only girl you want to talk to.

Kurt grabs me by the elbow just outside the entrance to the pool. Bertie slides between us, and his sneakers squeak and echo against the cold tiles.

"Remember…" The stern violet eyes watch me steadily. "You will want to shift the moment you're in the water. Don't do it."

"Kurt?"

"Yes?"

"*Obviously.*"

We're the last ones to sit on the bleachers, since I couldn't find a proper practice Speedo for Kurt.

"Thanks for joining us, Hart. Hart's cousin."

Thalia pulls at the strap of her bathing suit and makes a face. "It itches my shoulders. Layla gave it to me."

My heart feels like a Hacky Sack in use when she says Layla's name.

"Now, listen here," Coach says. He hooks his thumb on the loop of his jeans and stands like the Vietnam navy vet he is. "I don't want no funny business out there. This isn't synchronized swimming. It's a goddamn race. We still got ourselves an important meet, and while schoolwork is important, you can make it up tomorrow. The meet cannot be postponed."

The team cheers. Ryan leans close to me and whispers, "Yeah, I'd like him to try to explain that one to my mom."

Coach blows his whistle. Everyone lines up for basic diving drills. Since Kurt and I were last in and last to get ready, we're at the back of the line. "So if the calamari tattoo works, then why the worries?"

Kurt frowns at me. "It's an ancient and sacred cephalopod, *not* calamari. I'm simply advising you in case you get an urge."

The only urge I have right now is to punch him in his gut, if my hand wouldn't break on his stomach. I catch Layla looking over at us before taking a dive. She breaks clean through the water, her hair wrapped into a tight bun.

"She's got a fantastic stroke," Kurt says, his eyes following her across the length of the pool.

"The line's moving." I push him along.

"Good form, Santos," Coach yells.

Maddy goes, then Thalia, then Ryan and the others.

I let Kurt go first, mostly because I'm curious to see him swim, but also because my stomach is in knots. This is the first time in a week that I'll be getting back in the water. The faster the practice ends, the sooner I'll have to get to the boardwalk. Then I'll be on some ship on the way to some island inhabited by others like me. Or unlike me, if I'm the only truly half-human merman.

At the edge of the pool, Kurt shuts his eyes briefly, as though he's saying a prayer. He stretches his arms in the air, giving him the effect of being seven feet tall, and then he bends his knees slightly and dives cleanly into the pool. He's so fast that he gets about halfway without having to surface, not that he really needs to. There's an audible moment of awe as everyone turns to watch him. Even Coach's whistle is dangling from his lips.

I suck my teeth the moment Kurt pulls himself up at the opposite end of the pool. I can do that. I *do* do that. I take a moment to breathe in the water-laden air, the smell of chlorine, the cigar scent of Coach lingering around, the burnt sweetness of curiosity that breaks through all those smells. I envision myself in the water, thinking how much I've missed it, like half of me has been hiding for days. I push away the face of the silver mermaid lurking in the back of my thoughts. I think of the sea. I think of me in the sea.

Hey, this pool works too.

I dive, harder than I really need to, so I push myself more than halfway across the pool. I let my gills open, my eyes taking in the blueness of the tiles, the lights bouncing off the surface of the water. I let myself spin in one place, then surface to stroke. The gills recede and I turn my face to breathe. I've already reached the end of the pool.

"Twenty seconds!" I've never heard Coach scream like that. "You cousin here did nineteen, but he can't compete with us next week. Holy mackerel! You swim like that, boy, and we'll be Triborough champs for the first time since I took over the team!"

I don't try to hide my smile, and I welcome the pats on the back from everyone. Except Maddy and Layla, who pretend this isn't happening. I walk past them and splash them with the water dripping from my hands.

"You're such a tool, Tristan," Layla says.

"Hey, look, you're alliterating, Ms. Pippen ought to give you an A."

Coach blows his whistle again. "All right, enough of that. I have an idea. Say this is an experiment. Hart's cousin—what's your name again there, bud?—Kurt, that's nice—Say Kurt here is the controlled experiment, and you all on my team are the uncontrolled experiment. You all have to best him. Matter of fact, Kurt's sister came in at 20.5 seconds also, so she'll be the second round. Who wants to go first?"

No one raises their hands.

No one except for Layla, who shoots her hand into the air. Always with something to prove.

Kurt's usually somber face breaks into an amused laugh.

"What's so funny?" Layla puts her hands on her hips and stares right at him. If I know one thing, it's that I don't want to be on the other side of that gaze when she's angry. It's like laser beams trying to fry your face.

"Nothing, I—"

But she doesn't let him finish. She turns from him and gets into position. This isn't the best plan Coach could've come up with. It's one thing when we're racing each other. This is like putting us in the ring with Oscar De La Hoya and calling *him* a controlled experiment.

Layla stretches her body, rivulets of water still rolling off her tan shoulders. She's the same girl who followed me out to the beach to swim the Mississippi. A wild spirit, her dad calls her. Here she is, trying to best a merman at swimming without even knowing it. It's kind of hot.

The whistle blows, and they tuck their heads and push off. If he were any kind of a gentleman, Kurt would let her win. Something tells me that he's not the kind of guy who just lets things fly. He swims as he did before, all sinew and muscle, like he's blending into the water.

Layla is about a foot behind him, which, considering he's unearthly, is pretty damn good. The only time I've ever seen her swim this hard is when we were on lifeguard duty at the YMCA pool and a little girl fell in the deep end. Talk about motivation. Maybe Coach really knows what he's talking about, mostly.

They reach one end, and Layla flips backward. She pushes herself with everything she has and is neck and neck with him, stroke for stroke, as they race back to our end of the pool. Even the girls on the bleachers stand up to get a better look. Kurt finishes first, pulling himself out of the pool in one swift motion. Layla comes up not three seconds behind, gasping for air. She rubs the water out of her eyes and pulls off her swimming cap. Her hair is coming loose from its bun and floating around her like a lily pad.

"I'm going to feel that in the morning," she says.

"Ho-ho!" Coach looks at his timer. "Not bad, Santos. Twenty-two seconds."

Kurt and I reach out our hands to pull Layla out of the pool. She stares at them, then swims across the lanes and pulls herself out.

"I'm not putting too much stress on you, am I?" Coach asks Kurt in what he thinks is a conspiratorial, hushed voice but that we can all still hear.

"None at all, sir."

"That's a good boy." Coach slaps Kurt on the shoulder and is surprised that his hand hurts after doing so.

"Who's next?"

And like pulling big rotten teeth, one by one the team goes up against Kurt. Some of them, like Jerry, get about halfway across the pool before giving up completely, and others, like Ryan, try their hardest but come in well behind. And then there's Angelo, who's waiting to race against Thalia, because he thinks it'll be easier.

"Hart, you haven't gone yet."

I stand at the mark beside Kurt. "You tired yet?"

"I believe I've only warmed up my arms," he says, flexing his bicep in the air.

"I didn't take you for an exhibitionist," I go.

"It's not exhibition. It's allowing the general public a great privilege."

"I'll go easy on you, I promise."

"Please don't. It's customary for the guard to compete against princes and princesses."

"Shhh."

Kurt breaks into a rare smile. His eyes focus on the end of the pool where Layla stands by herself, wrapped in a red and black towel. She likes to walk around the pool between drills to keep herself warm.

Coach's whistle snaps me awake, and I'm already a second behind Kurt. I don't hold back, because I know he isn't either, not for the lowly humans and not for me. We are equals, mermano-a-mermano, racing across the pool.

Then it happens.

The tingle starts at my spine, like my calamari tattoo is running out of juice. It's a craving and burning all in one, spreading along my legs, my forearms. I reach the far end of the pool where Layla stands and grab the edge, shaking the cramp out of my leg. The feeling subsides as I push against the shift that wants to burst out of me. I look up at Layla, whose eyes are wide on me. I look down at what she's staring at and see the clusters of blue scales that have popped up along my wrist. I press against them and brush them away. They dissolve into sand. I turn around and dive back in, even though I know Kurt has already beaten me. I just have to get away from her. Pretend like she didn't see anything, even though I want her to see. I want her to know, even though it'll be dangerous.

"What the hell happened there, Hart?" Coach is on me the moment I surface.

"Cramp, Coach."

"Hmm. Don't scare me, boy. We only just got you back."

Kurt holds out his arm to pull me out of the water. I'm dripping, and I feel heavy, like my tail is showing.

It isn't.

Layla isn't standing at the opposite end of the pool anymore. She's nowhere around. I avoid Kurt's stare, because I don't know if he sensed what was happening. I don't know if anyone saw. Then again, if they did, they'd be a little more shocked than now. Shocked like Layla's eyes. Something in me broke, and as Coach blows his whistle to resume the races, I'm almost positive that I wanted her to see.

chapter
TWENTY-ONE

"A re you joining us?" Kurt hovers around the entrance that descends to the locker rooms.

"I'm going to hang for a bit. I'll meet you guys outside."

"You're sure?" I don't know what it is about Kurt. His seemingly all-knowing violet eyes, his I'm-103-and-I've-seen-the-world attitude. Or just that he can see right through me.

"I need to swim."

"Take your time. Your parents aren't gathering us for another forty-five minutes." He turns and follows the echo of the rest of the team down the stairs.

Coach locked the entrance to the pool, so the only way in or out is through the locker rooms. I grab a towel from the bin, leave it at the edge of the pool with my Speedo, and jump in feetfirst. I let myself float, close my eyes, and feel the shift. I don't hold my breath as I feel the quick burn at either side of my throat where my gills open, and my legs stiffen and cramp where my fins grow. I trace the splatter of blue scales along my forearms. I swim just an inch above the white tiles, flip and twist, then lie right in the center with my arms behind my back. So this is what it's like to sleep underwater. The surface of the water dances with the light, back and forth and back and forth, making its own patterns. I wish I could stay here all day.

Then there's a splash at the end of the pool. I push myself up, willing my legs to shift back. The split is the hardest, a burning that only lasts a moment but feels like forever. My thighs cramp up on the first couple of kicks. I swallow a mouthful of chlorine when my head breaches the surface, my neck stinging where my gills have closed like shutters.

"What the hell was that?" Layla surfaces when I do. She's in her bra and panties.

And I'm naked.

I grab on to the metal steps on the end of the pool. "A little privacy, do you *mind*?"

"Oh, who cares. It's not like everyone else hasn't seen it."

"Shut up, Layla. You don't even know what you're talking about." Why is she here? I thought they were all gone. My brain is a distorted jumble of curses and poor excuses. I grab for my towel and pull myself out of the water. Bad move, bad move. I try to rub off where my scales are still dissolving into sand.

"What the hell *is* that?"

"I don't know what you're talking about." If I've gotten one thing right from my experiences with the opposite sex, it's that I know how to be a jerk.

"In the water. You were—?" She can't say it. She knows how crazy she'll sound. "I thought I saw—"

"—me naked? Congratulations. Your wildest dream come true."

She grazes her hand across the surface, splashing me. She swims to the steps and pulls herself out. She slides to the towel bin and grabs one to wrap around herself. It's too late, though. I've already seen what I needed to see. It's different from seeing her in a bathing suit all summer or during meets. This is more intimate, all lace and good-night dreams. Her hair is dark with water, curling at the tips.

"Don't tell me I didn't see what I think I just saw. You ignore me for days. And your two new mysterious cousins show up out of nowhere with matching tattoos."

I breathe in her panic, anger, sadness. "It's a family crest," I go, pulling on my Speedo under the towel.

"More like the freaky-eye cult."

I gasp. "You told me my eyes were beautiful!"

"We were *six*."

"So?"

"And you told me I was your best friend. Or did your near-death experience make you realize that I don't matter anymore?" She's reaching out to me. She holds my wrists in her arms.

I think about the whirlpool in my dreams. The silver mermaid, her sharp white teeth and eyes. Opening my eyes after the storm and seeing Layla's face, the hot white sun around her skin. The smile on her face when she realized it was me. The times we snuck into the aquarium after hours on a dare, and her face at the sight of glow-in-the-dark sea horses. If she got hurt, it would be because of me.

"I—I *can't* tell you. I can't tell you what's going on. Maybe one day. But not now."

"You can tell me anything." Her hold tightens.

"This is different—"

"But—*why?*"

When I don't answer, she looks down at our wet feet. She's giving up on me, and I'm going to let her. She's about to say something else, but we're interrupted by the loudest crack of thunder, a reminder that I have somewhere to be. "Good-bye, Layla."

I turn from her and go back into the dressing rooms, breathing in deeply so at least I can sense her near me—lavender and salt and crushed flowers, sticky between her fingertips. *She loves me not.*

chapter
TWENTY-TWO

The farther we walk along the boardwalk, the more lost in the mist we get, and the less I can make out the outline of the Wonder Wheel or anything beyond a few feet or even my mom's red hair. This doesn't feel like my Brooklyn, my Coney, my home. Something in the air, the smell of the belly of the sea churning, is a different kind of familiar. My gills itch with expectancy, a longing for something I only feel when I'm in the water.

Funny how a few days ago I was diving off the pier just for the hell of it, and Layla was diving in after me just to show everyone she could. I wish I'd said something else to her, something that might make her still have a little hope in me. I'm losing her, and in the dark fog that hugs us, I fear I already have.

Thalia grabs hold of my hand, our feet crunching on the thin layer of sand on the creaky floorboards. She sighs, and her sigh sounds like a cloud deflating. I don't know what to say to her that wouldn't seem corny. She's wearing the red and black bracelet Ryan gave her after school, a skinny rubber thing with our team logo—the Guardian Knights. She lifts her hand periodically to look at it, as though she can read the time on it.

"Tristan." My name comes out in such a whisper that I can barely recognize it as my mother's voice. Soft thunder rumbles in the distance. "We're here." She holds on to Dad's hand and leans in to kiss his cheek. I can't see his face, but I know he's looking down.

"Ready or not," Dad says in the same way he always did when we played around the apartment, the park, or the white hallways of his office building.

My eyes focus for the first time on the small wooden ship bopping along the pier. Sheer and iridescent sails puff against the breeze. Two small creatures zoom back and forth, pulling on deep green ropes, pushing crates, and rolling barrels. A line of people are making their way onto the deck one by one.

"Solitary merfolk," Kurt answers before I can even ask. "They're not bound to our court in any other way than being of the sea folk. Still, they make their offerings when we're here, just to have our protection."

Protection? Protection from what? I'm about to ask, but we've already stopped walking.

Dad pulls me into a hug, and we clap our hands against each other's backs. We've never really had to say good-bye for anything, just the one time at swim camp, and we knew exactly where I'd be going then and when I'd be coming back. Something inside me falters, but when I let go and look at the ship, look out at the darkening skies, I know there are more important things.

Mom holds my face in her hands, our eyes mirrors of each other. "Don't forget. At the offering you must only give the contents of the front pocket. The side pocket is for my father—"

"Relax, I got it," I assure her while trying to reassure myself. I sling both my arms into the straps of the backpack she stuffed with goodies for our trip.

She sighs, letting go of my face and taking Dad's outstretched hand. They walk back down the way we came and fold deeply into the mist.

—

I've already tripped on a barrel and stepped on a barnacled claw foot. It isn't exactly the perfect start to a voyage. We aren't moving yet. Kurt and Thalia lead me through clusters of creatures who stare at the Coney Island boardwalk as though they're afraid they'll never see it again. I force myself not to look at it, because part of me feels the same way.

The passengers vary. There's a family of unbelievably hot girls with green faces and webbed hands. They wear little cut-off denim shorts and bikini tops, their oversized sunglasses perched on top of their heads like plastic crowns, as if they're just going on a regular family vacay to the Bahamas or Cancun, not a floating island off the coast of New York City.

Then there's a guy with the body of a man and the head of a gray and blue fish. A tiny light hovers over his face, and I realize it's part of him—like a shiny flashlight dangling out of his forehead. He wears a traveling salesman kind of suit, and the slits on his nose wiggle against the salty wind. When his shiny black eyes catch me staring, I'm afraid he'll flip me off, or worse. Instead he bows.

Here we go again with the bowing.

A boy runs past me; a woman with curling brown hair chases after him. She picks him up, and he struggles against her until she reprimands him in his ear. He looks like he's wearing a turtle backpack, but as we pass them I can see the hard shell is part of him. She picks a spot with an excellent view of the shore. Then I notice her arms. They have no bone in them. Where there should be fingers are tiny suction cups that shift back and forth from fingers to tentacles.

And then there's a guy. Just an average guy, a little older than me with dark jeans, black leather boots with archaic crosses on the shins, a long-sleeved black T-shirt, and disheveled brown hair. He wears a baseball cap to the side and chews on a coffee straw. He's leaning against the side of the boat, watching and holding a small cardboard box with MTA stickers on it. He winks at me as we walk past, which is weird, but finally someone who doesn't bow.

"Let's go meet the captain," Thalia says. In her ballerina skirt, she looks more like a regular girl than a sea creature. She leads us to the mast of the ship. Out here is just the horizon. Kurt knocks on the mast. There's a series of squeaks, like rope and metal being pulled. A deep voice comes out of the darkness and says, "Kurtomathetis, I was wondering when you would make it."

Thalia puts her hands on her hips and looks up at him. "But we're ahead of schedule!"

I follow their stare up and over the front of the ship. Where there would be some carving, like a dragon on the Viking ships they had at the Met, is a merman. From the waist up he has the V shape of a football player. His hair seems to be alive in full black curls. His shoulders have splotches of golden freckles where the sun hits the most. He bows his head with a kind smile.

Arion grabs the conch strung over his chest and blows it. The sails expand, and even though there is no strong wind just now, we start moving. The ship is alive with excited whispers. I hold on to the front of the ship, my legs feeling wobbly as we start moving. I'm really doing this. Oh, god, I'm really doing this.

"Lord Sea—" the captain says to me.

"You don't have to call me that," I shout over the small wave that crashes against us.

Arion looks taken aback. His dark eyebrows knit together, and his black eyes look over his shoulder at me. "What shall I call you?"

"Tristan is fine."

"Tristan." He tastes my name on his tongue, pronouncing it a few times before he's confident about addressing me so informally. "Son of?"

"David Hart?"

"Tristan Hart, son of David Hart. Welcome aboard."

I'm too stunned. "What are you?"

"A merman like yourself."

"But you're, like, attached to the ship."

We make a sudden turn to the left. "Whoa," he says. He raises

146

his hand and makes a pulling motion. A sail drops. He uses his left hand to slap at the air, like he's trying to parallel park. Behind me the ship's steering wheel mimics his hand movement.

"How are you part of this ship?" I ask.

"I have carried my father's debt to the king," he says. No big deal.

"What do you mean? What did he do?"

"I was a boy. It is so long ago I cannot remember. My father had the choice of being executed or indentured to the king. He was to serve millennia guiding the ship between Toliss and whatever coasts the Sea Court happens to visit. But my father grew old, and his sentence was carried over to me."

"That doesn't seem fair."

"That is the way it is, Tristan Hart."

Arion's baritone laugh sounds like the conch strapped to his chest. He touches the tip of his bushy black beard. He finds something in it, a tiny crab, and pops it into his mouth like a grape.

"Guess you never go hungry," I go. "But how do you sleep?"

"The sails, they're quite soft."

"Way to look on the bright side." I wonder what other kinds of punishments my grandfather has given out, and if I were king, whether I could ever do the same.

There's another bang, and this time the rain breaks. It isn't cold, thunderstorm rain. It's soft, like passing through a warm curtain. "We've crossed the wall." Arion calls out.

"Should we go below deck?" I instantly regret asking.

"We are of the sea, Tristan. No one objects to getting a little wet."

Thalia's laughter is contagious. Here the clouds break up. This is the first stretch of sky I've seen in weeks. Around me, the other passengers lift their noses to the sky or reach their hands over the side of the ship, where water will splash and lick their fingertips. Or tentacles, whatever the case may be. The only one I don't see in the crowd is the human guy with the cardboard box. Surely he did oppose getting a bit wet.

"Hang on tight, Lord Tristan!"

My stomach plummets with that tickling roller-coaster feel. I even let myself scream. A small wave pushes us past the wall.

"There's that," Kurt says.

And yeah, there is that. Behind us, the wall of warm rain stands still. It marks the last of the ugly rain clouds that have latched on to the sky for the past few days. I can see the horizon ahead, and it is grand. The sun has begun to rise on this side of the wall. It's been so long since I've seen the sky. I'm about to tell Thalia as much, but then—

That's when I hear her.

No. No, no, no, no.

"Let me go! Get your slimy hands off me."

No.

The sound of feet hitting wood.

People shoving.

The pulling and pulling of limbs.

"Intruder!" someone yells.

"Get *off* me!"

It's coming from the main deck. The crowd gathered there reminds me of when fights break out in school. Everyone gathers around in a circle watching the brawl. Layla is being dragged across the deck by two guys who are stronger than they look. Their bodies are wire thin, with mostly human faces, and the scalps of sea urchins. They hold her wrists and ankles and sling her onto the center of the deck.

I've never seen Layla's eyes this wide. One by one she stares at the faces on the ship until she finds me in the crowd. Tiny gasps of air leave her lips, like she's trying to breathe and hiccup at the same time.

A second set of footsteps rushes up to the deck. The guy and his cardboard box.

"Arion," one of the urchin guys says. "She is an intruder."

The black ropes that bind Arion to the front of the ship stretch, pushing him up so he can turn around and look down at the scene. He glances back at the island. The speck of land is getting bigger by the second. "State your name and how you managed to get on board."

"Layla," I blurt out. "Her name is Layla. She's my friend."

"Yours?"

"Yes."

She pushes herself up, standing with her hands down and out to create a barrier between herself and us. When did I become the us?

The urchin boy stands with his hands at his sides. Now I can see his face. His nose is like a button pushed down on his face, which from the temples up to the top of his hair is dark blue. He points to her without smiling. "It is against the king's wishes that humans enter the island. Unless, of course, they're for play."

The other boy, almost a replica, only more purple, smiles wickedly.

"P—play?" Layla's eyes remind me of the insides of a Magic 8 Ball, moving around dizzily, trying to predict what might just be unpredictable.

"She must be sequestered until the king can decide her fate."

The crowd gasps. The only human guy chews on his toothpick and scratches the back of his head, then puts his cap back on. He cranes his head to peek at the horizon. We are very, very close.

The urchin guys grab her, one by each hand. She kicks and screams, her eyes burning holes through me.

"Wait, wait a minute." I jump from the top deck, where I've been standing, to land on my feet. "She's off limits. Didn't you hear me before?"

The blue one puffs his skinny, nonexistent chest at me. "Yeah, I heard you. What of it? Rules is rules."

"You've got no authority, half-breed," the purple one says.

Half-breed? No one's ever called me that.

"Even though I am not *your* king, I'm still the king's grandson. I'm of the royal—royal f-family." I catch Kurt's eyes and take his small nod as a sign that I'm on the right track. "Unless *you* want to explain to the king how *you* let a human best you and board your ship."

The urchin brothers back down, but not without showing how deeply they'd probably want to ram their spiky little heads into my gut. The crowd looks pretty bored with us, and the group breaks up little by little. Some of them bow to me before turning away to mind their business, and others look down their noses—or the equivalent—at me, cursing me in grunts. Some are just completely disinterested and continue to stare out at the water.

Arion clears his throat. "Lord Sea is right. She can stay with him. The Sea King will decide her penalty—"

"*Penalty?*" Layla and I blurt out the word at the same time.

"Outcome," Kurt corrects, but that doesn't make it any better. My dream of her drowning flashes in my mind.

"Come with me." I shove the two urchin boys off her and pull her with me, tripping down the stairs and landing below deck. "What. Are. You. Doing. Here?"

She's shaking. She lets go of my hand and wraps her arms around herself. Her wrists are red where the urchin boys were holding her. Something in me is on fire. I want to hold on to her and tell her that it's going to be okay, even though I don't even know what we're going to see when we reach the shore.

"What am *I* doing here? What are *you* doing here? Where is *here?*"

"A ship? The water?" I reply.

"Do *not* mess with me right now, Tristan!" The low light of the gas lamps around us casts shadows over her face so that all I can see are cheeks, lips, eyes. She looks away, sniffling.

"Is this what you couldn't tell me? You joined a—circus?"

Wow, I wish I'd thought of that one.

"How did you even get on board? *Why* would you even get on board is probably the better question."

"To help you, *duh*? I thought you were involved in some Sharks versus Jets kinda crap."

I rub my palms on my face. "Well, there are sharks."

I lean against a stack of barrels. How did I even get here? I'm the worst at protecting the people around me.

The stairs creak under Kurt's weight. I recognize his sneakers as he makes his way down. He stands like a soldier, stone faced, arms behind his back. His stance totally clashes with the outfit and his windblown hair. His eyes scan Layla's face. "I can't promise that you will be completely safe. But, as you are important to Tristan, you are important to me. We will do all we can to keep you safe."

She takes a step forward, and the light from upstairs shows the red corners of her eyes, the dry trails of dirty tears. "I hate you," she tells me. "Who the hell are *you*?" she asks Kurt. "His Canadian-Irish-Italian cousin?" She turns back to me. "How long have you been lying to me?"

Seven days, six hours, and forty-five minutes, I want to say.

The ship shakes, and a barrel falls out of place, knocking me to the side. Layla falls forward and Kurt catches her. He helps her to her feet. *Don't worry about me, guys, I'm fine. Just almost got flattened by whatever is in those barrels.*

"We're almost there," Kurt says.

"No shit, Legolas," Layla snaps.

Kurt stares at her. I don't know if he's going to kill her or let my grandfather do it. "How much does she know?"

"Sharks," I answer.

He nods, even though it shouldn't make sense. "Very well, keep it that way for now. She needs to see for herself. Perhaps we can interest the king in her."

"Eww, no way!"

"Not like that, stupid." I try not to picture Layla in a metal bikini being offered as a trophy bride to the King of the Seas. "Wait, it's *not* like that, right?"

"Hmm? Oh, of course not." Kurt shakes his head in that way he does when he sighs *humans*. "Do you have anything to offer the king, besides your virtue?"

I don't know whose jaw drops lower, mine or Layla's. I can smell her anger like lit kerosene. She balls up her fists and steeps in her own fury. Upstairs the footsteps have faded. Thalia sticks her head into the opening. "We're here. Hurry up. *Vamos!*" She quotes my dad, and I can hear her scamper around on the deck.

Kurt grabs onto the ladder and stops halfway up. He bends down so he is face-to-face with Layla, their noses just shy of touching. For a moment, I think he's going to hit her. But then he says, "Whatever you do, do not leave Tristan's side."

I can practically hear her roll her eyes. Up on deck, the sun shines so brightly that I have to shield my eyes against it.

"Where did this come from?" I hold my arms out and welcome the sun against my face. My body is buzzing with excitement, like the first time I rode a wave, when I changed into my fins in the pool earlier, or when Layla gave me CPR the day I washed up from the storm.

"Welcome, young Tristan," Arion says. The ship bops in the still, crystal-blue water. I stand on the ledge of the ship to jump off. I fall on my ass in the water. The water is the Goldilocks kind of perfect. I want to splash around in it.

Layla and Kurt are already on the beach. The sand is white with black freckles. My flip-flops have come off, and they float on the surface. I grab them and make my way to my friends. Layla is staring at the golden specks on Arion's shoulders. Or maybe she's just staring at his shoulders. Everything looks too vivid here. His skin is more bronze than an hour ago, his hair slick and black, his onyx eyes like inky pools. Under the live black ropes that wrap around his tail, the scales glisten in black and white flecks.

"Holy-shitake mother-flower mushrooms," she says.

I turn to Kurt and Thalia, who stand in their wet clothes holding on to their shoes. They also look more radiant. This is what they look without their glamours, like the raw colors of a prism. Thalia is greener than before, her hair no longer a subtle black-green. She spins on the sand, the bottom of her dress puffing out in a circle. Kurt's tanned skin has a slight golden tinge. His violet eyes look more like crystal. I wonder if I look any different.

Layla's still staring at Arion, who bows to her. "I apologize for my crew. They're a bit angry."

"Are they also repaying sentences to the king?" I ask.

Arion laughs. "No, they're just urchins."

"Thank you, Arion," Kurt says.

"Give my best to the king."

"We shall."

I give him one final wave. The human boy stands waiting with his boots dug into the sand. He holds the cardboard box at his side.

"What's in the box?"

"A gift to the Sea King from the Thorne Hill Betwixt Alliance."

Kurt doesn't seem too pleased with whatever that is. "You know they'll give it to the elders before they give it to the king."

The guy pretends to ignore Kurt and holds out a hand to me. "Marty McKay." He looks at Layla. "First time on the ship, I take it?"

She nods, a sheer layer of sweat makes her glisten in the sun. "Aren't you boiling? It's like a million degrees."

Marty smiles. "I keep cool. You're in for a treat. You know, if the king doesn't get all off-with-your-heady." He traces his index finger across with his neck.

"Don't listen to him," Thalia interjects. "Our court is more civilized than whatever happens on land."

"Tell that to the guy stuck to the ship with electric tape."

Kurt points a finger at Marty. "I don't know who you are. I assume you're part of the peace treaty, but I will not have you besmirch the king on our own land."

"Whoa, easy. I kid. I joke. I make funnies."

He seems harmless enough. He has a good handshake, and as weird as this sounds, he smells clean—like clear water.

"Sheesh. Mermen. Feisty as hell."

"Hey!" I resent that.

Layla shakes her head, and her hair is wild around her shoulders, like whatever is going on in her head is spreading like wildfire. "Mermen?"

"Ta-da!" Marty puts the box on the sand and stretches his hands toward me. Jazz hands.

She laughs. "Get the—"

"—mother-flower out of here?" He picks the box up again. "I most definitely will not. Baby cakes, we're on an island that is quite literally stealing the sunshine out of our world with that misty curtain over yonder. The tsunami wave last week, the disappearances on the beach, the funny things you think you see from the corners of your eyes when you're out shopping for underwear?" He raises his eyebrows at her, and I'm about to take back my approval rating. "All of it is because the all-powerful, ancient-as-hell Sea King is having a fantastic feast in honor of his grandson." He stretches only one hand at me. Jazz hand.

Layla looks at Kurt and Thalia, then back to Marty. She stares at the white sand and the water stretching across the sand to wrap around her ankles before retreating back into the ocean. Her eyes fall on Arion's ship. She looks up at me with those golden doe eyes. Everything I've been keeping from her, from the moment I sprouted a tail, boils down to Marty McKay and his jazz hands. Finally she says, "I'm not speaking to you."

She doesn't have to whip her hair at me as she gives me her back. The wind does that for her. She grabs Marty's hand, and they walk toward the inside of the island.

"Do you even know where you're going?" Kurt calls after them.

Marty turns around, way too happy for a human on a deserted island full of supernatural creatures. But, hey, he seems like he's used to it. "Follow the yellow brick road, right?"

"He's funny," Thalia says. "I hope the guards don't kill him."

"If they don't," I go, "I think I will." It feels nice making empty threats. As king, I may not get that luxury.

chapter
TWENTY-THREE

The moment I turn away from the stormy horizon is the moment that this is for real. Arion's ship is a diminishing speck getting closer to the wall that hides the Coney Island shore—the pier where I put my hand under Catherine Valdorama's bikini top when we were thirteen. The pretty nurse who gave me my tetanus shot when I cut my arm on a broken beer bottle after diving for a volleyball spike. All of that seems like it happened to a different person.

Thalia tugs on the strap of my backpack, because I keep stopping to stare—at the violet flowers that bloom like stars and the sparkling white sand. I grab a handful of it and let it slip through my fingers.

Tall, slender trees form a path into the island. Their leaves are a raw green. I pull on one and rub the leafy skin between my fingers. There's a thin layer of water on them, and when I let it go, the other leaves spray me with a thin mist.

Thalia sings a wordless melody, and soon enough we all march to her rhythm as though she's our pied piper.

The trail leads us to the mouth of a river. There's an archway with pillars that would better fit an ancient Greek temple. But perhaps this is their temple, their church on the sea. I remember asking my mom why we didn't go to church like Layla and her parents, and she'd say, "Because we have this," lying out on the Coney Island sand with her toes tucked under the surf.

Little things like that make more sense now.

The pillars themselves are majestic: each has a long trident mounted on the front, like the tattoo that decorates my spine. I can feel the magic pulsing through my being, the ink mingling in my blood somehow.

Sea lions are sunbathing on stones the color of their skins, so they blend into each other. They raise their heads, and when they see us, their bodies shimmer and they become slender girls who dive right into the river. They bop in and out of the water, joined by young mermaids and iridescent fish and some things I don't even have names for. They simply follow us with their chimed laughter.

The ground beneath us glitters. The river ends in a waterfall that falls like silk against the boulders. Somewhere inside me, this place seems familiar, like something out of a dream that I can't remember. Layla and Marty have stopped here to wait for us. "I guess this is where the yellow brick road ends."

"At least we don't have to cross a field of opiatic poppies." Marty laughs curtly, then adds nervously, "Right?"

"Is there a shortcut?" Layla shields the sun from her eyes as she looks up to the top of the waterfall. The wall keeps going up even past the source of the water.

"Court is behind this wall," Kurt answers stiffly. "Just—stop asking so many questions."

She's about to argue, but she catches my eye, and I give her my most pleading look to let it go.

"The other way is through the tunnels underwater," Thalia adds. "But those are not for foot-fins. The only way is up."

Marty looks to Layla and mouths, *Foot-fins?* She shakes her head and shrugs.

I place a hand on the rough rock wall. Carved steps in the rock slope up to the top, as though whoever was sculpting the stairs wanted to keep them hidden. From this angle, it looks like they lead right up to the sun.

"At least you know there's only one way up or down." Marty swallows hard, tapping his fingers nervously on his box.

"I'll lead the way," Kurt grumbles.

"You okay?" I whisper to him.

He holds on to a root protruding from the earth and uses it to pull himself up, three steps at a time. His violet eyes glance at Layla, who looks as at home behind me as she does on the rock-climbing wall at the Y. "I have a lot of explaining to do," Kurt says.

"She's not your responsibility," I go. "She's mine."

"Still, I should know better."

I think if I pat him on the back sympathetically, he'll push me right back down the steps. I wonder what it feels like to always be so wound up. If Kurt is this way and he's doing all he can, what am I going to do with an entire civilization on my shoulders? For an ancient being, my grandfather sure has a lot riding on a teenage nothing from Brooklyn.

I stop to catch my breath and wriggle out the cramp in my fingers. I wonder if Kurt resents me for being such a pain in the ass and having to play baby-sitter not just to Thalia but to me too. And for real this time, I'm going to make an effort to be nicer to him.

"Surely you can keep up," he says when he notices I've slowed down behind him.

Maybe I'll start being nicer to him tomorrow.

⁓

The sun beats hard on the ground, which has thin cracks running all through it. From up here I can see the way the thin river snakes through the forest of misty-leaved trees, the pillars that mark the entrance, the shore where the tide has already erased our footprints from the shore, the horizon, the wall, the point where the clouds turn dark—and behind that, Coney Island.

"Quite a sight for someone who's never seen it before," Kurt says, pulling me up first, then Layla. She teeters with the newness of this height and grabs onto Kurt's shoulders digging into his skin with her yellow nails. Her eyes focus on the pitfall, the way the dark green of the forest melts into the waterfall so it looks like a cloud of mist. I can hear her gasp, and I don't know if it's because she's scared of falling, or because she's looking into Kurt's eyes and is surprised by their color. She looked at me that way once.

"Hot damn!" Marty holds the cardboard box over his head in a triumphant pose. "I'm the ultimate king of the world."

Thalia pokes him in the stomach, and he tenses up completely.

"No tickling unless we want me to plummet to certain doom."

And it is a most certain doom. Below us is a sight I have no name for—grotto, oasis, mermaid paradise? It's like someone took an ice-cream scoop and hollowed out the back side of a mountain and left this. A lake the size of two Olympic-sized pools is nestled in the ground. It's light blue at the top, and the bottom fades into black. Smooth boulders line the sandy lake that sparkles in the direct sunlight. When the shiny things move, I realize it's not the rocks that are glittering but the mermaids curled and napping in the sun.

I knock some loose rocks with my foot. They fall over the ledge, bouncing off the side of the cliff rock wall until they hit the ground. Heads snap up, one by one, like piano keys picking themselves up after a finger slides all along the keyboard. There's a section at the other end of the lake where the leaves are the size of car doors and hung with sheer draping like the sails on Arion's ship.

The mermaids below sigh and gasp. There aren't any OMGs or WTFs or Can-you-believe-its? These sounds are the highest notes on a violin, a melody that is so pleasant I never want it to stop. And for the first time, I wonder if this is what I sound like when I talk, even if it's just a fraction of this?

Kurt leads the way down. Along the side of the cliff is a narrow ledge that zigzags all the way down so we have to press our backs to the wall and walk sideways. The entire court is watching our descent, and suddenly I wonder if I'll ever stop feeling like a sideshow attraction.

I've grown up with pictures of mermaids in my mother's books, and I've been to the Mermaid Parade every year since I can remember. Lots of fishnets and seashell bras. Nothing like the girls clustered down there like handfuls of Skittles. They perch on flat rocks with their fins dipped in the water. Seal girls stand on the shore in their nakedness, hair flowing over their breasts. They wave at us and blow kisses. They push their hair away from their faces and gather it over one shoulder. They wink and let loose with their beautiful voices again. They shine like stars floating on the sea, tails licking at the water from their perches.

I wonder if anyone else's tongue feels as dry as mine.

When we hit the ground, Marty holds on to his box for dear life. "Remind me to bring a snorkel for the tunnels next time around."

We walk along the water. Groups of mermaids gather under the fan-like leaves of tall trees. I try not to stare, but this kind of weird is different than seeing a guy in drag on the subway: these are mermaids. Some have slender pixie faces with long ears that point out through their hair. Their fins fan wide and outward, elegant and in a burst of scales that vary from subtle yellows to pinks. There is a girl so small and purple that when she smiles her black teeth are jolting. There is a woman with long blond curls holding a baby mermaid in her arms. It wriggles—well, like a fish—and points at us.

I nudge at Layla and point out the baby. "That's how I was born." And she stares at the family too, wonder and confusion blurring her hazel eyes. She takes my hand because maybe she feels how freaked out I am, and maybe she is too, but at least we're together. At least I can share this with her. She points at the guards. "How come the gladiators are on feet too?"

"Something about a squid tattoo," I joke. "I promise I'll tell you later." She squeezes my hand in reply.

The soldiers wear metal shields that cover their chest and a chain-link skirt sort of thing that covers their junk, which I guess makes for an easy shift. They wear gold cuffs on each wrist. Walking past them is like casually walking past a line of armed marines. *Don't mind us, we were personally invited by the king; pretty please keep those sharp and deadly swords in their scabbards.*

Past the guards are tent-like sections housing what must be the court merfolk Kurt mentioned once, the ones who are allowed to have feet. These princesses aren't like the mergirls baking on the rocks. These sit up tall. Their scales form around their breasts. Their long hair is gathered and looped through all sorts of shells, dripping with pearls and golden baubles.

One is the most breathtaking of them all, a girl with white-blond hair twisted around an open conch shell. She holds my stare with her gray eyes. She sits at the foot of a guy who reminds me of a naked grizzly, all shoulders and chest and full beard. He crosses his arms over his chest and gives me his cheek. Well, that's not a good way to make friends, is it?

Past the row of decadent tents is a line of the others who were on Arion's ship with us. They stand on either side of the throne. They're holding gifts. I feel for the backpack my mom filled up for me.

And there is a deep *Ahem*, like the sea itself is clearing its throat.

I turn slowly, my eyes flitting from the gray-eyed princess to the rows of guards who kneel, to the merfolk in the water whose heads are bowed. Kurt and Thalia are kneeling. Marty takes a cue and does the same. So does Layla.

I don't know if it's the shock of his face or just because I'm stupid. But I just stand there. There he sits, like a statue that belongs in the middle of Central Park. He is taller than me, taller than anyone I've ever seen in my life. With legs like tree trunks and with his ankles covered in scales and tiny barnacles. They glisten with water and light. The hairs on his legs are golden against skin that is tanned like well-beaten leather, a lifeguard's tan like mine. He wears the same warrior metal as the others, but his armor looks worn from decades of sea air. The scattered scales along his arms and legs are the color of the sky just before twilight, a blue that is hard and endless.

The Sea King.

"Hello, Tristan." His is a deep baritone, a conch shell with an endless hollow. And my mind goes completely and totally blank, like staring at a test that I know the answers to but stayed up too late studying for and forgot.

So all I can say is, "Uhh. Hi."

And that's all I've got.

chapter
TWENTY-FOUR

My grandfather.

The Sea King.

White hair curls around his shoulders. He has a short beard, like General Grant and George Clooney, and I wonder if that is how I'll look when I'm his age. If I ever get to be a couple of thousand years old.

"You brought us something?" His turquoise eyes, framed by a strong brow and bushy gray eyebrows, look to Layla and then back at me.

"Uhh—" I bow awkwardly before taking a step forward. "No, no. She's a friend."

Kurt stands and walks over us. "It is my fault, sire. She—"

"No, it's *my* fault—" Layla says.

"Lord Tristan, I take responsibility—" Kurt tries again.

"I say they blame it on the urchin brothers," Marty chimes in.

To the right of my grandfather, a little green boy with webbed feet and a raw redness around his gills, like acne for merkids, blows on the golden conch strapped around his chest.

"Now," the king says. "You, girl, state your name and purpose."

Layla stands with her hands shaking at her sides, like the time her dad caught us drinking his imported Ecuadorian beer in their basement. My heart skips with the fear that she might not say anything. Or the completely wrong thing.

"My name is Layla Santos. I am—"

"She's my friend," I say. Kurt presses his hand on my chest, because I'm standing. He pushes me back down to sit and shakes his head. With his face all serious and the sun hitting right in his eyes, I can almost picture what he'll look like when he gets older. Kind of like my grandfather. He whispers to me, "Let her speak."

"Am—Tristan's best friend."

The court breaks into cafeteria-style jeering and cackling, only broken up by another honk from the little green boy.

"And how did you get on my ship?"

"I didn't mean to. Tristan and I were fighting at school, and he was all vague and *I can't tell you.* I thought he was in trouble. So when the—they—the urchin men?—were pulling up the ladder to set sail, I just jumped on and hid below the deck. It was busy, too many people moving around. No one noticed me."

"You thought my grandson was in danger, so you stowed away on a ship despite your own safety?"

She nods. I'm ready for him to laugh, to tell her she's a tiny human and squish her between his giant fingers.

He bends forward and down to her so that he can get a closer look at her face. Something passes over his turquoise eyes—amusement.

I recognize the way he goes from serious to smiles in seconds like my mom does. "You are a most brave girl."

Layla smiles at him, and the effect is the same that she has on anyone: it warms him. I can see it in his face. It looks like it's going to be all right, but someone in the crowd yells, "Intruder!"

And that's followed by "Land-dweller!"

"Skin-sack!"

"Trespasser!"

"Punish her!"

I turn around, but the taunts come from everywhere at once, so I can't point out the source. I shut my eyes against a sudden ache that goes away as quickly as it came. I can recognize the hunger in their gem-colored eyes. It's the same hunger as the silver mermaid in my dreams—empty, expecting.

The king taps his lips with a finger, thinking. "My dear, do you know where you are?"

She hooks her thumbs on the loops of her shorts. "Apparently, an island with mer—maids?"

"Merfolk, if you wish," he says shortly. "What you are seeing is not something we allow humans to walk away from. Not alive, anyway. It is how things have always been."

"What about him?" I point at Marty.

"He is not exactly—human—as she is," my grandfather says.

Not human? He looks human enough. Marty shrugs, standing there with his cardboard box.

"I would offer you a chance to stay and live with us, as you

168

don't seem much of a threat. However, I do not think that is an option for you."

She shakes her head slowly, panicked eyes searching my face. I'd like to try to explain to Mr. Santos—*Sorry, sir, but I had to leave Layla on a mystical island with my other half of the family because she just doesn't listen. Please don't take out that machete you have from your time in the Ecuadorian army.*

"Very well." He nods, and I get ready for him to trace his finger across his neck and a guard to take her away. Instead he says, "You will have to make an offering. As you were all late, you will be the last ones to offer your tithes."

I breathe a little easier. We sit to the right of the throne on a row of boulders and watch as one by one, everyone who was on the ship with us steps up to my grandfather's throne, bows, and presents a gift on a giant shell held on either side by boys who look like miniature versions of the gladiator guards, tattoos and all. The offerings are anything from jewelry trinkets to crayons to Pillow Pets to hammers to what look like pieces of bicycles.

I lean closer to Kurt, "What happens to all that stuff?"

"It gets distributed among everyone."

The turtle boy reaches up to the shell and drops in a toy, probably his favorite one by the pout on his face and the way he pulls away when his mom tries to put her arm around him.

It's our turn.

Marty, the human-looking non-human, hands the cardboard box to the king directly.

"Representing the Thorne Hill Betwixt Alliance, I, Marty McKay, present your Sea Lordiness with a gift."

One of the guards moves as though to take the box, but the curiosity on my grandfather's face radiates. He holds up his palm, and the guard returns to his post.

"May I?" Marty pulls off the red-and-white MTA tape and reaches inside the box. He pulls out a long, rectangular glass box. Inside is a cluster of neon flowers that glow in whites and pinks and purples, their stems twisting on themselves, alive.

"Orchids. They grow in salt water, best in the shade," Marty says.

The king's laughter is booming, wondrous. "This is most acceptable." A girl, a slightly bluer version of Thalia, walks up and carries the flowers away. Marty bows and steps to the side, which leaves just me and Layla.

I do as my mother said and unzip the backpack. I empty out the front pocket onto the shell tray. It's all computer parts and mismatched pieces of earrings and bracelets that my mom keeps in one of her treasure trunks. I unzip the small front pocket and pull out a captain's eyepiece. It's made of a bronzed heavy metal. I pull it to its full length and hand it to my grandfather.

He holds it to his eye on the wrong end, and I hold back a laugh, because I don't want to be the one to tell the old man that he's holding the glass by the wrong end. But he corrects it himself and jumps a bit when he holds it right at my face. He laughs, a rumble like thunder, and claps his thigh. "Tell my daughter she still knows me well."

Sure. Good. Glad you like it. I wonder what kind of grandfather he would have been if he were in my life. Would he have broken the fifty-year rule and come to see me sooner? Would he have dressed up for Christmas and been a wet Santa with treasures from the bottom of the sea? Would he have taught me whatever mermen teach each other? I absently run my hand along my smooth chin. He wouldn't have to teach me how to shave. But maybe how to catch a mermaid?

"And now," he says as he looks down at Layla. "For you."

The whispering and giggling starts again. How am I supposed to be their king when they clearly don't even like humans?

Layla digs into her pockets. She's got on these shorts that show off her golden, powerful legs. She pulls out a pack of gum. She pulls off a sliver and puts it in her mouth. She chews and chews and nothing is happening, so the laughter continues.

She blows a bubble between her lips until it gets as big as a basketball, and then it pops. Some of the court mermaids jump at the echo of the pop; they touch their coiled hair and fix their pearls as though they're appalled that she would dare frighten them so. Behind us the mermaids watching the spectacle from the fringes of the lake smile with approval, and part of my nervousness washes away.

Layla hands the pack to my grandfather, who takes it almost greedily. He does as she did, and soon all the wrappers are scattered around his feet. I think about when Layla and I had contests to see who could fit the most gum into our mouths, and our jaws would hurt from chewing so much. She smiles with her mouth full of gum now, the same way she did then.

My grandfather chews and chews. "Masticating food that never ends. Wonderful. It reminds me of eating various fruits all at once."

Marty leans into my ear and whispers, "I haven't the heart to tell him that there are zero fruit servings in that pack of gum."

When the king frowns, my heart sinks. "The flavor is all gone."

The mer-court jeers. My grandfather, the Sea King, swallows his gum and sits back, pleased with himself.

It's strange, almost painfully funny, how I have never known him, and suddenly, unexplainably, out of thin air, I love him. I see my mother in him, and I wonder if I'm in there too.

He bows his head to Layla, the lines around his eyes spread with a smile. "I accept your gift. And you are welcome as a guest of Tristan Hart."

She bows her head to him and links her fingers with mine. Everything about her is buzzing, and that makes me drunk and happy and dizzy. Since we're both alive, I guess this means *she loves me*.

chapter
TWENTY-FIVE

An orchestra plays cellos and violins that look like they were made from the mast of a ship and strung with gold, and trumpets and horns made out of endlessly coiled shells.

My eyes are everywhere at once—the girls jumping off rocks, the women holding merbabies, the princesses mingling in their private but open tents. I try to picture my mother sitting by the throne under one of those canopies with her hair done up in shells and pearls, watching as purple girls play the harp for her. I can't see her there trying to be a good and proper princess. I know she'd be in the middle of the lake, dancing, mingling, being the life of the party.

We pick food off opulent trays passed around by more pretty pink girls who might actually be boys. It's hard to tell. Layla elbows me because I'm not eating enough. She says it's rude to not eat everything they give you. Like the time her dad made some Ecuadorian delicacy, which was really just guinea pig, which, no matter how you cut it up and put it on the grill, is just a big fat rat. But I ate it then, just like I'm eating whatever this delightfully green chewy stuff is now. For Layla.

Marty sucks on the inside of a clam, which makes Layla wrinkle her nose.

"Unlike other fey," he says, "merpeople are the only ones whose food you can eat. Land fairies can keep you in their courts if you so much as lick honey from their spoons—or various other parts—"

Layla snorts, taking a sip from a fizzy pink liquid. Her eyes squint when she smiles so hard. I never noticed how long her eyelashes are, how black against the smooth honey of her eyes.

Marty hits me in the shoulder to get my attention. "Hey, Tristan, check this. What do you call a thirteen-year-old mermaid?"

I shake my head and Layla shrugs. "What?"

"A *mer*teenie!" He slaps his knee and wipes a fake tear from the corner of his eye.

Layla rolls her eyes but laughs as well. "Lame."

For the first time, I notice Kurt's scowl is missing. I spot him over by the tents shaking hands with some older men. "Who are those guys Kurt's talking to?" I ask Thalia.

Her yellow-green eyes narrow. "Ugh, that's Elias. He's the son of Ellion, herald of the East. They're nasty folk. Nasty, nasty."

"Tell me how you really feel," Marty coos at her, wrapping an arm around her shoulder.

I've never heard Thalia dislike anything, so in my book they're not good news. Elias is the grizzly guy I noticed before, bordering on steroid-big with hair and eyes as black as tar. At first it looks like he's wearing silver arm plates, but when he crosses his arms over his chest, I can see it's just his scales.

I scratch at my wrists where my own scales want to come out. I let them. One by one, they surface, starting at my wrist and ending in a splatter around my elbow. My grandfather glances over at me, a smile tugging at his severe mouth.

Layla is staring at my arms. She doesn't say anything. I can feel her amazement.

Elias is joined by the girl with the white-blond hair in a conch shell. She plays with the black pearls around her neck. Her skin is the white of clean snow. The pink of her lips form a tight smile. She bows at the men he parades her in front of, and then returns to the shade of her tent.

"That's Elias's *betrothed*." Thalia notices me staring too long. "I forget her name. She's the daughter of the North herald, but to settle her father's debt she agreed to marry Elias. It was a thing."

"Better watch out there, little mermaid, you're starting to talk like me."

"Look what I got," Layla says, holding up a small silver tray of what look like pink Jell-O squares. She and Thalia toss them into their mouths like they're catching grapes. I let Layla feed one to me just to be polite. My lips catch the tip of her finger, which tastes a bit salty. Her smile is happy, lazy. I think she might even be drunk.

The pink square is slightly sweet with the texture of gummy bears. "What is it?"

"The guy who handed it to me said it was jellyfish brains," Layla says, collapsing into a fit of laughter with Thalia.

"I thought we were friends. *Jerks*," I add under my breath.

"That's why I couldn't resist," she says. She and Thalia tiptoe dance along the hot ground, then finally sit at the edge of the pool with their feet dangling over the water. Thalia shifts into her tail so that it peeks out from her puffy tulle skirts, and her tail fins lick the water. She's the green of new grass. Layla asks her something and Thalia nods. Slowly, Layla traces her finger along Thalia's scales where her thigh would be. I can smell Layla's wonder, her own blend of blooming flowers.

"Pretty hot action over there." I forgot Marty was sitting beside me.

"Huh?"

"Don't act like you're not seeing what I'm seeing."

"Dude, what *are* you?"

"Oh, you remember that." He leans back on his elbows, his baseball cap shielding his face from the sun. "Tell you what. If we see each other again on land, I'll tell you." He puts out his fist and I bump his with mine. "There's a lot you don't know, dude. This is just the beginning."

"You ever been to one of these before?"

"Nah. But I'm neutral, and the alliance means keeping all the courts happy. It's a fairly new thing with a treaty signed in magical blood, fairy tears, unicorn horns—you know, that kind of stuff. Didn't really work for Versailles, but it's a wait-and-see."

I nod, like I know what he's talking about.

"I've seen things. Nothing like this before, though. Pretty cool, huh? It's like waking up one day and taking the blindfold off." He stands and dusts sand off his jeans, even though I'm sure he's got sand in places he won't be able to dust off for days. Trust me. "Now if you'll excuse me, I'm going to go let the mermaids seduce me."

It goes on for what seems like hours. The sun stays at a high point, like perpetual noon. Layla and Marty are welcome, and I guess I am too. The kids sure think I'm something special. The ones who can walk come up and poke me, and then run away. Girls walk up to me and bow their pretty little heads. It's like the mermaid version of the Lifeguard Catwalk. They walk past with their glittering scales beneath flowing skirts that look more like sheer scarves wrapped around their bodies.

My grandfather sits beside me. "I'm glad you are enjoying your people." He's been standing around just watching for hours and I almost forgot he was there.

"What happens next?"

"Are you in a hurry?"

"No, I'm just—wondering."

"How is your father?"

"He's good."

"And my daughter?"

"She's, you know, good?"

He chuckles. "How very...*good.*"

"Grandf—Sea King?"

He nods but doesn't correct me as to what I should call him. He waits for me to talk.

"I have about a million questions to ask you."

He smiles like my mom, all cheeks, even with his beard. "How about we start with one."

That's totally unfair. How about we start with how the hell is this island moving on its own? Or how come I can't turn into a whole fish like Thalia and Kurt, not that I actually want to? Or what happens if no one likes me? That grizzly Elias guy looked like he wanted to kick my ass, and I've never even seen him before. It's like starting high school all over again.

Finally I settle on, "Why didn't you come sooner?"

The blue of his eyes get dark like dusk. "Believe me, I wanted to."

"Don't get me wrong. I love my mom and dad, and my dad's sisters are okay. But it would've been nice to know that I at least *had* a grandfather. I don't know." I shake my head. I'm being stupid and sentimental in front of the king. I'm never like this. I take a deep breath to loosen the tightness in my chest.

He sets a firm hand on my shoulder. "Let me show you something."

"What?"

"Something you should've known much, much sooner."

chapter
TWENTY-SIX

He leads me through a passage behind his throne. I let my fingers trace the walls. The rock is ancient and smooth, shaped by water and glistening with dew. Tiny lights float in the crevices of the stalactites, which hang like icicles.

The air is cooler here. I can even smell the sea.

We take a right, the lights ahead of us like tiny beacons, and I realize they're leading us. We're in a cavernous room. There's a natural pool of crystal-clear water that looks cold to the touch. When I get up close to it, I can see something behind my reflection, a dark shape taking form. Suddenly the surface breaks, and I hold up my arms to shield my face. I push myself backward.

"Easy, boy," my grandfather says. I wish he wouldn't talk to me like a pet, but when I open my eyes, I realize he isn't talking to me at all.

"What is that?"

The king sits at the edge of the pool and holds out his massive hand to a creature I've never seen before. With bright yellow eyes and a long horned snout, it's completely familiar. A sea horse. But when it grunts, its arms come out like webbed paws and lead to a body that ends in a curling tail. It nuzzles into my grandfather's hand like a puppy and a horse all at once.

"This is Atticus," he tells me. "He gets lost in the lower tunnels and ends up here instead of Thalia's chambers."

I still can't pull myself off the floor. "When Thalia said she missed her sea horse, Atticus, I was picturing something— smaller," I say, careful of my words, because something in its yellow eyes tells me he can understand me. I have some food I've been stowing away in my pockets instead of eating, and I feed it to him.

"He is the last of his kind," Grandfather says. "Just like us."

"What do you mean?"

He walks across the room to the pool, where there's a tall golden chair with spikes that end in jeweled points. It doesn't look very comfortable, but he seems to like it. I notice the trident for the first time, softly glowing in its stand beside him. Not like the dinky little toy I'd pictured. It's practically as tall as he is. The fork crackles with lightning on its own. I want to touch it. I wish it were mine.

I take a step back and the feeling dulls a bit.

"It's calling to you," says the king.

"It's strange. Like I know it's mine." Then I look at his serious face and add, "Only it's yours."

He takes the trident with one hand. Even from here, I can feel it humming. The lighting sparks start at the forks and lead down its body of twisted gold that ends in a jagged and long pointed white crystal.

"What do you want with me?" There. I said it. It's only taken me all day. "Why me? Why not one of your sons?"

He sighs. I hate when people sigh, like they're deflating and giving something up. "Because I don't have sons."

"Oh."

"I have scores of daughters. I had a few boys, but I've outlived them all. My daughters have sons, but your mother is my favorite."

"You're not actually supposed to admit to that."

"Why ever not? I'm the Sea King. Maia was my favorite. When she chose your father—I almost killed him." The trident sparks some more, and I take a step back. "During our last visit, I let more of my people go on shore. The Betwixt Alliance had only just been born, a treaty establishing peace between the worlds, courts, and kingdoms. And everyone played on human soil. Maia always loved people. She'd lie on the beach and watch them. Their laughs, their loves, their deaths. We don't die easily, and when we do, we return to the sea." He coughs, and when he does, I see him shiver from head to toe. It's like watching a great statue teeter.

"Kurt said you chose me to run for king or something."

"To be king you must own the trident. The trident can be won during a championship, or it can be taken by killing the owner. You are my blood. And yet you are a stranger. If I simply *made* you king, I would be breaking the trust of my people. I would leave you with a broken kingdom. With a war you would not know how to fight. I cannot be like the kings of old."

Championship. Kill. War. The words are on the tip of my tongue like razors on their edge. "What—what if I say no?"

He scratches his beard, and I'm afraid something is going to crawl out of it and he's going to eat it. Instead he stands and holds the trident with both hands. He points it at the pool where Atticus was swimming minutes ago. "Do you know where you come from?"

It feels like a trick question. I come from my mom. I don't really want to have that conversation again in my life, ever.

"You come from the sea." The trident hovers over the pool, and shadows dance over the surface, until the water is reenacting his words. "Poseidon owned the seas, and his sons after him. They mastered the waves, opened whirlpools, and buried the monsters as deep as they could. There were three Sea Kings once, and each had a separate piece of the trident. The fork, the staff, and the crystal spike. Each king fought against the others, the sea folk dying as the battles waged. We slaughtered dragons, gorgons, and the fair folk who would have us cower to their wicked games. Our magics ebbed like the tides. Our numbers were depleted. Until one king united us all. He merged the trident. He tamed the giants. He made us all one."

"Was that you?"

The king laughs, and the sound echoes off the walls. He stands the trident up so the tip of the crystal hits the floor and leaves a tiny dimple in the rock. "That was my great-great-grandfather.

His blood is mine, just as it is yours. If you don't do this, then our line dies with me. You can go back to your human life. You might even lead the same life as your mother. But you will always get called back to the ocean, to us. You are ancient, and you are of my blood, the way I am of the sea. And that, that is why I have chosen you to be my champion. My blood, my grandson, my young Tristan Hart."

I leave my grandfather in his chamber and return to the court, where the sky has burst with sunset colors.

Silks are draped over the tent openings, and lamps are turned on. Some merfolk dive back into the water and go below wherever it is they go. Others curl up on their boulders and sleep. In the distance someone is strumming a small guitar. I don't know the tune, but I find myself humming. My entire body is humming. I've never even touched the trident, and I can still feel its power

Marty is sprawled on a bed of spade-shaped leaves. He's made a pillow out of a bunch of silk, his cap covering most of his face.

I find Layla and Thalia with their toes dipped in the pool. They stare up at me with sleepy eyes. "Where have you been, Tristan?"

"Yeah, you missed Marty trying to synchronize swim with his merteenies."

Sorry, guys, but I was busy learning my family tree and being told officially that I was going to be a champion. I reach down to the lake and wash my face.

"I met Atticus," I say.

Thalia squeals, then covers her mouth when she realizes she's about to wake the whole island. "Did you find your chambers? Kurt already went to his. You can stay in mine, Layla."

"Do you snore?" she jokes.

Thalia leads us back through the passageway, the mini-firelights hovering over our heads. Layla reaches for my hand, and I take it eagerly. She's my rock, and I'm a balloon getting carried away in the wind.

Thalia runs into an opening to the left, forgetting about us and jumping into the pool with her recently well-fed sea horse. I don't exactly know where I'm going. All the tunnels look the same. The cluster of lights gets frantic in front of my face. I try to flick them away, but Layla stops me. "I think they want us to follow," she says.

Oh, I knew that.

The light leads us right and then left again. There's only one opening here. I part the silky sheer curtains and walk in. It's a room, like any other room. The bed is made of more shipwreck parts, and when I touch the mattress, it is the softest thing in the world. Layla hits the bed first. The last time we slept in the same bed was when we were little. Before I knew we had matching parts, but maybe even then I sort of got the idea. She stretches her body, and the arch of her back lifts from the mattress and then sinks back down. I sit carefully. I'm afraid she's going to banish me to the floor. Then, her eyes flutter, barely awake, and she reaches her hands out.

"I thought you'd left me," she says.

I lie down beside her. I trace her face lightly with my finger. The slope of her nose, the dip of her lips. I stop at her jaw and then let myself trace her neck. She whispers something, and I wish it were my name. Her eyes open suddenly, bright against the hazy light of the stone walls.

"What are you doing?" She doesn't move. Neither do I.

"You had something on your face."

She smacks her cheek. "Is it gone? What was it?"

"This poisonous fly that you can only find or Toliss Island. Really, I killed it for you."

Just then she smirks. She's caught me. She presses a hand on my chest and pushes me away, but grips my T-shirt at the same time. "Tristan." I don't like the way she says this. No, let's just smile and stay in this moment, because whatever she's going to say, I'm not going to like it. "What's going to happen tomorrow?" She lies flat on her back, and I do the same. I follow the grooves of the ceiling with my eyes, trying to count the tiny chips that sparkle.

"I'm supposed to be a *champion*."

"So it's not just a feast in your honor?"

I shake my head hard. "Nope. I'm going to be introduced as the king's heir. Apparently he has no living sons."

"That's *so* sexist. Why can't there be a girl Sea Queen? Why—"

"Relax, it's not like that. He has daughters, but it'd be like making Hannah Montana president, you know? My mom was supposed to be queen. But she chose to stay with my dad."

Layla gets on her side. Even though the room is cool, I can feel the heat of her body "So, what? You're going to be this king? You're not going to graduate? You're—" she chokes. *You're never going to see me again.*

I didn't think of that. I mean, I didn't exactly get on one knee and accept, but when your grandfather is wielding a trident that crackles with lightning in your presence, you don't exactly want to disagree. "I can't exactly go back to the way everything was, can I? Now that I know what I am. How do I just sit in class and joke with the boys?"

"How are you supposed to be a champion? The only time you've ever fought is when Angelo and Jerry want to reenact WWF." She's sitting up now. Her voice goes up a few octaves when she's stressed.

"Come here." I pull her close to me so her head is on my chest and her hand is over my heart. I'm not as sure as I sound. Can she tell?

"Tristan," she whispers. "The day of the storm, I cried from the moment the wave hit you till the moment I found you. Please don't leave me like that again."

I hold my breath, because it's what I've wanted to hear from her since the moment I came back. My Layla, my girl. She's always been there; I just never saw her the way I do now. I kiss her forehead and feel her body soften against mine as she sinks into sleep.

———

First I think it's a trick of the light. There are so many moving shadows in this room that I can't tell. But then I see it moving. A hooded figure past the entrance to my room.

As gently as I can, I pull myself off the bed without waking Layla. I part the curtain, my eyes adjusting to the low light. I take slow steps and listen. The figure is walking quickly, and I can tell it's a girl—her hood swishes in the wind. Maybe she's trying to hide from something. Maybe she needs my help.

The tunnel makes a break to the right into a room covered with floating orbs of lights. There's a pool like the one in my grandfather's chamber, but bigger. The rock around it forms a perfect circle. Leaning over the pool is the hooded girl. Her slender hand holds something silver and dips it in the water.

She sees me and gasps, jerks her hand back, and covers her face with her cloak. She runs to an opening to the left.

"Wait!" My voice echoes off the stalactites. I turn to the pool, where the silvery head of a fish floats to the surface. The water is clear and bright, as though there's a light all the way at the bottom. The blood around the torn flesh of the fish head taints the water with blood, but the trail thins out quickly.

Maybe she was feeding Atticus. But why would she need to hide and run from me? I can see a gray shape behind my reflection again. This time it isn't the sea horse. I trace my hand on my chest where she cut me once before, only I thought it was a dream. I can't force myself to move. The dark melody of her voice vibrates through the water and fills the emptiness of the room. I can see her face, the white of her eyes, her cruel razor-sharp smile. She grips the bottom half of the fish and waves it at me, blood trailing from its end like dripping paint. I take one more step back and feel something hit me hard on my skull.

She licks her lips, and then there is darkness.

chapter
TWENTY-SEVEN

I wake up in my bed with the taste of iron on my tongue. My chambers are bright with floating butterflies. One lands on my arm, and I swat it away. It leaves a sticky neon trail.

"Morning, sire," someone says. She's the color of orchids with slick silver scales covering her breasts. Her hair is braided and twisted with shells, piled atop her head.

"Who are you?"

She bows. "Hannah. I've come to deliver your armor."

I feel the back of my head. There's nothing there. Yet I know I didn't dream being hit hard.

Hannah holds up a gladiator outfit like the guard was wearing the day before. I think I'll pass, but I say thank you anyway. She bows low and gives me her white smile. I jump back when I notice how sharp her teeth are.

"I'm sorry, sire." She stands back up. Her teeth are fine. It's me. The dreams have started again. I have to talk to my grandfather. Maybe he knows the deal with this sea witch and can tell me I'm not crazy.

"No, no, it's me. I'm just a little jumpy." I take the clothes from her and set them on the bed.

"You'll be fine," she says warmly. "My mother used to be your mother's handmaiden. She really loved her. Your mother was a kind princess, the loveliest of them all. Not like these other girls."

I laugh at that. "Thanks. Have you seen—"

"She's getting fitted for something a little more fitting for the tournament announcement."

"Right. Good." I don't know how to tell her to go away. "I'm just going to get dressed."

She looks startled, as though I've just caught her doing something she shouldn't be doing. And that's undressing me with her eyes. I know that look. I give it to girls all the time. Hannah bows again and this time winks at me. "Are you sure you won't be needing any help?"

I cough into my hand.

"I'm sure Lord Sea will be fine, Hannah." Kurt saves me. He stands at the entryway wearing a chain-link metal skirt. His violet scales decorate his forearms.

Hannah bows her head low as she walks past Kurt.

"Unless you want her to stay," Kurt says with a mischievous grin.

"Really, I'd like to live another day." I go over to the pool of water and splash the cold and salty water on my face.

"What's that you got there, Kurty?"

"Don't call me that."

"Just trying something new."

Kurt holds a long wooden box with moss growing over it, looking like he went to the bottom of the sea and dug it out of a pirate wreck. Really, he shouldn't have. "I am to give you this as a symbol of your house. It will let the court see you are the true heir of the king."

I set the box on my bed. "You haven't seen Layla, have you?"

"She's got a new dress," he answers.

"Yeah, I heard that. But where *is* she?"

"You asked if I saw her, not where she was." He can't keep the smirk off his face. "Come, open it. There won't be any food left if you don't hurry up, and then you have to be judged—I mean, presented—before court officially."

"You know, you could be a little nicer to me." I flip the lid open. "Now that I'm going to be a champion and all." I'm expecting the thing to either blow up or glow. Everything seems to glow on this island.

"Holy—"

"It's been handed down in your family. Only a son of Triton can touch it."

Nestled in the box is a dagger about two feet long with a double-edged blade that catches the light of the room. The handle is dusty gold with swirling black pearl as an emblem. I can sense it humming. It's not the smelling thing; it's something else—like feeling power that's as old as the earth. The way I felt the power of the trident without even touching it.

"What happens if someone else touches it?"

"It burns them," Kurt says casually. "Now, here's a shoulder strap to sheath it. Look how nicely it matches your new armor."

I think I might let him hold my new dagger just for fun.

———

The hush over the court reminds me of the silence during a meet, just before I dive. Bodies rustle against each other, lips whisper behind cupped hands.

Here, the sun is shining. My stomach rumbles because I missed the seaweed buffet while I tried the armor on. It's only a skirt underlined with leather so you can shift into your tail without ripping your clothes. Even without a mirror, I decided to change back into my cargo shorts.

Kurt crosses his arms over his chest, glaring at me with annoyance as I take my place beside the king. Beside him is Layla in her new mermaid-woven dress. The rosy silk clings to her body like a second skin, and it's so translucent that I can see her muscles flex beneath it. Somehow she looks like she belongs here more than I do.

When my grandfather snaps his fingers, the little green boy with the golden conch comes running. He blows into the conch until the whispers die out and all you can hear is the breeze in the trees and the trickle of the waterfall behind the wall. The Sea King stands to his full height. He's quite spectacular to look at, with his mane of white hair and turquoise eyes. His voice is amplified in the silence. "Today is a day like no other," the king announces. "Today I welcome home a lost son, Tristan Hart, my *grandson*."

There's polite applause and some overly enthusiastic cheering that I bet comes from Marty's section of the crowd.

The king looks around at the crowd, one by one. He licks the salty wind off his lips and says, "We are the keepers of the deep, ancient as the belly of the sea, a remnant of every era of this world. And yet our numbers fall to others who will have us drown in our own waters, our magics all but lost as we war among ourselves. We are forgotten. But we are not gone, and we are not going just yet."

At the last bit, the heralds stare sheepishly at their scaly toes.

"I presume some of you wonder why we've returned to these shores eighteen years too early. I have no living sons. My reign is ending, like the remnants of a storm, and soon I will return to the waves that created me."

Across from me, the grizzly silver merman Elias whispers something into his girl's ear. I want to throw something at them to make them shut up and pay attention.

"I give you my trident." He holds up the spectacular golden shaft. It crackles and sparks and radiates its own light from the quartz. "He who holds the trident is the King of the Seas. For millennia, there hasn't been a championship for the throne. The last one to win it was my great-great-grandfather, Pelagios. In my time, a champion will win my throne. Each champion will be selected by his regional herald. With one exception. I will select my own."

The green boy with the conch scuttles back out, his webbed feet slapping on the ground. His voice is high pitched and amplified for someone his size. "From the West Sea, Dylan, son of Ammon." A tall, broad man steps forward. His hair is like raw gold with streaks of silver. His skin is slick with a golden tan, and he has patches of scales along his ribs. He wears a small gold band across his forehead with carved symbols I have no name for. He holds a young guy's arm up in the air. The guy is a younger version of the herald. Ammon and his son. Their tent roars with applause as they walk before the throne, beating their chests like something out of *Clash of the Titans*.

If there were ever a time for me to shit my pants, it would probably be now.

"From the South, Adaro, son of Leomaris." Father and son strut out with their fists in the air. They have long black hair and skin like sienna chalk. Their scales are a cluster of reds and oranges. Adaro bows and presses his fist to his chest like an oath.

I hate the way Layla whistles for him, as she did with the guy before that. I know she's just having fun. But she should only be whistling and cheering for me.

Adaro bows to the king before standing beside Dylan, two warriors with their arms behind their backs and chests puffed out with pride.

"From the North, Brendan, son of Finbar." The loudest cheer erupts as this guy walks out with his father. They're the tallest of the bunch and not as abrasively muscular as the other champions. They at least smile instead of roar at the crowd. The father has cropped gray hair, more GI Joe than the other gladiator-like heralds. His son, Brendan, has a shock of bright red hair that reminds me of my mom. A woman with the same red hair, piled in a sophisticated bun and decorated with starfish and pearls, walks behind Finbar. The slope of her nose and her sharp cheekbones are so much like my mom's that a pang of nostalgia hits me like a shock. She waves at her son, who shakes one fist in the air. He could be one of my friends, and I can already tell he's not taking this as seriously as the rest.

I motion toward the red-haired woman. "Is she—?"

My grandfather nods once. "Mm-hmm. She is my daughter Maristella."

The green boy then announces, "From the East, the herald competes as his own representative, Elias, son of Ellion." Elias and his fiancée stride out of their tent. They remind me of Jerry's parents during parent-teacher conferences, the way they walk side by side but look in opposite directions. Elias is all roaring chest-pumping, and his Snow White mermaid stands there barely holding his hand like if he were going over a cliff she'd definitely let go. I sort of like her. Despite getting the fewest cheers, Elias takes the most time walking back and forth in front of my grandfather, who frowns at the display.

The boy with the conch blows on it lightly and clears his throat. *Oh, shit. I'm up.* But—I don't have an entourage. I don't have my dad or a fiancée to walk me in front of the court and show off my goods. Compared to everyone else, I'm actually wearing too many clothes. Maybe I *should've* worn the metal skirt after all.

"The Sea King's champion for the High Court." Somehow, people are already cheering. "Tristan Hart, son of David Hart."

Am I supposed to prance around beating my chest like a chimp in front of my grandfather? Right now what I'm least prepared for is the cheering. They're actually cheering at me. Granted, I can make out Thalia and Layla and Marty, and if I listen hard enough, I can even hear Kurt hollering. But then there's Hannah, and the boy with the turtle shell and his mom, and even my mother's sister is clapping with a smile on her face. I find Layla's face in the crowd, her skin glowing in the light. She cocks her head to the side and blows me a kiss the way she always does before a meet, and deep in my heart this all feels right.

My grandfather grabs my hand and holds it in the air, just as the heralds did for their kids, and suddenly I wish my dad were here to see. I haven't won anything yet; I've just been introduced to a court of sea creatures, but they're not booing. At least not yet. Maybe I can do this. I pull off my shirt and strap the dagger to my bare chest. I'm not rippling with the muscles of the other bros, but I've got a pretty hot body.

Finally, the boy with the conch steps forward and blows the horn. I take my place beside Elias, who isn't shy about the way he snarls at me.

The Sea King stands again. "The five champions of the High Court," he says for a final round of applause. It dawns on me that if I have to fight any of these guys, I'm done for. I can hold my own in a fight against some asshole after school, but I'm not at Thorne

Hill anymore, and Elias could crack my skull open and use it as a serving bowl if he wanted to.

"The challenges that await our champions will try their strength, their minds, and their hearts. They will come face-to-face with the darkest parts of their souls as they go in search of the power of the Sea King." The king holds the crackling trident over his head. When he releases it, it levitates and spins slowly over his outstretched palms. "This is the power of the Sea King, a gift from the gods."

The trident breaks cleanly into three pieces and sounds like knives sharpening. The three-pronged fork crackles with thin fissures of lightning at its tips. Its handle fits into a long staff made of braided gold. The bottom is a long and jagged spear that appears to be made of quartz or some kind of cloudy glass; it has a brass handle. Each piece hovers in the air over the lake. They each spin in their own contained tornado until the force is too much and they're sucked down into the lake. Down, down, down into the blackness of the bottom.

My grandfather dusts his hands and sits back on his throne. He glows a little less than before. The effect isn't instant, but it's noticeable to me.

"Where have they gone?" someone gasps.

"Each piece has been sent to an oracle. There are five remaining sea oracles on this plane. The champion who retrieves the trident rules this throne."

"What if no one champion gathers all three?" Adaro asks.

The Sea King leans forward slowly. "Those with a single piece will return here, and a final duel will occur."

So much for not having to fight the guys directly.

"What is today?" Grandfather turns to the green boy, who whispers in Grandfather's ear. "Ah. The next full moon is just over a fortnight away. Leave at sundown and return with your findings at the next full moon, or not at all."

"But sire," the herald of the West speaks up, "the oracles shift their locations every so many years. Their last known locations may have changed."

"I never said it would be easy," the king says with a tiny wink. "You all have excellent resources at your disposal."

Wait a minute. I don't have a strategy. I don't have resources. What was my grandfather thinking? What am *I* thinking?

Before I can say anything, my grandfather pats me on the back as if he's done it a million times before. "Now, let the festivities continue."

chapter
TWENTY-EIGHT

I t's still daylight, but the sun is sinking, allowing the pale blue sky to burst with the first signs of pink and yellow.

Kurt is at my side. We sit alone watching our companions eat and drink the strange new flavors, dive into the cool water, and laugh. "Congratulations."

"Where the hell have you been all day? Shaking hands and kissing babies?"

He looks a bit embarrassed. "I've been asked to give accounts on what your character is like."

"Did you tell them I took you to the mall and fed you swine, because that's what I do to all the merpeople who come out of my faucet?"

"I was gracious, I promise."

"Can I ask you something?"

"I believe you already have."

"Don't hang around Marty so much. You're starting to joke like him. But seriously. What's a fortnight?"

Kurt laughs, actually laughs. "Fourteen days."

"How was I supposed to know?"

"The important thing is that you know now. You must also know the king would like to speak to us privately before we leave."

"Is he going to give me a cloak of invisibility or something useful? I mean, all I've got is you and Thalia. If I can get her to sit still for more than a second."

He doesn't acknowledge me. Not just because I'm being a smart-ass, but because Elias is standing in front of Layla and Marty with his finger pointing in their faces. When he yells, he spits. The music stops, and everyone drops their instruments, their food, their turtle-shell Frisbees to hear what the yelling is about. Marty stands in front of Layla to block her and shoves Elias right on the chest. Elias shoves him back, sending him splashing into the lake.

We rush over to them.

Kurt becomes all political etiquette and calm. I pull out my dagger. "What seems to be the problem?"

Elias points at my friends. "These humans have stolen from me."

"Do not forget that *she* is my sister and of the court. The boy is of the alliance, and the girl—the girl belongs to Tristan—who is a champion—" As well-spoken as he is, Kurt really does seem to be making all of it up.

Layla stands but wobbles. "I don't belong to anyone," she says indignantly. "This is the twenty-first century."

Elias is the first to laugh "There! She denies being his. Therefore, she is a thief."

"I am not!" She's drunk. She's drunk, and now she's going to get herself killed.

"They've stolen drink from my family's tent."

Thalia gets in between Elias and her brother, holding a long, thin glass full of bubbly green liquid. If I didn't know better, I'd say it was champagne with green food coloring, like we tried to do last St. Patrick's Day. "*This* is of the court, not just for you and yours."

"The human girl is not of the court, which makes her a thief. Guards!"

The guards trot around us. "Whoa, whoa! Easy." I look to my grandfather, but he shakes his head as if he can't help me. "Is there a different way to resolve this?"

Kurt leans in to my ear and whispers, "Elias is very influential. He'll argue his way into having her beheaded. Your grandfather is no longer truly Sea King, and other than some loyalty, he doesn't have the same power he did before giving up the trident. Elias knows that."

"You're not so scary." Layla presses her finger on Elias's bare chest.

"This is ridiculous," Elias says, exasperated because the guards can't move in on her and the king can't take sides.

"I can take you," Layla says again.

"*Shut up*," I say between gritted teeth. "Do you have a death wish? I can't save you."

"Since when do you save *me*?" She turns back to Elias. "I challenge you to a race. Little ole human me versus big ole champion-of-the-wicked-East you."

The crowd eggs them on. It's like I'm watching a fight break out in the cafeteria because someone stared at someone else too long.

Elias turns to the king. "She is a disgrace to our people, and the only way is to punish her."

"I wouldn't think a guy your size would be afraid of little me." Leave it to Layla, standing up to guys three times her size. When I was in middle school—tall but really skinny—the ninth-graders picked on me, and Layla once kicked a kid in his shins with her little cowgirl boots. That's when I knew I couldn't live without her. But this isn't a junior-high bully we can just run away from. This is a holier-than-thou merman who doesn't like either of us breathing the same air as him.

"I take your challenge as an insult. Disgraceful. The champion of the *king* brings humans among us. He does not deserve to be champion." Every other word is laced with a kind of hatred I don't recognize. People usually like me. I mean, I'm a pretty nice guy.

"He cannot help bringing humans among us," Grandfather says, "as he is half human himself."

I realize he's just made a joke, and so does everyone else. He may not have his trident, but he's still seen as king, and the crowd laughs at his joke. See, my grandfather is a pretty nice guy too.

"I've seen her swim, sire," Kurt says, his face turning red suddenly. "She is exceptional, even for a human."

Layla crosses her arms and bobs her head at me.

"You have a courageous heart," my grandfather commends her. "But it is also a foolish heart. If you lose, you will be set on a sailboat without an escort to face the sea on your own. Should you win, you will be an honorary member of this court. No harm can come to you by my people."

"As long as they are still your people." Elias growls loud enough so that only we who are nearest can hear him.

"I'd like to take her place in the challenge," I say.

Kurt shakes his head. "You can't. It's done. They've accepted."

"What happens if Elias loses?"

Thalia shrugs. "This never happens. If he challenged another merman and lost, he'd have his fins stripped and he'd be left out in the sea to die."

My laugh is bitter, nervous. "Comforting."

Layla pulls on the straps of her dress, and the silk pools around her feet. She's down to her bra, the same lacy pink-and-black thing she was wearing when she decided to surprise me in the pool.

I hold my hands out to them. "Are you sure there isn't anything to be done?"

Kurt and Thalia shake their heads. Even Thalia's pretty smile is a tight line.

I follow behind Layla. "Why, why, *why*, couldn't you have just let me talk?"

"You don't talk for me, *Finn*. Don't you believe in me?"

"It's not that, Layla. I do." *I just can't have anything happen to you.* I leave it unsaid.

"Not enough, I guess."

I grab her wrist. My whole body is hot. I don't know what to say to her now. *I love you? Please don't die?* She's almost a better swimmer than me. On my bad days she beats me. But this guy is a full-blown merman. The whispers of the court surround us like a swarm of mosquitoes. She pulls her hand free from my hold and practices her breathing. Just like at any other meet.

I rub my hands over my face. This is happening.

This is happening, and I'm not doing anything to stop it.

chapter
TWENTY-NINE

They dive at the same time.

There is one giant intake of breath from all of us that makes the hair on my body stand on end. She hits the water. A clean, perfect dolphin dive. That's what Coach calls her, his pet dolphin. I don't know how the water is, but it looks warm at least. She doesn't come up right away for breath. Her body is a blur beside Elias's.

My heart feels like the time I spent an entire homeroom making a rubber ball, twisting and snapping rubber band after rubber band into a tight ball the size of my fist. My heart is a ball of twisted rubber—and that's how every girl wants to make a guy feel, right?

She's falling behind Elias. Not by much, but enough to keep even my grandfather at the edge of his throne. She comes up for air, and that's the beauty of it: he doesn't have to. She's going to lose. And she's going to die. And it's all going to be my fault.

Her arms are like hummingbird wings flitting through the water. She's almost a foot away from him. They reach the rocks. He flips right around, a smile visible when he breaks the surface just for show. My own gills burn.

"Will you *stop* pacing?" Marty pulls on my cargo shorts. "It isn't going to help."

Maybe not looking might somehow make this nauseous feeling go away. I pick the spot directly across from me where the herald tents are. Alone, while her future husband is racing my best friend, the Snow White mermaid lies on heaps of blankets. The servants who surrounded her moments ago are gathered at the edge of the lake. She leans her cheek on her fist, bored. That's when I see it. I mean, see *her*. In a second, her gray eyes glaze over with a black shadow and her lips mouth a single word, a word I can't even begin to guess the meaning of.

The crowd gasps and squeals as Layla speeds up. One, two, three, four strokes, and she's reached the other side of the shore.

Elias is only a second behind her, but it's clear to everyone watching that he's lost.

The court is a mess—girls, kids, fathers—*laughing*. My grandfather is still and pulls at the tip of his chin hair. He makes a motion to reach for something at his right, his trident, and then realizes it isn't there anymore.

Elias has lost. He's lost to a human girl, an intruder, and the court is laughing at him. I look for his fiancée, but she isn't there anymore, and I can't find her in the crowds of the court.

In the lake, Layla cries out and cringes. She has a cramp and grabs on to the rocky ledge. Kurt and Marty are weaving their way through to help pull her out of the water as Elias turns his blood-shot eyes on my friend. My Layla.

Brow tight, lips curled in a growl, hands outstretched for her neck, he is literally a creature rising from the lake to attack her. I can't say I do this without thinking. I think he's going to hurt her. I don't think about what this might do to my standing as a champion. I run and dive into the lake, close enough to him that my splash distracts him. Elias turns to me full on.

The shift comes naturally. It starts as a tingle in my spine, right where my tattoo is, and it travels all the way down. In two strokes I adjust to one tail movement instead of two kicking legs. One, two, and I have my arms around him. One under the right arm and one over his left shoulder. I squeeze him and he pushes hard against me, so we sink into the water.

He's physically stronger, and we go down, down, down. We hit against a wall, and I let go of him. He charges at me with arms outstretched, full speed, Superman underwater. We're locked in a wrestler's grip, forearm to forearm.

Something in me is awakening. I don't know what to call it. Instinct is too simple. It's older, more primal. It's more than defending a girl I'm possibly in love with; it's knowing that I *can* beat him. I push as hard as I can through the water. I can feel every fiber in my body, every bone in my tail, and he cannot overpower me. Something in me knows nothing can harm me. I am untouchable.

And then there is the darkness. We're so far from the surface that the light doesn't reach us anymore. He breaks my hold and hits me right on the jaw, sending me slamming against a boulder. His hands close around my neck so my gills can't take in water. I hold my breath, but it isn't enough. I wrap my tail around his, and even though I can't see his face, I can still see the whites of his eyes. His grip loosens, and his eyes roll back into his head. He lets go completely, falling down into the pitch-black. Did I do that? I couldn't have. I wouldn't know how.

My stomach contracts and there's that nauseous feeling again. My head feels like it's splitting open. I reach for Elias's hand and try to pull him up to the surface, but he's as heavy as he looks and my muscles feel like elastic that's given out and snapped.

I shut my eyes against the throbbing pain in my head, and I know this is all happening because of her. I can see her face again. Smiling, waiting in the black coldness of my dreams, the silver mermaid. Waiting for a moment like this.

chapter
THIRTY

It's daylight.

I'm drooling all over my arm in Ancient History. The teacher, Mr. Van Oppen, leans his Hugh-Grant-looking self against the chalkboard. He has a funny accent I can't ever guess right and the kind of hair that flops everywhere when he runs his fingers through it.

The girls are crazy about him. I'm talking Indiana-Jones-writing-on-their-eyelids-and-hanging-around-after-class-washing-the-eraser-board-for-him kind of crazy.

"And what year did Alexander the Great conquer all? Come on, now, it's not like it's in front of you on the reading assignment from last night, hmm?"

Silence.

A sliver of light peers through the blinds and hits me right in the eyes. Mr. Van Oppen pulls on the string to make the shutters stay shut, and my eyes are unblinded. The lights in the classroom are so bright that I can't imagine how I fell asleep in the first place.

He taps my desk with his long, skinny index finger.

"Mr. Hart?" He never calls anyone by their first name.

"'At the age of nineteen / He became the Macedon King / And he swore to free all of Asia Minor / By the Aegean Sea / In 334 B.C. / He utterly beat the armies of Persia'?"

"Very good, Mr. Hart. I see you've been listening to your Iron Maiden, hmm?"

The class snickers.

"What made him a good king? Ms. Shea?"

Maddy sits with her legs up on the chair. She's wearing a tiara from her Sweet Sixteen party, which was really just me, her, Layla, and some of her drama club nerds at Ruby's on the boardwalk, because her mom wouldn't let her have a party. The tiara was my will-you-be-my-girlfriend gift, along with a few other things I fished out of my mom's junk trunk.

Maddy pops a big, green bubble-gum ball and rolls her eyes. "Down with kings! Alexander the Great was such a poser. Did he even fight? No. He just got people killed, and killed a whole bunch of other people who didn't even want to be ruled. He killed them right there and then—dead. Dead, dead."

My head pounds at the temples.

There's a knock on the door. Everyone looks at me, then at the door. Then me again.

I stand and bump into the desk next to mine. It's Layla's. She sits with her hands tied and propped on the desk. She has her head down like she doesn't want anyone to look at her face. "This is all your fault, Tristan. All your fault," she says.

"What the—" I grab her hands and start trying to undo the ropes, but every time I get one knot undone, another one pops up in its place.

Maddy gets up and out of her desk, and everyone goes, "*Oooooooh.*"

She stands over me and says, "You always picked Layla over me. Now you got her dead. All you do is hurt people, Tristan Hart."

"The *door*, Mr. Hart. The *door.*" Mr. Van Oppen walks around and sits on his desk. "Everyone else turn to page 1001, the future—the destruction of New York City by a little merman."

"Wh—"

"The *door*, Mr. Hart. Answer the *door.*"

I can't shake the numbness spreading through my body. I turn the knob, and when I open my eyes, the silver mermaid is there. She bares her shark teeth at me. The hallway is full of water. She moves her hands to try and grab me, but she can't breach the glass wall between us. I shut the door in her face and press my back against it.

Mr. Van Oppen stares at me with a furrowed brow and a crooked smile. "My, my. And here I was wondering what all the fuss was about. Hmm?"

chapter
THIRTY-ONE

When I breathe, I breathe hard.

Breathe like I haven't had any air in years. Layla's face is right over me. Her eyes are wet, and she wipes her hand across them. She brings her closed fist right down on my chest. Déjà vu.

"Easy, girl," I hear Marty say.

"Where am I?"

"You're alive is what you are," Thalia says. She's in between shifts. Her deep green scales cover her breasts, and she's still wearing her puffy pink skirt. She's rubbing a black paste onto my chest where I've got more long red scratches.

"You're in the king's quarters," Kurt says from somewhere. I recognize the bed, the throne across the room, the empty stand where the trident used to be.

I stretch my arms out and feel the sheer blanket, too fine to be silk but the softest thing I've ever felt. Then I glance at Layla's face again and think of the kiss I stole from her. No way, her lips are definitely the softest.

But other memories push past that one—the silver mermaid, over and over again. She's here. She's somewhere on the island.

"Elias. That shark mermaid was down there. Where's my grandfather?"

"The king is calming the crowds," Thalia says. Her cuteness is replaced with that all-knowing, kick-ass attitude she doesn't always let peek through. Shit must be serious then.

"Elias's followers want your fins stripped on a platter."

"He's not back?" Of course he's not back. I remember him trying to choke me, then letting go and sinking into the abyss.

I can see it in their faces. They think it was me.

"I didn't kill him! I didn't!" I sit up, past the ache in my legs. "The last thing I remember is trying to reach for him. He was beating me, and then he just started—sinking. Then I got this feeling like my brain was ripping in half. I saw her, the silver mermaid. The shark mermaid from my dream! It's like she was inside my head."

Heavy footsteps enter the room. "Why didn't you tell me of this, Kurtomathetis?" The king's voice booms through the glittering stone walls.

"I didn't know—"

"Do you know how severe this is? How dangerous she is?" His face is red. His white mane curls wildly around his leathery shoulders.

"Wait, hold up. Rewind." I cross my hands in a T for time-out.

Grandfather walks over to his chair and sits. He slumps in his chair like he's beaten, like with every minute the trident is gone, more of the power he's held for centuries is washing away.

212

Layla and Thalia link arms at the edge of the bed. Marty leans against a wall, looking exactly the way he did when I first saw him, coffee straw and all.

"Tell me, Tristan," says the king, "when did the mermaid first come to you? What did she look like?"

"The day of the storm. I have zero memory of surviving except for this dream. She comes at me and attacks me, but this shark wearing some kind of helmet comes and saves me and drags me to shore."

"That explains the missing sharks on the guard," Kurt says.

"Indeed," my grandfather responds.

I tell them about all of my memories of her, the storm, the hospital, the dreams, the tunnel and pool right here in Toliss. "And when I was fighting Elias, it felt like she was trying to get into my mind. It's always like that, but there's a barrier and she can't ever break through. Who is she? What does she want with me?"

"She is my sister." My grandfather leans back on his tall golden chair and concentrates on the fireflies. "She is Nieve—a murderer and a deceiver. She's a sorceress and a traitor to the throne. When we were young, she killed my mother's newest babe out of jealousy. She was banished for two hundred years by my father, who feared the harpies' fury if he killed his own daughter. Then she was released, and she tried to become part of us again, but there was something rotting inside her, so she never could. Her blood is wrong, poison. When Father made *me* king in her stead as eldest, she killed him. So I locked her up below the sea, and she's been there for centuries."

"Why didn't you just off her?" Marty asks. I'm afraid my grandfather is going to turn around and drown him or just smack him, but he doesn't.

"Because I am an utter fool." He sighs long and hard. "I am foolish to think our kind can change. I am foolish to think that my people can find their way in this new world when I've clung to my father's tradition for so long. My father could not kill his own daughter, no matter how dreadful she was. She was still his. I knew I should've destroyed her when I took the throne. But there is no greater crime than killing your own family."

"But she killed her own sister and her father!" Layla yells.

"And she was punished. The Caves of Tartarus were supposed to contain her."

"Now she's out," I say, and I'm surprised at how even my voice is when I'm actually trembling. "So if my dreams weren't dreams, and someone was feeding her in the pool, then we're not the only ones who know she's out."

"Traitors in my own kingdom." Grandfather shakes his head. "Kurtomathetis, send guards to the Narrow Caves and report."

"Thalia, the two of you will remain with Tristan and guard his family." He looks at Layla and his face softens. "And friends, naturally."

"What should I do?" I stand with empty hands, unknowing. "She's definitely coming after me."

"When you were born I bound you. You have my protection. I released most of it so that you could shift into your true self, but my power is still there. Only when I am truly no longer king would she be able to harm you. Now that I no longer have the trident, my magics will ebb.

"You must find the trident. You should be king, as it is our family's right. No matter what blood you share. It is your birthright." He nods to the dagger slung over my shoulder.

"That was mine when I was your age, before I became king." I wonder about the things he's had to do with it, the things I'll have to use it for. "It was my father's and his and his and his. Well, I can go on for quite a long time. It was a gift from Triton."

"*The* Triton?" Marty goes, the excitement in his voice so rich that it's like he's the one getting the present.

"Yes, *the* Triton," Kurt answers irritably, returning from the tunnel.

"Son of Poseidon, god of the sea," Layla says.

The merpeople stare at her.

"What? My mom's Greek," she says, rolling her eyes.

My grandfather rummages through what looks like a bunch of junk. Now I know where my mom gets it from. "Now, where is that—ahh—yes, this'll do—Miss Layla?"

Layla rises slowly from the bed. She stands in front of him with damp curls and clothes. "Yes?"

"Because I am a merman of my word, and a king is only worth the promises he keeps, this is a token from my court. So that harm may never come to you by me or mine. I'd say you've earned it, quite surprisingly. My grandson is honored to have you as a companion."

Both our faces go red.

"You should tell *him* that," she says half jokingly.

He puts something in her palm, and she closes her fingers around it. She doesn't look at it, but she smiles her brilliant smile and thanks him.

"Marty, thank you again for the gift."

"Aw, King. No shiny dagger?"

My grandfather frowns at him for a moment before turning to us one more time. "Now, a fortnight will come and go, so I suggest you head back. As king, I cannot interfere with the champion, so I suggest you learn as much as you can from Kurtomathetis."

"I've got to grab some of our belongings," Thalia says. "Layla and I will meet you at the ship. King—" Just when I think she's going to bow down and curtsey, she runs up and gives him a tight hug. He holds her and smooths her hair like a father would to his own.

We start going down one tunnel together, but the girls make a right and we keep going straight toward a tiny white light.

When we've reached the mouth of the tunnel, it is dusk.

"It's a wondrous sight," says the king.

"Does this mean we get our summer back?" It's a tiny thing to look forward to.

My grandfather laughs. "Yes, the wall is down."

"But won't humans be able to detect it?"

He shakes his head. "The barrier is still there, but you can only see it if you're on the other side. Magics of that size are gradual."

Marty points to the shore. "Well, there's our ride. I can't wait to get this sand out of my—shoes."

I laugh. "Yeah, shoes."

He gives one low bow to my grandfather, takes off his baseball cap, and shakes his matted brown hair. "From the members of Betwixt, a gracious farewell. From myself, a wicked awesome good time." He jogs back to the ship, his boots sending up clouds of sand behind him.

Kurt and I turn to my grandfather. I don't know what to say, really. I want to stay longer and ask him to tell me everything. I've never had a grandfather. I've watched Layla with her two grandfathers, both of them tiny and wielding their canes like angry swords and giving her money to put into a college savings fund. When you grow up without grandparents, it's like you're missing a link to a past you didn't even care you had until you have to sort through it to understand who you are. I want to know, and there is too much to know.

My grandfather's enormous hands come down on our shoulders. "You're both in very good company." He walks back through the trees until my eyes can't follow.

chapter
THIRTY-TWO

H *er name was Lola—"*

We're sailing in the warm night breeze. Marty's singing at me.

"She was a showgirl—"

Layla and Thalia are getting navigation lessons from Arion, who is clearly smitten with the two prettiest girls in the whole world.

"Marty?"

"Yeah?"

"Don't forget who has a new, shiny dagger in his backpack."

Marty makes a zipper motion over his lips and leans back against a wooden barrel, wriggling his toes. His heavy, black leather boots are beside him, along with his shirt and his hat. He calls out, "Hey, Arion!"

Arion pulls on the braided ropes and sails, and swings as close to us as the black ropes that bind him will allow.

"What is it *now*, Master Marty?"

"I like that. *Master Marty*. Sounds official. So you got any more of that seaweed ale? It's not so bad now. The grassy aftertaste kind of goes away."

Arion's cool composure is evaporating. His bushy black eyebrows furrow. "There's more below deck. Please, have as much as you'd like. Just beware of the urchin brothers."

At the mention of the little urchin guys, Marty shakes his head and leans back. "I think I'm good. Are we there yet?"

"Soon. Very soon," the captain says, turning back to his post. I think he mumbles something like *Not nearly soon enough.*

"Yo, Kurtomawhatsis?" says Marty.

"Just Kurt is fine," Kurt says.

"What's your story, man? Why does the king trust you so much?"

Kurt shrugs. "My father was on his council. My father built the Glass Palace. My mother was part of the queen's court when she was still alive. She was like a sister to Lady Maia, Tristan's mother."

"Ahh. 'Splains it."

"What's *your* story?" Kurt asks in return. I don't know if it's the seaweed ale, which is as good as it sounds, or if he's just gotten comfortable, but Kurt is almost friendly. "What are you? I can't smell you, and the king already asserted that you're not human. You're no vampire or werewolf. You're no fey. You're not a witch."

"There are a bajillion otherworldly creatures out there, Kurt, my man. Maybe I'm a mega-vampire-werewolf-creature mix with fairy powers!" Marty tries to stand, but we hit a small wave and he falls back.

"Not nearly as cunning," Kurt whispers to me. "Besides, the ale affects you like a human."

Marty taps his temples with his index finger and winks at us. "Smart man."

"But you're *not* human," I repeat.

"Yes, Champion Tristan Hart."

"Stop drinking that shit. It got Layla in enough trouble."

And there she walks into the conversation. My foot tastes rather nasty.

"How was I supposed to know I was drinking a mermaid roofie? I won, didn't I?"

I think of Elias's fiancée. The black film over her eyes. Kurt said not all mermaids have powers. Maybe it was just the light. But how else could Elias lose?

"I thought you were dead meat, ladybird," Marty says, pulling her down so that she sits on his lap. I don't know what it is about Marty, but he's easy to be comfortable with. She doesn't even smack him the way she would've smacked Angelo or one of the boys.

"I don't know what you were thinking," Kurt says, "challenging Elias like that. And you. You're a champion. There are things you're not supposed to do. It's a wonder the entire court didn't get into an uproar."

"Oh, they had an uproar," Layla goes. "Your grandfather just put an end to it right away. After two of the guards pulled you out, another two went back to look for Elias. No one knew what happened. His girlfriend was screaming, '*I want him dead! I want revenge!*' about you and went crazy."

"She's hot, too hot for a creep like Elias," Marty says.

"Does she have any magic?" I wiggle my fingers.

"No. It would've been common knowledge if her family still had magics. The king decreed that those who still do must make it known." Kurt eyes me curiously. "Why do you ask?"

"No reason."

Thalia swings from the mast deck to the main deck on a rope. She crashes between her brother and me. "She's not very nice. Then again, I wouldn't be nice either if my father had promised me to marry Elias."

Part of me feels ashamed. I know I didn't like Elias. But I didn't kill him. He was alive. I know he was. Hell, if he hadn't passed out, he would've probably killed me.

"Did you tell them what you are yet?" Thalia says, looking from Marty to us.

His eyes go wide and he stares at her. "That's so uncool, ladybird."

Thalia giggles, her green hair flying all over my face as we ride against a small wave and strong wind.

"Well?" I'm waiting.

"I'm not going to tell you." Thalia puts a finger to her lips.

Marty looks more relieved.

"It's not my fault I'm cleverer than you all." Thalia stands. She holds on to the side of the ship and looks out at the night. The barely there sliver of moon casts a silver glow on the water. There's a dark mound out there that must be Coney Island. She looks back at us over one shoulder and winks. She pulls her shirt over her head and pulls her puffy skirt down. I look away because it's just weird looking at her like that. She steps on the rail and jumps over. I catch a shimmer of green scales and the translucent tip of her fins.

"I love skinny-dipping." Marty stands, pushing Layla to the ground. He's undoing his belt buckle.

"Whoa, whoa. Technically she's dressed, as far as mermaids go," I say.

Kurt shakes his head. "No, some of us wear more clothes than others. Purely for decoration, like the princesses. But it's bothersome when you're in and out of the water."

"See, that settles it."

"Marty, gross!" Layla shields her eyes as he drops his jeans and boxers, which are white with little red kisses. There's a second splash.

Suddenly I nudge Layla. I think of her face sleeping, the way she pulled me closer and lay on my chest. "Remember when we went skinny-dipping off the pier this winter?"

Layla shakes her head and tries to suppress a laugh. "I don't know who had a bigger heart attack, the police officer who found us or my mother when he told her."

She hugs her knees and stares at her toes. It's like we're in my living room again, talking smack about the girls she doesn't like and letting a movie run in the background for white noise. Her hair tangles in the breeze, and when she looks up, I can see her eyes are glazed over. "What's going to happen now?"

"Guess I have to search for an oracle and get the trident pieces back." When I say that, it doesn't sound so hard. Then I let my mind go dark. "What if the others get to them first? They have entire kingdoms as a resource. I have you." I nod to Kurt. "No offense."

"I'm not hurt. You're right. I'm but one source of knowledge. We also have your mother and Thalia, who has her own resources, believe it or not."

"And me," Layla adds.

"You're not in this. I can't have you almost killed *again.*"

She picks at the chipping yellow nail polish on her toes. Her lavender scent is thin in the sea breeze, but it's still there. Her lips are pursed, stubborn, decided. She's all *You're not the boss of me, Tristan Hart.* "Remember when you had that harebrained idea to sail off to the Mississippi like Huck and Jim?" she says.

"Yeah, I needed someone to make me some sandwiches while I sailed."

"Shut up." She gets up in my face. Her pretty hazel eyes stare me down; her hair gets blown right in my face. I could kiss her now if I wanted to. "I went because I knew you wouldn't make it a day without me," she says. "Plus, it's not a Coney Island summer without you. So I'm in. Because you're the biggest jerk on the planet, but you're my jerk."

"Don't spare my feelings." I press my hand to my heart and change the subject. "So what'd you get?"

Her expression flits from confusion to *duh.* She pulls out a thin gold chain with a shell dangling from it. It's a simple little thing; it looks like a spiral that starts off small and ends in a horn-shaped opening.

Kurt nods, Mr. Know-It-All. "*Spirula spirula.* The symbol of your family. May I?" He takes the necklace from her hands and undoes the clasp. He kneels behind her, and she gathers her hair away from her neck and lets him put it on.

I was going to do that.

Maybe I wasn't, but if she'd asked me to, I would have.

Arion clears his throat. "Sire, we've reached the shore."

I run up to the mast deck and grab on to a rope. The mist that's been clinging to Coney Island for the last couple of days is still there, but it's thinning. Luna Park isn't lit up, which is weird for this time of year, but the rest of Brooklyn is there. The entire city is still awake in its own way. The dark shape of the south pier comes into focus. The urchin brothers are flashes of blue and purple, running along the deck and up on the sails, getting ready for us to stop. My stomach flips like when I'm at the top of the Cyclone, and just like that we've landed. There's a hard splash when the anchor drops down.

"Honey, we're home," Layla says, sneaking up behind me and leaning her head on my arm.

"Yeah."

"This is where I leave you, sire." Arion's black ropes bring him down to where we stand. His black and white scales shimmer in the hazy yellow lights on the pier. "Should you need me, I am but a call away." He pats the golden horn hanging on a leather strap across his chest.

"Thanks a lot, man." I hold out my hand to him. I don't know how merpeople say hi and bye. I guess I should add that to the things I still need Kurt to teach me.

Arion stares at my hand like he doesn't know what's required of him.

Layla laughs. "Look, Arion." She slaps my hand, our fingers hooking in the universal *Hey, man, what's good?* hand slap. I guess it's not as *universal* as I thought.

"Ah." His booming laughter echoes as he does as Layla shows him. "My very best." He can't help it; he still bows.

chapter
THIRTY-THREE

I run to the window and pull open the curtains. There's sun! No more fog. Summer in Coney Island is here, like my grandfather said it would be.

"I don't think I've seen you that happy since you were eight and there was a blizzard." Dad stands in jeans and a white T-shirt. As he takes a sip from his coffee, the smell wafts toward me and my stomach grumbles.

"Hungry?"

"Ugh, merpeople are not known for their culinary skills. I ate jellyfish-brain Jell-O."

"Blech." He waves me toward the kitchen. "Kurt's in your bathroom, and Thalia is in your mom's. I think she's using my shampoo to make bubbles."

"Those darn mermaids." I find two cold slices of leftover meat-lover's pizza, which I devour in five bites.

"Don't get too full. Mom wants to make pancakes."

"Did I mention they make these green biscuit things like pancakes, but they're like mushy shrimp and seaweed?"

He sticks his tongue out in distaste and spreads open the newspaper.

"Sorry we woke you last night when we got home. I had no idea what time it was."

"Yeah, yeah. You kids spoiled the wonderful evening your mom and I were having."

"Ugh, disgusting." I put my fingers in my ears, but I can still hear him laughing. I grab a glass and some OJ.

"Oh, come on, son, your merbaby zygote didn't make itself."

Orange juice comes out of my nose. It burns, and my dad just rustles his newspaper so he can read it better.

"You've got juice all over your face," Kurt says.

Dad leaves the *Brooklyn Star* open on an article that reads "Vampire Puppy Sequestered" with "Rise in Missing Teen Boys" right across from it.

Mom walks in wearing one of those long summer dresses that reaches the floor. "Did you see what your dad made for you?" She points out a huge map on the kitchen wall behind me.

"Dad?"

"Well, your mom said there could be maps involved. I figure it's the least I can do to help."

There are geographical maps of the world. One of all the continents, smaller ones of the magnified continents, one for North America, and one of New York City. There's a cluster of push pins at the corner of the NYC map. I grab a blue one and push it on our street. *Here.* "Command Central."

Mom pulls out the box of pancake mix and a frying pan. "Now, from the beginning."

———

I don't spare any details. From Arion and the urchin brothers catching Layla on the ship to how my grandfather split the trident into three. But not the part where I fall asleep with Layla. I keep that to myself.

I forgot to tell Kurt and Thalia to leave out the part about Nieve, because it's just going to freak Mom out. So, of course, Thalia blurts it out. "Aunt Maia, what do you know of the sea witch Nieve?"

My mom's fork grinds against the plate. "My father imprisoned her. She's in the caves."

Thalia bites her lip. I guess every family has the crazy relative no one wants to talk about. In our case, we have a crazy shark-mouthed sea witch who likes to kill her family. "She's been attacking Tristan."

"*What?*"

"But only through my dreams," I add. Sure, that makes it better.

Dad looks confused. "Who is she?"

"A wretched woman with the powers of the greats. We've never been able to prove it, but she killed my mother. I know she did." Mom's fist is white around her fork as she holds it. Her turquoise eyes catch me with a fury I've never seen come out of her. "Why didn't you tell me?"

"Why didn't *you* tell *me?*"

"How long have you been seeing her?"

"Since the day of the storm. I hadn't changed yet, so how was

I supposed to know I wasn't just going crazy after having survived something like that?

"Did she hurt you?"

"She definitely had the opportunity, but it felt more like she was playing with me."

Mom shakes her head silently. "She was rather good at trying to make others insane." Mom pushes her plate away. "She'd delve into your mind and make you see things that weren't real. You'd be defenseless if she could get her hands on you."

"Wait. He gave me a dagger." I run out to the living room and unzip my bag. The black sphere in the center of the handle swirls slowly, like it's in a time of its own.

Dad chuckles. "It's no lightsaber, but it'll do the trick. Let's hope you don't have to use it too soon."

"It's curious," Mom says. "Nieve has been in the caves so long that entire generations don't know of her. How does she know of Tristan?"

"There's a traitor on the island," Kurt says. "The guards are spread out, and more are being called. Maybe she's not only after Tristan."

"She always wanted my father's throne."

"In which case, none of the champions are safe."

I draw Nieve's likeness on a napkin with black marker, a crude shark mermaid. I secure it on the map off the coast of Coney. "If the next full moon is on June 26, I have seventeen days as of right now. A little more than a *forknight*, or whatever it's called. If I were a sea oracle, where would I be?"

I wish I had a sound track of crickets playing in the background, because that's what this silence sounds like—crickets. Dad pressing the pages of the *Brooklyn Star* flat on the table, Mom fuming in my direction with her arms crossed over her chest, and Kurt and Thalia eating as much syrup as we have stored in the pantry. Right, my champion team.

"Oh!" Mom gets up. "When I was girl, my sister Alcyone and I used to play around one of the oracle's caves. She was a mean, nasty old thing. One time—" She looks about the room. "You don't need to know about that part. Another time, our cousin Lucillia dared us to take something from the oracle. She's the youngest of the ten sisters and was born without the sight. She has minor magics and can read corny shells, but that's about it.

"*But* she has a wonderful collection of the rarest pearls and jewels. There was one that was my favorite. It was a pretty, slightly pink pearl from the Arctic. They only form there, and only when two clams get stuck together and—you know. I'd notice it every time my mother sent us to deliver news or food—because it's always good to be on friendly terms with an oracle, no matter what her level of power is."

"So you stole it?" Dad's smile is from ear to ear.

"Do you think she noticed?" Thalia asks.

"It was one of her favorites." Mom shrugs. "I'm sure of it. She wouldn't know it was me, because there was no way she would've been able to see it happening."

My stomach twists. A pretty pink pearl. Oh god. Oh god. Oh god.

"But how do you find her?" Dad asks.

Mom puts her finger on her lip. "The last I remember, she was off the Canary Islands. But that was five h—" Mom notices my dad's cheesy smile at the fact that she's about to reveal how old she is. "A long time ago."

Kurt stands in front of the map, hands on his green cargo shorts. I don't know what he sees. I see a bunch of places I've never been to. That's the thing about growing up in Brooklyn. Everyone is from everywhere in the world, so it always feels like you've already been there. Angelo and his big Italian family, Layla and her Greek and Ecuadorian parents, Jerry and his Puerto Rican parents. Bertie and his crazy Jamaican grandmother who likes to chase us off their front porch with a broom and call us *batti* boys.

Kurt points to the water near Florida. "There's an oracle here."

"How do you know?"

"Because I do." His reply doesn't come out snooty, but there's more than he's saying. Knowing Kurt, he's not going to give anything away. Keepers of the deep. Right. More secrets. "I mean, I've been there."

"How long would it take to swim down there?" Dad asks my mom. "I mean, it's a little over eight hundred miles on land, but then if you consider—" He stares ahead, mumbling, which he does when he's solving my math problems. "Maybe seven days without stopping."

"You're forgetting the channels," Kurt says.

"You lost me at *channels*," I go.

"When you get deep enough, there are currents that break through the water and form paths that run all over the earth." Mom walks around the table and points to New York. "If I remember correctly, there's a channel south of Staten Island that leads to the Great Coral Caves. Is that where the oracle is, Kurt?"

"She's there. It's only been a few years."

"A few human years or a few mermaid years?"

He sighs, exasperated. "A few human years. Thirty, maybe. She should still be there. If we find the sightless oracle and give her your pearl as a gift, especially if she coveted it as you said—"

"Let me go get it," Mom says.

Oh god. I should tell her. No time like the present. "Mom?"

"Yes, honey?"

"Was the pearl strung on a thin silver necklace?"

"Yes, it was in my treasure ch—"

"Well—"

"Please, please tell me you gave it to Layla," she pleads.

The knot in my stomach is tighter. "Actually, I gave it to Maddy."

"Tristan!" She reaches out her hands as if she could wring my neck, which she should.

"I didn't think it was important. You have so much stuff in there, and remember when I was trying to get Cindy Rodriguez to go out with me and you let me pick something out so I could give it to her for Valentine's Day? And the tiara for Maddy's Sweet Sixteen?"

She grunts and balls her hands into fists. Dad flips the pages of his newspaper, his way of telling me, *Don't look at me, son. This is your mess. Fix it.*

Kurt shrugs. "So get it back from her."

Even Thalia laughs at the suggestion. "From what I've gathered from the girls at your school and her general disdain toward you, you'll be lucky if she hasn't already burned it, sold it, or simply thrown it out."

I shake my head. "She doesn't throw things out. She's super sentimental. She keeps everything that means something to her."

"That girl is going to need counseling because of you!" Mom starts throwing dishes into the sink. They fall so hard that I cringe, waiting for one of them to break.

"I'll get it back." I guess we really are going to school today. "Don't worry." But even as I say it, I'm not sure I can convince myself.

chapter
THIRTY-FOUR

Dad honks twice as he pulls away, leaving Kurt, Thalia, and me staring at the steps that lead up to the school entrance guarded by clashing angels.

Some kids are jaywalking away from the school. It's the first sunny day in a week, so half the school must be doing the in-'n'-out, walking into the building just for show before turning right around and heading to the park, Coney, the mall, or if you're my friends, the kosher Mexican restaurant on Sunset with the hot Mexi-Jewish girl behind the counter.

I'm thinking about how I can get the pearl back from Maddy when she won't even talk to me. Adaro and the others are probably halfway around the world, and I'm back at high school. Some things just aren't right.

Someone shouts my name across the street. Kurt and Thalia's hands hover over the daggers at their waists, which they say are glamoured from the human eye. My dagger is in my backpack, because I may have seen a lot of shit in the past couple of days, but this whole glamour business still gets me.

"Ryan!" Thalia shouts, forgetting about the weapon and taking a step forward.

Wonder Ryan runs against the traffic. Thalia's face is as bright as the noon sun when she sees him. I'm surprised they aren't running toward each other in slow motion.

"Hi!" I know his hello includes me and Kurt, but he only looks at Thalia. He's wearing a T-shirt the color of asphalt and new jeans. His hair is messier, not as slicked to the side as usual. "I missed you."

"So did I."

"Yeah," I smirk, "so did I."

Kurt shoves me away toward the entrance, and we share a laugh. I'd never admit that watching them makes my insides feel like beef jerky, like I'm shriveling up because I don't have someone looking at me like that. I can only think of one face I want to see. And when she comes into view, my heart sinks, because she's getting out of a white BMW with tinted windows and a license plate that spells PUMPITUP. Suddenly I remember Alex, the orange guido from the beach who helped find me. Fire creeps over my skin. Even my dagger tucked into my backpack hums as though it feels how ticked off I am.

"What's wrong?" Layla asks, slinging her backpack over one shoulder.

"Nothing," I say with a shrug. If she's not going to tell me that she's seeing someone then fine. "Did you get in trouble?"

"I told my dad I was with Maddy. Her mom unplugs the phone at night, so it's not like they called. Still, he was super mad."

"Hello," Kurt says, all stiff and merman-y.

She smiles at him and says, "Today might be boring, after yesterday."

"I look forward to human pleasantries, actually. First, Tristan needs to acquire something from the angry blond girl."

Before Layla starts breathing fire at me, I go, "I'll explain." The school bells chime and we ascend the steps.

"Hey, Tristan," a girl calls out to me in the hallway. I don't know her name, but I wave.

Ryan slaps my arm, "Dude, Coach said he's going to pull us out of class again for practice. Luis texted me the announcements already."

"Isn't it great to be in charge?" Layla asks. They all fall into a giddy stride walking into the school. Though arriving back home didn't feel any different, coming back to school does. There's something different about the walls, the lighting, the way my classmates' emotions fill the sterile air. Or maybe it's just me and my guilt pangs over having to break my ex-girlfriend's heart all over again.

⌒

"You're officially being weird," Layla tells me, gathering her hair into a bun for practice.

"I'm a weird guy," I say, stretching my arms to either side, "in case you didn't notice."

"You know," she smirks, "I still haven't seen you as a mermaid." Her laugh is small, forced. Her nervousness smells like birthday candles after they're extinguished.

"I'm all man, lady," I try to joke, but it comes out angry and she shrinks back. "I'm sorry."

She dismisses me with her hands and says, "Whatever," before diving into the pool.

What the hell happened? A few hours ago she was all over me and now...What did I do wrong?

Coach blows his whistle. "Chop, chop, Hart! Meet is tomorrow. Gotta be ready!"

I nod, scanning the team one more time for Maddy to come strolling in with her white T-shirt over her bathing suit. She doesn't. She wasn't in school all day either.

I dive when the whistle blows again, the water being my only comfort against the dark thought looming in the back of my mind—the thought that it's only my first day as a champion and I'm already failing.

———

The hot dog is cold and the bread is stale in my mouth, even after I drown it in ketchup. Bertie and Angelo have found a reclining chair with wheels and are taking turns pushing each other across the room, because there are only two lunch monitors and they keep disappearing.

I lower my head to whisper to Layla. "Have you talked to Maddy? She's not in school today. I need to talk to her."

Layla shakes her head sadly. "I bet she's just cutting class, her and her new bad-girl self."

I hesitate, breaking my hot-dog bun into crumbs. "Do you remember that necklace I gave her?"

"Yeah, that little pink pearl. She loves it."

"It belongs to one of the oracles. I need it back."

She exhales loudly. "You know, just when I didn't think you could sink any lower with her."

"Me?" I yell indignantly. "You've seen what I've seen. I wouldn't do it unless this was serious."

She shakes her head. "I don't know if she still has it. Knowing her, she hasn't thrown it out. Did you try her phone?"

"I tried. It goes to voice mail, and she doesn't text back." Layla pushes her tray of food away from her in disgust, and my heart darkens like the clouds that are no longer clinging to the sky.

We sit in silence and watch our friends decide to hang out on the field after class, because Principal Quinn is supposed to be in meetings all day and Ryan has keys to the sports equipment. Kurt avoids looking in my direction, feeling a little guilty that he's having so much fun.

<hr />

The target rings are lined up in the middle of the field. Each one has a different teacher's picture taped at the bull's-eye. Most of the arrows are horribly off, if they make it to the rings at all. There are only seven guys on the archery team, and they take great pride in teaching everyone else. I'm okay at it, but I've never gotten a bull's-eye. Ryan, having taken archery since he was in junior high, is the captain of the team.

I take a seat near the bin of arrows.

Thalia giddily unzips the oversized purple backpack my mom gave her this morning. She pulls out a finely crafted bow and a set of arrows. I know this is a terrible idea. I would never, ever bring weapons to school. But Kurt insisted we have to always be prepared.

"That is a beauty," Ryan says. His blue eyes are practically sticking out of his head when he sees the arrows. "You guys are certified, right?" And I quickly say yes before it becomes an issue.

"Our father was an expert archer," Kurt says. He holds the brass bow, which looks light as a feather as he weighs it against his palms. "He made this for me."

Thalia doesn't join them and instead stays sitting between me and Layla. "You're not going to try?" I ask.

"I find that it might hurt Ryan's human ego if I were to best him." She leans back on her palms. Even knowing what she is, she is a wondrous sight. Her hair is free and flowing around her face with a life of its own. She crosses her legs and wiggles her ankles so that the glitter of her slippers catches the stadium lights. I wonder if she misses her fins. I've only changed a few times, and already something deep inside me is urging me to find a river, or even a bathtub, and sink in.

"I very much miss Atticus," Thalia sighs. "But I like it here. Don't tell Kurt."

"He looks like he's having more fun than he'd like to admit," Layla says. I follow her eyes to where Kurt is taking aim.

"Kurtomatheis wouldn't know how to have fun if it were pulling on his fishtails."

I laugh hard at that. I bet Kurt can hear what we've said, because when he lets his arrow go, it misses Principal Quinn's picture and hits the outer ring.

Ryan gets a bull's-eye on the picture of Mr. Van Oppen. Thalia shrieks and claps her hands. The other guys go, one by one. Some of them get close, but none of them are as accurate.

Jerry throws his arms up, letting the school's bow and arrow fall to the ground. "This is whack! I'm going to check on the freshman lunch period, if you know what I mean."

"Yeah, all your little boyfriends are waiting," Angelo calls out after him, and is answered by Jerry's middle finger. Bertie isn't too far behind Jerry after he fails for the umpteenth time at getting his arrow to go anywhere other than the grass.

"Know what?" Layla goes, pushing herself up, her arm brushing against mine and sending pinpricks down my spine. "I'm gonna go play with sharp objects too." She runs up to Kurt, who shows her how to stand, his hand carefully guiding her hands into position. He whispers something to her, and she smiles. She lets go and hits Ms. Pippen right at the center of her third eye. Layla jumps up and down and throws her arms around Kurt's neck.

"She's lovely, you know." Thalia nods at her.

"Who?"

"You know who. Layla. *Duh?*"

"Yeah, well." I grab a handful of the fake grass and pull hard on it. "This whole Maddy thing isn't going to make me look like Champion of the Year in her eyes."

"If I've learned anything by watching human interaction, it's that they're always angry at the person they feel they love. It's easier to feel anger than love. Love makes people sick. Anger just consumes you so you think you're not feeling anything."

"What about mermaid love?"

"Mer-kin, maybe all immortals, don't necessarily fall in love. Forever is awfully long, and the oceans are vast. You never know who will, how do you say, rock your boat?"

"Maybe that's why I have the reputation of being a man-slut."

"Surely, it has nothing to do with the fact that you're also a sixteen-year-old foot-fin."

She cups her hands around her mouth and hollers when Ryan gets another bull's-eye. He drops his bow and arrow. He runs over to us, gets down on his knees, and kisses Thalia on her sweet full mouth. At first she's surprised. Hell, I'm surprised. So is everyone who's looking at them from the bleachers. A camera flash goes off somewhere. Layla giggles behind her hands, and some of the guys whistle with their fingers. All except for Kurt, who shakes his head disapprovingly.

Thalia rests her hands around Ryan's face, bringing him in, and neither of them seems to notice the crowds. I want to look away, but it's not like anyone's been kissing me lately. I glance at Layla to see if maybe she's looking at me, but her face is tilted to the sky, where a gray patch of clouds is floating over us. When I relax my eyes, the clouds look like grizzly bears. I shut my eyes to get Elias's face out of my head.

Just then Ryan stumbles out of their kiss. "Cool. Okay. Good." He jogs back to the targets with a new strut.

"Tristan." Thalia bites her bottom lip. "Will you make me a promise?"

"What is it?"

"Will you let me stay? If you're king? Would you let me stay here like Aunt Maia did? I could never ask anyone else."

A king keeps his promises, my grandfather told me. I guess I should be careful of the promises I make.

A fat drop of rain hits me right in the eye. The knot in my stomach that started in homeroom is growing with the darkening gray clouds. I point at the sky. "I thought that wasn't supposed to happen anymore."

She stands with her hands over her eyes like visors. "It isn't. Something is wrong." She breathes in long and deep. "Do you smell it?"

I smell damp air. Mist rises around us. Clouds roll in front of the sun, and everything inside me turns. Just like before the first storm, the first wave.

Angelo is the first to run past me, yelling something about his hair and how he'll see us losers back in the lunchroom. Ryan holds out his hands and cries out with excitement. It's something that comes from deep inside him, as if he's waking up for the first time.

The sky turns black, the wind pushing the clouds fast across the sky. The only light comes from the stadium lights and the lightning cracking open the sky. Car alarms go off all along the block. For a moment, it feels like the earth is shaking around us, but it's actually the metal fence around the field that's shaking.

I grab Layla by the shoulders. "Please go inside. Please."

"What's wrong? What's happening?"

Thalia's glamour is fading slightly, or maybe she's just green with sickness as her yellow-green eyes widen at what they see. She points at the other end of the field. "There!"

Three of the ugliest creatures I've ever seen are ripping the fence open. Damp air mingles with the scent of sea sludge, like a manhole just threw them up into the street. The tallest one has the head of a hammerhead shark on the body of a human. Yellow eyes glow on either side of his head. His gills open at the touch of rain, and a smile like crushed glass grins right at me. Beside him is a creature that is blue from head to webbed feet. His elbows end in long red spikes, and his mouth opens to rows of canines. The smallest one of the three is round with the head of a blowfish whose cheeks constantly puff in and out.

Kurt takes aim with his arrow and shoots before I can even blink. The creatures are fast, and Kurt only grazes the blue one in the arm. They jump high and scatter around us.

"Layla, please do as I say!" I fumble to unzip my backpack for my dagger.

"No!" Kurt shouts over me.

"What do you mean no?"

"They'll follow her. Chase her. They're fast, whatever they are."

"You mean you don't know?"

The round one shows himself in front of us. He breathes hard and puffs his body out. Shit.

"Get behind the targets!"

I pull Layla down, shielding her with my body behind the wooden target. The needles hit like darts into the wood.

"Lord Sea, stay down," Kurt says. "Thalia, aim!"

She reaches for a bow, stands quickly, and lets the arrow fly.

Ryan has his back against the target. "What the hell! What the hell are they?"

I peek around the target ring. They're just standing in the shadows waiting, like this is a game.

"Ryan," Kurt says as he kneels and pulls his arrow into place. "You can hit them. Go on. On my count. One."

"Two."

Thalia's hands tremble as they search her backpack. She pulls out two slender daggers and throws one to Layla, who catches it in midair.

"She can't fight." My voice is frantic, and I hardly recognize it. This is not how a champion should sound.

"She has to."

Layla pulls the dagger out of the sheath and holds it up, her knuckles with a vise grip on it. She nods surely. This isn't like fencing during spring recess. This is something else, something we've never faced before.

"Three!" Kurt and Ryan shoot. The creatures spread out instantly, howling as Ryan's arrow pierces the hammerhead in the arm. The creature howls in pain, but just for a moment, before pulling the arrow out with one tug, dripping black blood and red flesh.

"Holy shit!" Ryan says, holding his chest as if to keep his heart from coming out.

I want to tell him it'll be okay, but even I don't know that. As Kurt yells something over the thunder, the creatures charge right at us. I shove Layla out of the way, so the blue creature pushes the target on top of me. The ground is muddy and wet. I slip when I try to push the wooden target off me. The blue one does it for me. He pulls the red spikes out of his skin and stabs at the grass around me. I kick his gut with the full force of my legs roll over, and reach for my dagger.

Up close, his eyes are dirty yellow. His permanent smile reveals bloody gums. He raises his fists in the air and brings them down hard on the ground, shaking the field right under me. I swing and catch him on the side and he winces. The barnacles around his neck suck at the air like suction cups. Layla runs around us, and as he reaches out with his spikes, she brings the dagger down through his back.

The creature's body shakes, and black blood dribbles out of his mouth. The body goes limp over me and falls slack on the ground. I take his red spikes and stab him through the chest to make sure he stays there.

"Where are the other two?" I push myself off the ground.

More car alarms go off after another blast of thunder. The few students who didn't make it inside are screaming behind the bleachers. Up inside the school, crowds are gathered at the windows.

Kurt and Ryan hold their arrows at the ready. The five of us stand in the middle of the field. The other two are still out there. I breathe in air heavy with their stink.

"There!" I turn and the guys let their arrows fly up at the fence where the hammerhead has climbed. He ducks to the right and jumps on the ground and charges at me. For all their strength and speed, they're really uncoordinated and stupid. His yellow eyes are focused on me and only me. I punch him with all my strength; my knuckles come away bloody from the sharp scales of his cheekbones. I slash my dagger out with both hands, but he jumps back from every swing.

Kurt's voice thunders over the car alarms, the screams, and the clapping thunder. "Tristan, get down!"

I throw myself on the ground as he takes one clean shot. The creature falls backward with Kurt's arrow pierced right through his throat. A guttural wail sounds through the field. Layla runs up to me and helps me stand. She takes my hand and examines it where my knuckles are cut open. "It's just a surface scrape."

Ryan stands over the blue guy's body. He taps it with his foot. It doesn't move. He bends down and uses the tip of an arrow to prod at the still body. "What are these things?" He jumps back as the body convulses and then starts to decompose into the grass, stinking of rotting fish.

"Ugh, that's disgusting."

"Let's get back inside," I say, holding my hand out for Layla to grab. She raises the dagger in the air so the rain will wash away the slick, black blood on the edges. Kurt's violet eyes are luminous in the darkness. I wonder if mine look the same way. I can tell he's still listening for the other creature, because I am too.

Thalia stands nervously just inside the gate leading back inside the building. Her voice is small as her eyes flicker around the field. She pushes her wet hair away from her eyes. "Come, Ryan."

He cups his hands at the sky and lets the rain pool in them, then washes the black blood off with it. He walks toward the entrance with his blue eyes focused on Thalia. His face registers shock as Kurt raises his bow and arrow at him. Kurt's face is stone. Ryan holds his hands up in the air.

"What are you *doing*?" I yell at Kurt. But then I see what he's doing. The arrow is pointed past Ryan to where the third creature, the blowfish, stands a few feet behind our friend.

"Ryan," Kurt says. He raises his arrow a little higher. "Don't. Move."

I don't know what I can do with just a dagger. If I throw it at the creature, I could very well miss and stab my friend. I do know that none of these creatures want my friends. They want me.

And before I can say *duck*, before I can even raise my dagger, the creature puffs out his face and snaps his neck in my direction.

I raise my hands to cover my face, and my entire body is a scream as Layla jumps in front of me, arms wrapped around my neck, mouth open in a pained gasp as the needles pierce her back.

chapter
THIRTY-FIVE

The rain beats hard against my neck.

Layla's eyes are wide and staring right at me. She's still standing. I'm afraid to hold her too tightly.

Behind us the creature falls, an arrow pierced though his throat. Layla's knees bend. She says my name. The thunder is loud, and the rain is like pellets against the ground, but I know she says my name. Her weight goes slack, and I keep my hands under her arms to try to keep her up.

"Help me." I don't know if I've actually said it.

Their footsteps splash against the ground. Thalia is at my side, helping me lay Layla facedown on the ground.

"Do something," I say. I look up at Kurt, who stands over me. Doing nothing. He could've shot sooner. Why did he hesitate? Why did I just stand there?

"There's too much poison," he says helplessly.

I take my dagger and, as gently as I can, rip the thin cotton of her T-shirt. The needles go right through it, and I can't take the shirt off without hurting her. I drop my blade on the ground. Run my hands through my hair. Press against my skull as if I can make all of this go away. Thalia is pulling out the spikes and sobbing at the same time. Layla's back is like a dark board of tiny red dots where blood pools out and is washed away just as quickly by the rain.

My knees are raw from kneeling on the turf. I hold her hand in mine, but there's no pressure, no weight. My body is cold. My skin is numb in the rain.

"That's all of it," Thalia says, holding out a handful of black needles. They're slick and black and don't look like much.

"Wake up," I whisper in Layla's ear. I flip her over in my arms so that I can look at her again. I never used to understand what people meant when they said they felt small against the rest of the world. But I do now. Her body is motionless in my arms. Her lips are purple. Her eyelids are wet. She looks the same way she did when she was sleeping in my chambers on the island, when we'd fall asleep in my living room when we were littler, when we'd lie out on the beach at noon and I'd wear my black sunglasses so she wouldn't see that I was looking at her. Something inside me breaks over and over again, and I don't know how to stop it.

"Tristan."

The rain stops. The clouds push away. I can feel the warmth of the sun against my skin. When I open my eyes, it's still dark out. The light isn't coming from the sky; it comes from Layla. The necklace my grandfather gave her glows under her shirt. *No harm can come to you by me or mine*, he'd said.

Her lips move again. "Tristan."

She smiles at me, and I try not to hug her too hard. I'm about to say something, anything, when a rough voice cuts through the field and yells, "Hands in the air!"

At the entrance of the field are maybe half a dozen cops. The creatures have completely washed away. The targets are all split into pieces; there's a huge hole at the gate and arrows all over the grass.

The officer repeats himself, and this time they all cock their guns.

chapter
THIRTY-SIX

An EMT drapes an itchy blanket around my shoulders. I'm shirtless with a bandage around my ribs, where apparently two of them are broken.

The rain has stopped, except for the thin sheet of mist that clings low to the ground. The EMT hands me a cup of black coffee. I shake my head at the bitter hotness that burns my tongue.

Detective Donovan has his hands in his leather jacket, nodding periodically as the hysterical girls give him their versions of what happened. Regular, end-of-the-year fun. Three monsters break through the fence. The girls giving their witness accounts point at me. Detective Donovan comes over to me, finally.

"Hurts?" He nods at my bandaged hand.

"No," I lie, and squeeze it for show.

"Are you up to giving a statement?"

"Like the girls said," I tell him. "We were hanging out on the field. These guys just came through the fence. Attacked. We tried to fight them off, and they went away."

"Guys?" The question lingers as he chews his gum. "The other students say they were *creatures*. That they looked like sharks and"—he stops himself, because he might just be too professional to even utter this—"creatures from the blue lagoon."

"I'm pretty sure it's the black lagoon," I say, regretting my smart mouth. "I think they had masks on."

"The girls say that they *melted* into the rain."

I shake my head, thankful that Ryan had been smart enough to put our weapons away for us, thankful that Layla was alive in my arms. She'd just left with her parents, wearing my shirt because we had to rip hers. "It happened so fast. They ran away after they heard the sirens."

I can smell Detective Donovan's doubt and his irritation, like dirt in my mouth.

"You kids involved in some kind of gang activity?"

"No, sir."

"You don't go here, do you, son?" He turns to Kurt. Thalia sits beside her brother. The blanket slips from her shoulders and onto the floor. No one moves to pick it up.

"I am not your son, sir, and no, this is not my school. We're Tristan's cousins, visiting students for the remainder of the summer."

"Some summer," he scoffs. His dark eyes squint, like if he looks hard enough I'll cave and tell him I'm a criminal.

An argument breaks out over in the parking lot. "Ma'am, please stay behind the tape!"

"Don't you touch me. I need to see my son!" My mom pushes

her way through. She pulls me into such a tight hug that I spill coffee on myself.

"Sorry! Sorry. Oh my goddess—"

"Ma'am, are these your niece and nephew?"

"Yes, why?"

"They have no identification."

"Well, yes, it's all at home. I didn't anticipate they'd need their passports in case there was an attack on the school." She sniffs down her nose at him. "Dad's waiting in the car around the corner. Most of the streets are blocked off."

"Tristan," Detective Donovan tries once more. His hard mask falls, and his frustration peeks through. "Do you remember what these men *looked* like? Anything that can help us? Any of you."

What am I supposed to say? There's no Sea King, so the nasty things that live in the ocean have come out to play? I'd be halfway to the nuthouse before anyone can say, *Are the men supposed to be so shiny?* "It was dark. They came out of nowhere."

"Are you finished?" Mom asks Detective Donovan.

He nods. "I'll be in contact. Here's my card. If you remember *anything.*"

I want to tell him that they can't help me and I can't help them. Instead I take the thin white card and pocket it so he'll at least get off my back. We follow my mom through the crowd. People stand on their porches and stick their heads out their windows. There's a PIX 11 camera crew and a lady TV reporter in a pale pink suit, who looks sternly at the cameraman. Everyone she interviews points in my direction. This is so not good.

I can see Ryan getting into the back of his parents' car. He looks behind one more time so he can wave to Thalia, who gives him a sad smile. I put my arm over her shoulder. The lady in the pink suit bum-rushes us, and suddenly between the sidewalk and our car, I have a hot white light on my face.

"How do you feel about people calling you the hero of the night? Is there a connection between this attack on your school and the missing boys throughout the city?" I swat the microphone away from my face and shut the door. As the reporter smacks the glass with her hand, my mom hits the gas.

chapter
THIRTY-SEVEN

Neptune's Diner is buzzing with families and early bird couples. Old Ukrainian waitresses with graying buns and faces that would scare you out of changing your order bus their tables as quickly as they serve them. We've got pancakes, French toast, eggs and sausage, and about ten side orders of bacon.

We skipped dinner the night before, everyone staying in their own section of the apartment. I sat in front of my Command Central wall, staring at maps that didn't tell me anything useful. Thalia went right to my room to call Ryan and convince him he didn't see exactly what he saw.

Dad slaps his newspaper with the back of his hand. "Who even took this picture?"

Under the caption "Local Heroes Fight for Fellow Students" is a crude picture of us fighting the sea creatures. We don't look like we're winning. I stuff my mouth so I'll have something to do.

Dad shuts the newspaper, stopping short of crumpling it into a ball and throwing it across the diner. "I can't believe they would keep the school open today."

"We have to go. We have to find Maddy." And I have to see Layla. She was dead in my arms, and then she wasn't. If anyone knows what it's like to think you've died and come back, it's me.

Kurt clears his throat. "How do you know your previous paramour will be there? She wasn't there yesterday."

"It's okay to just say *ex-girlfriend*, you know."

A different waitress rounds our table. But when I look at her again, I see she's not a waitress. She's wearing an apron with the picture of a cupcake haloed by stars with the logo "Erica's Cupcakes" in neon pink. She glances behind her nervously. There's something familiar about her, only I can't sift through my mind fast enough. She bows lightly at me. Kurt looks up at her, wearing the same expression I am.

"Have we met?" he goes, Mr. Smooth Criminal.

She smiles, tucking her long brown curls behind her ear. That's when I notice a tiny suction cup protrude from the side of her wrist and then sink right back. I jump back, rocking our booth, which alarms the early bird couple behind us.

"I didn't mean to frighten you, Lord Sea."

"Will you guys stop calling me that," I hiss.

"Pardon again." She looks back and waves at the cook visible behind the line of yellow order tickets. He winks at her and flips a pancake. "I've been looking for you. Your whereabouts are more secret than the Glass Castle."

"Who are you?" Mom asks, pushing herself erect.

The lady shrinks back a bit. "My friends call me Penny. I wish to speak to Lor—"

I hold up my hand. "Call me Tristan."

Everyone scoots over a seat to make room for her.

"You were on Arion's ship," I say. "You were with the turtle boy."

She nods happily. "He's my son, Timmy."

Timmy the turtle. No wonder merpeople are known for their cruelty.

"I remember you," Thalia says matter-of-factly.

"My son is rooting for you as champion."

"How did you find him?" Dad says, staring at the spot on her wrist where the suction cup rises again. His eyes are full of wonder, and I suddenly wish there were more people like my dad out there. "Is there a mer-tracking device on you we should check for?" He reaches over to me and digs through my hair until I pull away.

"My boyfriend," she nods toward the kitchen at the cook. "Timmy got your picture from the papers and put it on our refrigerator. Right next to his Batman and Superman magnets."

"That's real—neat?" I say, wishing I could find that part of me that's funny and quick and always ready to make girls laugh. But it's like that half of my brain is asleep, and all I can think about is Layla almost dying because of me. "Why were you looking for me, Penny?"

"I'm technically not supposed to do this," she says.

"Because you're landlocked, and the landlocked have no say in who becomes champion," Kurt says.

I try to kick him under the table, but I miss and hit the metal pole. Anger flashes over Penny's delicate face. "Yes, I'm landlocked. Which means I'm powerless against the merrows attacking our shores. Killing on land. The longer there is no Sea King, the longer those on these shores will be subject to the creatures who wish there were no Sea King at all. Believe me, just because we pay tithes for protection doesn't mean there aren't those who would rather have no king at all." She leans closer to Kurt, practically yelling in his face. I don't exactly blame her.

Mom and Kurt start talking over each other, but he lets her go first, always the gentleman. "What do you mean, the merrows? They're not allowed to grow past their infancy."

"What's a merrow?"

Penny takes the crumpled newspaper from the table and opens it to the pictures of the attack at our school. "These are merrows. This is the first time I've seen them, but I've heard stories of those that grow to full size and live in swamps and small lakes. When they came on shore, they had no fear of being caught. They tore through cars. Some got lost in the subway and got run over by trains. Can't say they're very smart, but in numbers they would be a challenge. The alliance isn't happy."

"Guys, what *are* they?"

"Wait a minute," Thalia says, eating the last bit of French toast. "Merrows are tiny, and they're disfigured. Those creatures were fully grown."

"Which would mean that those responsible for disposing of the merrows aren't doing what they're supposed to," Kurt's says gravely.

I smack my hand on the table. "Hi, champion here. Would someone mind telling me what you're all talking about?"

Penny takes a deep breath. "Sometimes a mermaid gives birth to a deformed child, not fully human or mer-kin. It has no reason, no sense of speech. There was a time when they tried to acclimate them into families. But they were too wild, and it often ended very bloodily. Before King Karanos—your grandfather—King Erebos decreed that the merrows born at court would be killed instantly. King Karanos thought it was too cruel, so instead he had a prison built for them where they would be left alone.

"What about the ones *not* born at court?" I find that the question leaves me slowly. Mostly because I already know the answer, but also because I don't want to hear it.

Penny looks down that the table. She picks up the salt shaker and holds it. "Sometimes the families would not want to travel that far and would simply leave the creature at the edge of a precipice. It is considered a curse to raise a merrow."

"I see," Dad says quietly.

No one touches their food anymore.

"So these creatures," I say, "these *merrows* that are supposed to be dead, are now fully grown and attacking people."

Penny shakes her head. "Not people. They're after you. Whatever gets in their way is just collateral damage."

"They've never attacked before?" Dad asks.

"They're not equipped to survive on their own," Thalia says. "If they're living to that size, then someone is raising them. I've never seen one before—"

"Nor have I," Kurt adds.

"The Sea King does not want to be like his father. From what my grandparents told me, King Elanos had the wrath of the eye of a storm. Your father," Penny turns to my mom, "wanted to be loved by his people, and now it's going to haunt him."

"Nieve is raising them," Kurt says. I can feel his mind turning. He's coming up with a plan. I have no plan. I'm just trying to take this all in. "I'm sure of it."

"What else do you know, Penny?" I ask.

"I'm not connected to the underground as such. This was my first tithe to the king. I was born on land, but my mother taught me the basic rules to keep my family protected."

I chew on a piece of bacon, just for the taste of salt in my mouth. "Why are you doing this? I mean, if you have no connection to the court, why would you even care about the championship?"

"Because unlike other merpeople, you know what it's truly like to be part of both worlds. You could change things. Change things for real. Like I said, my boy is rooting for you." She stands and presses her hands on her apron. "I have to get back to work. Remember, Tristan, it's not just my boy and I rooting for you. You'll find our kind is all behind you, not just in the seas." With that and a small wave she's gone.

I try to give her the best smile I can. I don't want to disappoint her by letting her know I'm no closer to piecing the trident back together than I am to graduating from high school.

chapter
THIRTY-EIGHT

The minute I step into school, I remember being on that field. I remember Kurt pointing his arrow past Ryan's head at the creature. I remember standing there waiting for its poisonous needles to hit me and then feeling Layla jump in the way. The way her body stiffened around me as the poison worked through her body. I shut my eyes against it. I decide nothing like that is ever going to happen again, because I'm going to find Maddy. I'm going to get the pearl, and I'm going to find the oracles.

I try to replay what Penny said at Neptune's Diner, but I collide into someone. Someone who is really pissed off.

"What's your problem, man? Can't you see where you're walking?" Angelo shoves me into the locker. It doesn't hurt, but the dagger in my backpack hums. "What's up, pretty boy? Need me to teach you how to talk?"

I wave Kurt off, because he's ready to jump right in there. We're gathering a crowd, people snapping pictures and running videos with their phones.

"Relax, man." I put my free hand on his shoulder. This is Angelo—pervy, wassa-matta-wit-you Angelo. Angelo who was born with a head of hair full of industrial-strength hair gel and a gold Italian chain, who always has your back unless he's the one messing with you. He's the asshole of your friends, but he's *your* asshole friend.

He grabs my hand and puts me into an *I'm-not-kidding* headlock.

I can feel it in my spine, the magic that's tattooed in my blood, in the ancient-as-hell dagger sheathed on my back. I elbow him and flip his arm around. I push him against the lockers, but not enough that it'll hurt him too badly. Just to show him that I can. "What's the matter with you, bro?"

His eyes are glassy. I wonder who else has suffered his wrath, and it's not even first period. I let him go, and he shakes his head as if he's been sleepwalking. "I don't know, man. I feel, like, jittery, you know?"

I let the tips of our foreheads touch like we're in a huddle before a meet. "Nothing you could've done."

"Yeah, but you're my boy. We're a team. My team needed me yesterday when you were getting attacked by some punks."

"We took care of it," I say. I don't know if I'm saying this for his comfort or for mine. It's even worse because beneath his trademark dude-scented body spray is the smell of his guilt, like wet dirt being turned in a grave.

"All right, you vultures. Get out of here!" Layla's voice breaks up the crowd. She doesn't always wear makeup, but she's wearing it now. It looks pretty on her, but I can tell that she's trying to cover up the puffiness from crying too long.

"Thanks," I say. I feel stupid standing and waiting for her to say something else. To tell me it's good to see me. Maybe this was what it felt like when she thought I was gone. Like I'm freaking thirsty and no amount of water will fix it. Only her. Only Layla can fix me.

She shuts her eyes and shifts the weight of her bag. "I don't know about you losers, but I'm grounded till I'm married and popping out babies. In that order."

"I'm free third period." Angelo raises his hand. Normally, Layla would punch him in the gut, but today she's going to let it slide. The bell rings, and everyone scatters except for us.

"Are you okay?" I ask, taking one step toward her.

She nods once but doesn't look at me. "Maddy's in the fourth-floor bathroom with her friends. She invited me to hang. I just don't like smelling like smoke."

"You need to go get her," Thalia tells me. She links arms with Layla and gives me a reassuring smile. I want to stay with Layla, but I want to go get the pearl. I leave them at the entrance of homeroom and keep walking straight ahead to the next stairwell. I look back once to see if Layla is looking too, and she isn't. She's pulling farther and farther away, and I don't know how to get her back.

———

The fourth floor is the ghost floor.

It's the only part of school, other than part of the basement, that never got renovated. You instantly know where the bathroom is, because all you have to do is follow the thin trail of smoke. The thick wooden door has a little W tacked on like an afterthought. I press my ear against it, but all I can make out is mumbling, some laughter, more mumbling.

"Knock, knock." I push open the door slowly.

There's a sudden rustle of kids gathering their things together and putting out their cigarettes.

"Chill. I'm not Quinn."

"Sorry, we thought you were Umberto," one of Maddy's friends says. She relights the end of her cigarette, and the little red light flares with every pull. "He came by before to clean the bathroom and gave us a five-minute warning."

Umberto is pretty easy to bribe as long as he knows he won't get caught.

Maddy sits between two other girls. One girl has a short black bob and wears tons of pearls around her neck. The girl on the other side is less dramatic, with long chestnut hair and rectangular glasses. She digs her hand into a bag of neon sour worms. I can smell the sour sugar from here.

Maddy stands, clearly uncomfortable that I'm in her space. "Are you lost, Tristan?"

"I was looking for you."

"Why?"

"Because I need to speak with you."

The girls scoff and snicker and grin at each other. *Am I really that bad?*

She looks like a blond Wednesday Addams with that dress and those stockings. She shoves me with her shoulder on the way out.

"Guess I deserve that," I grumble.

We stand just down the hallway, where the cigarette smoke only lingers.

"So talk." She cocks her head to the side, so her braids look like uneven weight balances. I wish I had practiced. I wish I knew what to say that would make her hate me a little less. I came to school to find her, and now here she is.

"How long have we been friends?" I start.

"Since we started high school." She doesn't even hesitate. "Why?"

"I know what I did was stupid. It was wrong. It proves that I'm an asshole."

There's a tug of a smile at her lips. "Keep going."

"And I'm sorry I'm the reason—"

"Trist, don't flatter yourself. I know it looks like I changed drastically after we broke up when you kissed that skank at the beach, but that wasn't why. Not entirely. I'm tired of being the *Amish* lady's daughter, the girl no one can believe you'd ever date."

My stomach turns into nuts and bolts. "I wish I could change what I did, but I can't. The truth is that you deserve better than me. I was so caught up in how sweet you are, and how honest and different from other girls. I thought, why not? Maddy's pretty, thoughtful—"

"Plus, I blew you."

My voice cracks, "Yes, you did. And, thank you. It was nice. Great, I mean. But, you know—"

She sighs. "Spit it out, Tristan. Do you want to be with me again? Is that it?"

Fine, now or never. "The necklace I gave you. It wasn't mine to give. It was my mom's. A real important family heirloom, and she asked me about it yesterday. So I kind of need it back."

She stares at her Converses. They're all drawn on with black Sharpie. The laces on her right side are untied. I bend down and tie them for her but keep my eyes on her face. She has no idea how much I have riding on this. How much I actually need her to help me now. How I really wish I'd never hurt her.

"Tell your mom I'm real sorry," she says. "I'll pay for it. I lost it. I—" She doesn't finish. She walks away.

It feels like the hallway gets longer and she'll never reach the bathroom door again. When she does, she glances over her shoulder to make sure I'm still crouched here.

I am.

chapter
THIRTY-NINE

I take the stairwell down one flight of stairs, but it's blocked by three couples making out. They don't even budge as I step between them and down to the third floor. Someone slams into me, pushing me against the hallway door.

"Watch it!" Some guy holds on to his pants as he runs away from two bigger guys. The halls are filled with more students cutting class than usual. A poke on my ass cheek makes me jump. When I turn around, I see it's a girl I hooked up with once at a party, maybe during freshman year—Samantha? She walks around me and stands in my way. She puts her index finger on my chest. Her eyes are glossy. Her smile is wide and manic. She leans close to my ear at the same time that I lean away.

"I haven't stopped thinking about you, Tristan."

"Thanks, Sam."

"It's *Jessica.*"

"Thanks, Jessica. Listen, I have to go." I try to step around her, but she blocks my way.

"I was thinking we could, you know, hang. You're always so busy that I never see you around."

The smell that comes from her is like rotting fruit and the spearmint gum she's chewing. I try to cover my nose politely. "Okay, how about I call you tonight?"

"Okay!"

"Good. I'll talk to you later, okay?"

"I'll be waiting!" She blows me a kiss as I run the other way, slowed down by the crowded hallway of students. Another girl calls out my name, but I keep moving forward. I make a left into the stairwell, where more couples are grinding against each other. I mean, damn, there are plenty of dark corners in this old school without having to do it all together.

A loud pop crashes against the wall, right over my head, and breaks into itty-bitty pieces. It's a peppermint ball. Or it *was* a peppermint ball. Then another. And another, until one finally hits me square on the forehead.

"I hate you!" she says. It's Diana, from the tennis team. We dated briefly last summer. Her serving arm was impressive, but she never, *ever* stopped talking.

She's holding a bag of assorted candy and chocolates, the big ones you get at Coney Island for $4.99. "Why didn't you call me back?"

"Diana, look, I'm sorry."

"It's Deanna!" She throws the bag of candy on the floor and runs up the steps.

Okay. I *have* to find my friends. This is beyond my level of strange.

I skid on the tiles when I round the corner to History. They're gathered around the door. Layla is leaning against the wall. She smiles the way I haven't seen in days. Her head is cocked to the side, and she's twirling a silky strand around one finger until it makes a coil of its own. She's flirting. She's flirting with Kurt, whose shoulders are relaxed and easy as he mimics the movement of throwing a lance. She laughs, but when she looks down the hallway to where I'm walking, her laugh goes away.

I've used the word *killjoy* plenty of times, but I never thought I'd feel like one.

"Well?" she says. I have her and Kurt's undivided attention. For the first time, I notice that the couple making out in the corner is Ryan and Thalia. Guess he can't ask too many questions if he can't form a coherent sentence. Not that either of them seems to mind.

"She says she doesn't have it."

"Oh," they both say.

"Yeah." I walk past them. I'm not going to add to my recent Strange Encounters of the Mer-Kind, because that'll just add to the list of things I haven't figured out. I can smell their disappointment, like flowers wilting in heat. An outstretched hand stops my forward motion.

"Must be careful, Mr. Hart, or you'll walk right past my classroom for the third time since your miraculous return." Mr. Van Oppen stands in white slacks and a dark green blazer over a crisp white shirt that looks like it resists wrinkles. He's the only dude I know who can pull off all of that, plus a blue scarf tucked just so around his neck and into his collar. When he smiles, it's sort of slanted, revealing teeth that look like he drinks too much coffee. His blue eyes are ringed with dark circles. I can picture him walking around his apartment, smoking cigarettes that he rolls himself and wishing he could burn our weekly essays.

I take my usual seat against the wall. This is the whitest of all the classrooms. The shutters are pulled tight, and there are curtains that don't let in any light. It's one of the few rooms that's air conditioned, so it always gets the most requests for transfers.

There's a small gasp behind me; it comes from Thalia. I guess even mermaids can't resist his strange charms. She uses Ryan as a shield and pulls him to the back of the classroom. Van Oppen is ruffled himself, like he can't resist *her* mermaid charm.

The last time I saw Mr. Van Oppen was in my dream, something I would never admit to anyone. Layla sits in front of me, right at the front. I can smell her lavender shampoo and something else.

"I forgot your cousins were joining us, Mr Hart," Mr. Van Oppen says.

Kurt walks in slowly. He sits beside me. He sniffs the air, and by the subtle growl on his lips, I can tell he smells something he really doesn't like. Everything about him, from his shoulders to the way he balls up his hands into fists, screams *tense.*

"Where was I? Oh yes, Helen of Troy." Van Oppen clears his throat and looks paler than usual. He stands over his desk and rifles through a stack of papers.

Bracelets jingle all over the class as hands fly up. The girls know to answer just by the way he looks at them, all *Yeah, that's right, I'm calling on you.*

A girl with purple-rimmed glasses leans forward so hard that I think she might teeter toward him. "Well, there was this thing on the History Channel about how this lady was trying to prove Helen of Troy was really real. But some text is missing. Or was it a building that was missing? I can't remember."

"Ah, yes, the best thing about history is perhaps also the most frustrating. There are some things you can't prove. Because the evidence has crumbled or washed away, or in some cases, it's been hidden."

"So was she real or what?" a girl in the back asks sweetly.

The girl beside her says, "I'd like to think she was. It's romantic that they went to war over her."

"Kingdoms go to war over less," Kurt says darkly.

"You're right," Van Oppen says. He stands in front of Layla and lifts her chin with his finger. If he weren't my teacher, I'd shove him off her. "Was this the face that launch'd a thousand ships, / And burnt the topless towers of Ilium? / Sweet Helen, make me immortal with a kiss. / Her lips suck forth my soul: see where it flies!" He hands her the handouts to pass along, and I can swear I can hear their tiny hearts fluttering all over the classroom.

"That wasn't in the reading," someone says.

"No, it was written by Christopher Marlowe. This story has fascinated people so much that they've spent their whole lives trying to prove it could've been true. They don't have much to go on, but they chase all over the world for clues. Sometimes its something as small as a rumor about a distant island claimed to be the home of the oracle that warned Menelaus about protecting Helen."

That's a thought. I raise my hand. "What do you mean, Menelaus and the oracle?"

"I'll forgive the question, since you had a concussion for a few days. I'll assume *that's* the reason you don't remember the reading on it."

"Uhm, thank you?" I go. "So what did Menelaus *do* to talk to the oracle?"

Mr. Van Oppen bares his teeth in a curious smile. "I do not wish to fill your head with fodder, Mr. Hart. The Greek oracles were girls chosen for their beauty. It was their burden, but it also was a great honor. The oracles would sit in a room with burning herbs and stones, the smoke so potent it would make them hallucinate. This would be translated as the prediction or sight. Hardly more than a girl's delirious ramblings. It'd be like the president taking advice from a socialite tripping on acid, which, well—never mind."

"So you believe Helen might be real but not oracles?"

"I did not say that, Mr. Hart. I merely stated what I know about village oracles in ancient Greece." I just remembered why I always fall asleep in his classes or take extended bathroom breaks. "Now, if you're asking me about real oracles, that's a different story."

Maybe it's his sharp blue eyes, maybe it's that he dresses like something out of a Jane Austen novel, or maybe it's the slightest trace of an accent. Whatever it is, the class is transfixed by his words.

Kurt shakes his head at me. It's not like I'm going to pull off clothes to show my Spider Man costume and reveal my true identity or anything.

Thankfully, Layla asks for me: "Did he just go up to an oracle and ask?"

"If only it were as easy as that. It's not the high-school cafeteria where you ask Lourdes for extra fries and she gives them to you. You present the oracle with a tribute, and if she's in a good mood, then she may give you an answer."

"What kind of tribute?" I go. And they say you'll never learn anything useful in high school.

People start to whisper. *He's so weird. Good thing he's cute. Can you believe those are his cousins? I don't care what anyone says, green hair is so clichéd.*

"Half your herd of cows. Your second wife. The blood of a virgin. The usual."

The sharp whistle of microphone feedback slices through the loudspeaker. A small voice announces that all after-school activities are canceled. I know we have a meet tomorrow and all, but my head's not in it right now.

Just then a sweet, soft hum fills the room. At first we look to the speakers, because it's not the first time the announcer has left on the microphone while he's jamming to his new-millennium pop collection. This time it's different. The temperature in the room rises. The sound is like a lullaby, a pitch that wraps around you and leads you wherever it wants.

Van Oppen smacks a book against the desk. "Whoever that is, please turn it off. Now!"

But it isn't coming from in here. It's coming from the hallway. There's a hole in my stomach when I fear that somehow Nieve has found a way to get me, that my dream after I fought Elias is coming true. I grab my bag for my dagger at the same moment that the door flies open.

My breath is caught in my throat.

I hold on to my desk, because I feel as if I'm trying to wake up from a nightmare.

She fluffs her messy white-blond hair, stepping into the room in a slinky black dress under a bright pink motorcycle jacket and heels that look like they're made of sequins and glitter.

Elias's fiancée.

"Hi." She leans against the doorframe. Her gray eyes find mine without even searching the room. "I'm Gwen. Tristan's cousin."

Part III

They say the sea is cold, but the sea contains the hottest blood of all, and the wildest, the most urgent.

—D. H. LAWRENCE

chapter
FORTY

Gwen.

So that's her name. So sorry about your future husband, Gwen. It wasn't my fault. There's this sea witch, you see?

"Don't forget about us." A sharp soprano voice echoes through the hallway. Behind Gwen is a cluster of girls, girls I've only seen as mermaids.

The court princesses are at my school. It's one thing for me to have this secret I can barely keep from my friends; now I have to deal with the rest of the school. I'm halfway sitting, halfway standing. "What are you guys doing here?"

"Come, now, Tristan." Gwen steps forward. "That's no way to treat your family." She hands Van Oppen a piece of paper, along with a smile that would have most men on their knees pledging their love for her. Not me, of course.

From where I stand, it's just a blank piece of paper, but he nods with a tense smile and tucks it in with his other papers mumbling something that sounds like "more of them."

As the princesses walk in, there isn't a single person who isn't staring at them. The glamours may disguise their naturally raw colors and their flawless faces. But nothing can disguise their hourglass figures as they move through the desk aisles like snakes in the desert.

There are four of them, from the princess with a lush head of chestnut waves who wears a shirt so tiny she might as well be wearing two clam shells on her breasts, to the one with ivory skin and plum-purple hair gathered in a bun. Like Thalia, nothing disguises the slight point to their ears or the gem-like eyes that glance giddily around the classroom.

"Dude," Angelo goes, "can I come to your next Christmas party?"

Sure, if Christmas is going to be ten thousand leagues under the sea and Rudolph is going to be a sea horse named Atticus.

Gwen takes the empty seat behind me just as the bell rings. I get up right away, because part of me is afraid she's going to take out a knife and stab me in the back. She thinks I killed her fiancée, and now she's going to try to kill me on my own turf.

My classmates stand aside to let Gwen leave first. I lean against the lockers just outside the door, and she stands in front of me. The metal bits of her leather jacket *clink, clink*. The gray of her eyes is harsh, and they're set on my face. Still, when she smiles, everything about her softens.

"I'm guessing this isn't your first time on land," I say.

She shakes her head slowly. "I've got a few years on you, foot-fin."

"You're not allowed to call me that."

"I can do whatever I want." She crosses her arms over her chest, which pushes her cleavage up and out. Not that I'm noticing or anything.

"What do you think you're doing here?"

She shrugs. "It's tradition for eligible princesses to seek a champion for courtship. Brendan and Dylan are being visited by *dozens* of mermaids from every inch of the seas. Technically, I'm betrothed, so I don't have to be here. But my fiancé's gone missing because of some half-breed claiming the throne."

Fine. If she wants to go that route. "I'm flattered you've chosen me to rebound on, especially after what *you* did to your champion."

If she weren't already so white, I'd say she goes pale at that. But the shock that registers on her face is all the proof I need that she helped Layla win, that *she did* something to Elias, which makes her guiltier than it makes me.

"That's right, Princess. I *know*."

She purses her full pink lips, seething. For a moment I think she's going to hit me, but she just turns on her heel and struts down the hall as if she's done it a hundred times before.

When the other princesses come out, they walk past and touch my face and poke my abs and my butt. The one with the plum-purple hair tries to go right for the goods, and then the princesses disappear. They mingle into the flow of students. Angelo pushes past me, hot on the trail of a girl who could probably eat him alive in a second, not that he'd complain.

At the first glimpse of Kurt's face, I throw my hands in the air and yell at him. "I have to *court* the princesses? Why didn't you *tell* me?"

He seems as surprised as I am. "I honestly didn't remember that part of the championship. I didn't think they'd be interested in you."

"*Thanks*. I really feel the love, bro."

"That's not what I meant. I meant that you're human. *Part* human. I should've taken into account that you're the grandson of the king. The princesses are sort of—"

"Shallow?" Layla suggests, seemingly too happy at my misery.

"I've swum in deeper puddles than them," Thalia snarls. "They don't want mates, they want meals."

"Cool, so mergirls are easy," Layla says. She shoots a finger toward me. "Hey! That explains you."

When I don't laugh, she pats Thalia's shoulder. "No offense."

"None taken. I absolutely loathe those girls." Her cheeks puff up. All things considered, Thalia is pretty cute when she's angry.

"They don't seem so bad," Ryan says, strutting out of the classroom and slinging his arms around Thalia's waist. He picks her up, and they're suddenly in their own world, away from the merrows, the princesses, the sea witch, and my championship. They're in high school.

Layla looks away from them guiltily. I wonder if she's thinking about Alex. Maybe she's thinking about Kurt. She sure isn't thinking about me, the way she keeps avoiding my face. "Maddy really said she doesn't have it?"

I nod. "Yep."

"Explain to me why you can't give the oracle something else." Layla reaches over to my chest and picks off a bit of lint. She smooths the fabric on my chest, absentmindedly, then pulls her hand away like she didn't realize what she was doing. I wonder if she can feel my skin grow hot at her touch.

Kurt answers, "That seems like the best idea, but all the other champions will be taking similar gifts—from family jewels to promising their firstborn children. This is specific. The Venus pearl is something that was taken from her."

"So then *don't* give her something else," Layla corrects herself. We're in front of Ms. Pipper's English class.

Jerry runs out of the room. "Pippen's a no-show."

"Again?" Thalia goes.

"Figured I'd wait a few more minutes in case the sub shows and I can get attendance in, but she's not here either." Angelo runs past, saying something about "red-hot girls in school in the caf." He jets down the hallway, chasing the hot mermaid trail.

———

Under the cacophony of students shouting, singing, or just being general pains in the asses is the same lullaby hum of the princesses. If I weren't so irritated, I'd say it was the greatest thing I've ever heard—it makes your heart sigh and burn all at once.

We take a smaller table away from the swim team. On a regular day it would be considered a huge diss to leave your team's table. Today they're all fawning over my mermaid cousins and don't even notice. That explains the way everyone was behaving in the halls before. Well, except that you never really know with Angelo. If I don't do something, the whole school may end up either making out or duking it out.

Over at the swim team's table, Gwen and the mermaid princesses have formed a makeshift court with Gwen at the epicenter. Their shoulders peek from their sheer dresses, and their legs—which would normally be hidden beneath layers of scales—are crossed and exposed by the slits of their skirts for the enjoyment of every guy, girl, and pervy lunch monitor in the cafeteria. Their gem-like eyes, so much like mine, watch their surroundings carefully.

"I'll be right back," I say, ignoring Kurt's warning not to do anything irrational and to remember this is all court politics.

Gwen settles her stormy gray eyes on me. They're lined with black makeup. She arches an eyebrow, which is kind of funny, because she's so blond and fair that it doesn't look like she has eyelashes or eyebrows unless you're up close. "Have you been formally introduced yet?"

I smile as charmingly as I can. "Can't say I have."

"That over there is Violet, Adaro's cousin. She's got the prettiest purple hair in her region. This is Kai, Brendan's aunt. She's a bit shy, but she'll come along. And that's Menana, a freshwater princess from the Rocky Mountain lakes. She's like our very own Pocahontas." They wave with their fingers, some more interested than others. Then again, I shouldn't mistake interest for amusement.

I feel like I'd rather take my chances with Nieve than try to calm down a horde of mermaids. Like my dad says, hell hath no fury like when your mother doesn't get what she wants. And here I am with a pissed-off wannabe queen and her posse.

Bertie notices me for the first time. His eyes are glassy, but there's a joker smile plastered on his face. "Man, I wish I were part of your family."

No, you don't.

"I need you to please call them off, Gwen."

"Whatever do you mean?" She stares at me so innocently that I almost want to believe her.

"I'm half human. Not half stupid." Most of the time.

"You're not king, Tristan Hart."

"My grandfather—"

"Your grandfather isn't king anymore either. So for now we're all free to do as we wish."

"Yeah!" Angelo pumps a fist in the air. "Who made you king of the world, bro?"

"If you want to do it that way…" I grab Gwen by the waist and throw her over my shoulder. She beats her fists against my back, but she's not trying very hard. I take her to a corner of the cafeteria and set her down. She smooths out her dress and her hair, but doesn't hide the smirk on her face. The table whistles and cheers at us.

"The way I hear it, my ex-king grandfather makes everyone with powers reveal themselves. From where I'm standing, no one knows about you and your little voodoo tricks."

She looks like a girl who's just been caught smoking and I'm threatening to tell her dad. "It's not voodoo. Voodoo is filthy, unnatural magic. I'm organic." She presses her hands on her chest. She really needs to stop doing that.

"I don't get it. Why did you help your future husband lose to a girl?"

Her full pink lips curl into a smile. "He's—a jerk, as you people say. Why did you help *hurt* my future husband?"

"He was alive, Gwen. Something was down there with us, and it got him. Look, I'm sorry about Elias. I didn't think it would go down that way. But this is now. We're not on Toliss. You're on my land. I've got enough to deal with without worrying about any of you drowning my teammates."

"I thought you were all swimmers," she purrs. She looks off to the left and chews on the inside of her lip. I get the feeling she could do anything she wants right about now, like blow my head off or set me on fire with the heat in her eyes. I can smell her power. I didn't know that power had a scent, but hers does, like firecrackers being lit. Instead she sighs softly. "I'm sure Elias just took the tunnels out of the island to avoid the humiliation of losing to a human."

"So here's hoping he's out there trying to beat me." I cross my fingers in her face and repeat, "*The princesses.*"

She traces a finger along my jaw, and all of my parts tingle. She's truly beautiful once you get past the immense bitch part. "Maybe they're wrong about you. Maybe you do have it in you after all." She saunters back to the girls and whispers to Violet of the purple hair. There's a collective sigh from all of them, and suddenly the air feels lighter. The humming dies down. All around the cafeteria, kids who were kissing, fighting, standing up and shouting, look around as if they've forgotten what they were doing and why.

I nod thanks to Gwen, who gives me her cheek.

"Congratulations on your first political negotiation," Kurt says as I sit beside him.

"She really gets under my skin," I say, reaching over to Layla's plate of fries.

She pulls it away and my fingers grab at the air. "Seemed like more than your skin."

"I don't like my girls with a side of crazy, thank you." Even though the effect of Gwen is still lingering in my pants. Stupid mermaid princesses.

"I don't get it," Layla goes. "Why are they here if none of them even look your way?"

"I resent that." I grab one of her fries while she's not looking.

Thalia taps her finger on her lips, thinking. "The way I see it, the entire courtship is a way to throw the champion off his course. Think about it. You're competing against their brothers and cousins, so why would they want you to win?"

"On the other hand," Layla says, squinting at me the way she does when she thinks I'm being a creep, "if you were to pick one of them, then she'd no longer be a princess, but a queen. And why do they affect everyone so much more than you guys do?"

"Because Thalia and I are here to help Tristan. They're here to play."

"So here I am with my school full of mermaids, an oracle to find, a throne to win, and the person who stands between me and the oracle is my ex-girlfriend, who says she lost the *one thing*

I've got going for me as far as offerings go." I rub my face with my palms, unable to stop the feeling of premature failure from spreading through me. "Anyone have any spare cattle?"

"No way did she lose it," Layla says. "She was still wearing it the day of the storm."

I didn't notice. I never notice. That's my problem.

"You could always—" Thalia shifts uncomfortably and puts her fry down. "You could always *woo* her again."

"No!" Layla's punches me hard on my shoulder.

I think of Maddy's face when she asked if I wanted her back. Despite everything I'd done, she'd still say yes. I think about Jessica and Deanna in the hallways. Until they approached me minutes ago, I'd totally forgotten about them. I figured they'd move on to someone else. How was I supposed to know I affected them that way?

A cheer erupts at the other end of the table. Angelo picks up Kai, a pretty little thing with shimmering pink lips and eyes like a powder-blue sky, and her long blond curls curtain around his shoulders. He sits her on his arm just so he can prove how strong he is.

"I thought *she* called them off," Layla says.

"Jealous?" I snort.

"You wish."

I do, and she knows it.

"He's acting on his own Angelo dumbassery right now," I go. "So, Plan B. The oracle you visited was in the Fancy Corals or whatever?"

The familiar Kurt sneer is back. I was starting to miss it. "*The Great Coral Caves*. And yes. She's there. You and I can go together. If we leave now, we'll be back by morning."

"*No!*" Thalia shakes her head. "The merrows are out there looking for Tristan. It would be unwise to swim alone through the channels. They're dangerous enough."

Kurt considers this. I don't think he's ready to fight those things again any more than I am. "Perhaps you're right. What about the landlocked waitress from the diner? What if beneath her enthusiasm for you as king, there was something else. What she said was curious."

Layla raises her hand. "Some of us weren't at breakfast."

"She told me her kid, the little turtle boy, is rooting for me."

Thalia stifles her laughter. "Honestly, Tristan. It was just this morning. What she said was: *You'll find our kind is all around you, not just in the seas.*"

I'm so hungry I can't even think. "I thought she was just being nice."

"We're never just nice," Kurt says. "Our kind never says what they mean to say directly. It's vague, but what if she was telling us there is an oracle right here in New York?"

"Hold on," Layla says. "How do you know she's not tricking him and making him look around the city when there isn't even an oracle here? Why would she care? Kurt's right. There are tons of people like her, right? What if she's one of the bad ones?"

There are tons of people like her. That thought is enough to silence us all, because we know it's a long shot, and I'm going to just have to take it anyway. I don't know if it's the vibes coming from the rise in mermaid activity around me, the power of the dagger in my backpack, or what. But something in there is clicking. I wish I could tell everyone, *Look, I'm not just a pretty face.*

"There are tons of others like her!" I point to Kurt, who looks surprised that I point to him. "Use your mighty-merman powers for a sec. How do you think the other champions are finding the oracles?"

"Same way we are: hearsay, family witches, hired guides, seers—" He pauses and catches my eyes with his violet ones. "Of course."

"You said Ms. Pippen's a seer," I go, a little too smug that I've come up with it before him.

"She hasn't been in school for two days," Thalia says, bursting my cloud of mojo.

"That's not a coincidence."

Layla scrunches up her nose. "Ms. Pippen's a what?"

"A psychic in your world. I noticed the first day we were here."

"Oh—"

"So then, let me give Maddy one more try—" Before Layla can punch me again, I add, "I'm just going to talk to her, not *woo* her. That's where you come in, Thalia. You stay here with Ryan and convince him he should throw a party."

"How am I supposed to do that?"

I try to keep the sly grin off my face. "I'm sure you'll think of something."

"Really, a *party?*" Layla gives me attitude.

"There's a madness to my method. I've got this. You, me, and Kurt, we're going to have a little search party on the boardwalk. There's someone I think can help us. And if that doesn't work, we'll have to find a way to get us all to the Coral Conclaves." I point to the swim team table, where Angelo is the center of attention. "Because I am *not* going to share my school with a bunch of bored, wannabe mermaid queens, and especially because I *never, ever* want to see Angelo do *that* again."

chapter
FORTY-ONE

D o you think this is a good idea?" Layla asks. We're feet from
the entrance to the school. Behind her, Kurt squints against
the sun.

Angelo runs past us as if his pants are on fire, which, given today,
they probably are. "I also invited all of your hot cousins to come
to Coney Island. Why aren't you being more hospitable, bro? Plus,
they say they packed more bikinis than actual clothes."

Layla rolls her eyes. "Now that you put it *that* way."

Angelo presses his palm over his chest. "Don't worry, Layla.
You'll always be my first love." He puts out his cheek so that she
can kiss it.

"Gee, th*aaa*nks." She stops an inch short of pressing her lips to
his face. "On second thought, I don't know where that cheek has
been all day long." Laughing, she walks right past him, stepping
from the shadow of the school into the light.

"Oh, come on!" He runs out after her. "It's not like I'm *Tristan*."

"Not cool, bro! Not cool!"

"See you suckers at the Wreck!" He takes the steps three at a time. It's surprising he doesn't miss a step at the speed he's going. He crosses the street, where a bunch of cars honk at him. He throws his middle finger in the air and howls at them, jumping into a red car with black flames painted on the side.

"Are werewolves real too?" I wonder. "'Cause that's just not normal."

"He's euphoric," Kurt says. "He's had the most exposure around the princesses other than—well—you."

Layla looks surprised that he points to her and then blooms into a playful smile. "I guess mermen just have no effect on me."

I stick my hand out in the air and go, "To the subway, Merman!" in my most dramatic cartoon superhero voice. It's wasted because the only one who laughs is Layla. Kurt watches me with the curiosity I give rats on the subway, and I wonder if we'll have enough time to introduce him to my comic books.

———

The train station is aboveground. Across the platform is a wall of graffiti that stretches all the way down to Coney. We weave through the late beach crowd, the kids with red, sticky Italian ices, girls reading while two guys try to beat box battle beside them. Watching Kurt fumble with the turnstile and having it hit him on the back is the highlight of my day.

The car we board is fairly empty. A group of extremely loud kids hang out on the opposite end from us. They swing on the metal bars and dare each other to race between cars when the doors open.

"What are you thinking, *Kurtomathetis*?" Layla stands beside him, holding on to the bars with both hands so she looks extra long.

Even his shrugs are proper. "It's amazing really, the way these lines represent your city. It's like the channels under the sea, the veins in our bodies connecting everything."

She looks like something is caught in her throat. Her hand goes right to the protective shell that hangs just under her clavicle.

I could be all poetic and stuff. If I wanted to.

At the next stop an older lady sits beside us in our corner, clutching her frilly purse. She snarls her thin lips at me, just like the old lady in the elevator at the hospital. Unbidden, Nieve's face comes to mind. Her irises, like the white of lightning, her blue lips and bloody gums. My temples burn as if someone is holding hot pokers on either side of my head and digging in.

"Tristan!" Layla kneels in front of me. She puts her cool hands on my face. Even with the air conditioning pumping from the vents, I'm sweating.

The old woman pushes past us and gets off when the train stops and the doors open. Well, that was that. The sensation subsides.

"I wish I could stop seeing her."

"Nieve?" Kurt looks around the car as though we'll be attacked any moment.

What I don't say is that I can feel her getting stronger, that the white of her eyes pulls me in and I need all the strength I have to shut it away.

The conductor shouts, "West Eighth, New York Aquarium! Next stop, Coney!"

"This is us," I go.

The kids on the other end of the car shout over something funny someone says. The doors chime open, and we leave them to their unbridled, unworried laughter.

chapter
FORTY-TWO

The last time I showed up at the Wreck was the week before the storm. Ryan wouldn't let up about my making an appearance, because if there's someone you want as your wingman, it's gotta be me.

The owner's son, Jimmy Haggerty, mops the bar with a rag that looks like no amount of bleach will ever get it clean. He nods at me in that way guys do, while drying a glass with the same rag.

The Wreck is the coolest place on the boardwalk, hands down. Angelo and the guys have taken over an entire corner of the place. There is a Mount Everest order of hot wings so red they almost glow.

Kurt takes in the room and says, "Thalia would enjoy this. It reminds me of Tortuga Cove. Except that there are no pirates here."

A man in full pirate costume walks in. Pirate Pete and Captain Loveday are part of a tour about the heyday of Coney Island, when the streets were cobblestone and lit up like Vegas. When there was a hotel shaped like an elephant, and the best rickety roller coasters in the entire United States.

"I retract my statement," Kurt says, breaking into a rare smile.

"Were you really so hungry you had to make a pit stop?" Layla asks, taking a seat closer toward the entrance.

"Relax," I say. "I have a good feeling about this."

Her face becomes an instant smile, the way she used to smile at me before—everything. She squints, and the black fringe of her lashes looks like it's nestling the gold of her eyes. The sun breaks behind me and lights up her cheekbones and the rich browns in her hair. I smile back, even though I don't know what we're smiling about.

Then she says, "Marty!" and her chair flies back as she practically flies to him.

Marty pulls up a stool beside me. He shakes Kurt's hand and avoids my eyes when he holds out his hand to me.

"Fancy seeing you here," I go, leaning casually against my chair. "On land. Out here in the world."

He slumps down. "Dammit! Shouldn't you be in school right now?"

I sit up straight. "Guess today's just my lucky day." I add, "*Na-na-na, boo-boo*," in a hushed voice so just he can hear it.

Marty fixes his cap from side to side. "Okay, I promised I'd tell you what I am."

I'm unable to keep the smugness from my face. "Let's have it."

"Not here, bro. It's one of those believe-it-or-not things." And even though he says that, he leans into Layla's ear and whispers. She stares at Marty with a sort of wonder that is rare for her lately. It was the same expression she had when she saw the Sea Court, when my grandfather gave her the shell around her neck. I wish she'd look at me that way, but all I get is *Tristan Hart, her best friend, who kissed another girl while he already had a girlfriend.*

I turn to Layla. Trusted lifetime best friend. "Come on, spill it."

Kurt comes to my defense. Trusted merman sidekick. "Now, that's hardly fair to Tristan. He's been very patie—" Layla cups her hands around his ear and whispers to *him*!

"Interesting." Kurt tilts his head at Marty, who in turn takes off his cap and bows like he's just finished an encore. "I never would've guessed. Though it completely makes sense."

"That's not cool, guys," I say.

Toward the back of the bar, Angelo and the guys have massacred half of their wings. The princesses look at them with something that crosses between hunger and disgust. Maybe with a splash of fascination. I wonder how come Gwen isn't with them.

"Trust me. You're new to this world. You have to see it to believe it, dude." Marty puts his cap back on. I'm about to argue that Layla isn't *even* part of this world and is more human than I am, but I don't feel like getting her right hook again. Marty calls out to the bartender, "Hey, Jimmy, let me get five bucks of the Rocky Mountains to stay and the Andes Picante wings to go."

I pull out the black leather wallet my dad gave me when I turned fifteen. Behind my ten-dollar bill is a photo-booth picture I'd forgotten about. It's me and Layla from the summer before high school. I'm holding my finger in my mouth like a hook. My face totally is leaned into Layla's. She couldn't even hold her funny face without cracking up. I push it down before she can see me looking at it.

"Put your pretzel monies away, Little Prince," Marty goes. "This round's on me."

Kurt, the rigid MerWonder, scratches the back of his neck and glances carefully around the room. I hate when he does that. He says, "This is all great, but we have some pressing—" But he doesn't finish. The distinct sound of a gunshot jolts us. We duck, but the screams come from the boardwalk.

I grab my backpack and run out the door, pushing past the crowds of onlookers. Straight ahead, where there are scattered rainbow-colored beach umbrellas, people grab hold of their things and run away from the beach. Memories of the day of the storm fill my head. I realize it's just a world of people who run the other way.

I search the clouds for a bit of black, anything that might suggest it was thunder and lightning and another wave. But the sky is an endless blue.

Emergency 4x4s honk at the traffic of people on the boardwalk. Farther away, police sirens wail. The crowd parts for a man with a bald head that's been slicked with suntan oil. In his arms is a heap of tattered bloody clothes.

He's struggling with the weight of a boy, and when he almost trips, a hand breaks loose from the pile of clothes and dangles, cold and blue.

The man's leg goes weak, but he balances on one knee. I reach forward to help, but I'm not fast enough, and the boy hits the ground with a wet thump. The corners of his lips are white and cracked. His eyes are open, staring at the sky. The smell of copper and salt hit me like a sucker punch. Down where the boy's leg used to be is a mess of sand and bone and loose skin.

The man leans down and uses two fingers to shut those dead, gaping eyes.

"What happened?"

When he speaks, his voice is a low growl. "I was just sitting. Reading. Beats me if I'll find my book in that mess now. Saw the top of a shark. But it was deformed." He hovers, his palm over his head to signal where the dorsal fin might be. "Then the boy—" He breaks off and stares back down at the dead boy. I realize my hands are shaking at my sides.

A set of hands comes down on my shoulder. It's Marty. He leans close to my face and whispers, "Come on, man. We don't want to be here when five-o shows up." My body is numb as we weave along the Coney Island boardwalk, away from the mangled body on the ground.

chapter
FORTY-THREE

We sit in a straight line, our feet dangling over the edge of the pier. This is where Coney Island turns into Brighton Beach.

"That was awful," Layla says, her voice catching in her throat.

"The merrows." Kurt says what I've been thinking but don't want to admit to.

I remember when Layla would curl up in bed because she didn't want to touch the edges, as if whatever was in the dark would reach up and snatch her. This is the same, except now we're all scared and pull our feet away from the water and set them firmly on the ground.

"Is this all because of the nasty sea witch who's out to get you?" Marty has a way of making even the worst things sound harmless.

"Yeah, that one. Apparently she might have an army of mutant merpeople called merrows."

I wait for a smart comeback that doesn't come. Marty tosses the bottle cap into the water. It skips once, twice, sinks. "Aw, sh*iiit*."

"What?" Layla gets ready to stand and run.

"I forgot the hot wings."

She sucks her teeth and smacks *him* for once.

"What? I paid for them."

"I'm falling behind," I say. "The other guys are halfway down the Pacific, and I'm still on land, watching people die around me and not doing anything about it." I punch the wood and regret it. The scabs over my knuckles crack and bleed. I look at Marty. "That's where you come in."

"Me?" Marty tilts his cap from side to side.

"You know everyone."

"Not every—"

"What do you know of a psychic who teaches at my school? Ms. Pippen."

"Wait, wait." Marty dusts sand off his black jeans. "Olivia Pippen?"

I stand to face him. "So you know her?"

Marty hesitates like he shouldn't have said anything at all. But he can't take it back.

I repeat, "Dude, do you know where she lives?"

He holds his hands up in the air as if he can conjure up a force field between us. A few more steps back and he'll fall off the pier. "Guys, I'm neutral. I can't—" He looks to Kurt. "You *know* I can't put anyone in danger that is part of the alliance. Besides, we used to have a thing."

"She's my teacher. I'm not going to *hurt* her. I'm just going to ask her if she knows of any oracles and where their locations might be."

Marty relaxes but doesn't look like he's going to cooperate.

"Hold up. You guys had a thing?" I can't help it, I sound super impressed.

He shrugs and smiles at the clouds. "Man, she's an incredible woman. But the seeing thing freaked me out. I mean, I'm not a dog or anything. I wasn't afraid she'd see me doing something I wasn't supposed to do. But check this: I have a lot of friends in dangerous jobs. Every time I'd introduce her at a party somewhere, she'd run out crying because she'd see them *die*. It puts strain on a relationship."

I give him a well-deserved hand slap and hoot. "You're kind of the Man."

"Hello?" Layla knocks at the air. "Murder, mermaids, mayhem? We can talk about Marty's sexcapades later."

Kurt raises his hand. "I vote *Not* on that last bit. But any information would be helpful. If not," he says to Marty, "I hope you're a good swimmer."

I wasn't about to make the threat, but Kurt's voice is steady, borderline deadly. I'm even afraid of him a little bit. Marty twiddles his thumbs nervously, taking one last look at the rippling water below. Sure, it's not exactly making him walk the plank, but after what we've just seen, the water doesn't look very appetizing.

He deflates and says, "I'm not going to tell you where she lives. But I will tell you where she's going to be tonight." He rubs his hands. I still don't know *what* he is, but I hold up my hands to shield myself in case he ends up being some kind of wizard who shoots fireballs when he rubs his hands together. If things like that exist.

Which they probably don't.

Probably.

Hopefully.

"If it's another overnight trip, my dad's going to shit bricks."

"Actually, it's a club." He winks at her.

A club doesn't seem so bad. "Where is it?"

Marty flicks the beak of his cap. Now that he knows we're not going to torture him for an answer, he's all chummy again. "Let's just say, it's *right* in the middle of everything."

chapter
FORTY-FOUR

The middle of everything is at Bowery and Twelfth Street.

Between Arcade Island and a long stretch of graffiti-covered wall is a door I've never noticed before. There's a black and red star over the metal door, which looks like it's been hit with a hammer too many times.

"What is it?"

"Like I said, a special club, lounge, bar. Whatever you kids are calling them these days. We call it Betwixt. Ground rules: try not to look people directly in the eyes, bump into anyone, spill anyone's drink, or make out with a girl who is someone else's date. *Tristan.*"

Layla elbows me a little too hard on the side.

"So it's just like being in the school cafeteria," I say, and reach for the handle. Only there isn't a handle to reach.

"After me." Marty bangs his fist on the metal once.

Nothing happens.

"Nothing—"

Marty puts his finger to his lips. "Shh." He makes like he's going to reach for a handle that isn't there. And then his hand goes *right* through, followed by the rest of him.

"Ohm—" Layla starts and finishes with a shriek as Marty's head pops right back through. "Someone has to hold Layla's hand because, well, it's not her fault she's all human."

Layla scowls at him. I reach for her hand, but she grabs Kurt's instead. He's standing closer to her, I guess.

Marty looks to me. "Knock once, wait for the knock back. A headless monkey could do it." He disappears.

"Here goes everything." I knock. The wait seems even longer than when Marty did it. Or maybe it's because I'm afraid it's not going to work for me. What if half of me gets stuck because I'm half human? And if so, which parts—

Then I hear it. The knock back. Only I can't seem to make myself move. I feel someone's hands push me forward at the same time I take a step in. For a moment, I feel weightless and cold. Two heartbeats later, the warmth rushes back. I stumble and trip down the steps. At least I land on my back and not my face.

Marty's talking with a guy who's almost seven feet tall. His red spikes graze the ceiling. He glances at me with a set of red eyes and a nose that looks like he gets into a lot of fights. "More convenient than a buzzer," I go.

The red-haired giant looks away, bored.

"Tristan, that's Ignacio." Marty nods at the red-haired giant. "And this is Lisbit, my future wife." He leans against the wooden podium toward a girl with a slender pale face. Everything about her is pointy, from her chin to the upturned tip of her nose to the black points she's painted over her eyelids.

"The little merman," she says. Her voice is deep and smooth. "It is wonderful to meet you. Hang on." A second knock echoes in the room. It feels like it's coming from everywhere all at once. She opens a silver box in front of her and pushes the red button. I stand aside, waiting for the tumble that never comes. Kurt takes one step in, balancing perfectly at the top of the steps. He holds on to Layla's hands as she passes through. I can see her shiver with the sudden coldness of the metal door. She gasps when she looks down the short steps. She pulls herself up straight and they stand facing each other, holding hands.

"How did you know not to fall down the steps?" I say, unsuccessfully keeping the annoyance from my voice.

He shrugs. "It's only logical not to rush right into unfamiliar territory."

Naturally.

Lisbit's eyes flare as she stares at Kurt. She glances at Layla, who lets go of Kurt's hands and stuffs them in her back pockets. Layla looks from Ignacio to Lisbit's gold shorts to the lights floating all about. They're like the ones on the island but smaller. She reaches out and touches one, then pulls her finger back with a jerk. "Ouch, they're hot."

The corners of Lisbit's plum-painted lips lift in a sly smile. "Curiosity killed the human girl. Be careful you don't go doing that in there."

Ignacio unlocks the door behind him. This one does have a knob. He steps aside. I hold on to the knob, tense at the thought that my hand might go right through.

I turn it.

I push it.

The music blares.

First thing's the stage. Red velvet curtains are draped open to frame the band. Hundreds of floating lights cluster above a four-girl band. They are red and black and white versions of the Beach Boys—but girls. In skin-tight polka-dot dresses, they *ohhh* and *ahhh* to the swaying crowd. Their logo, "The Vampirettes," is centered on their bass drum, enclosed by a set of red lips with two glossy fangs.

"Are they really vampires?" I hear Layla ask behind me. Her voice is a mixture of wonder and dread.

"What do you think?" Marty answers suggestively.

To the left are seating areas of couches and tall circular tables with barstools made of a curling black metal. To the right there's a bar with hundreds of glass bottles in all heights and shapes. None of them have labels on them. Some are full of a familiar fizzy green liquid. A thin green girl with paper-thin wings retracted against her shoulder blades pours a goopy red liquid and what must be champagne into a tall, skinny flute glass and slides it to a girl about my age.

"That's a bloody mimosa." Marty puts an arm around me. "That's Rhine, the bartender. She's a pixie. The guy bartender, Adam, is just human. He's part of the Coney freak show upstairs." He points to a guy covered in tattoos, from the top of his bald head, down his shirtless torso, and down to the tips of his fingers.

We weave across the dance floor. Behind me, a girl with feathery wings and owl eyes is bouncing around and twirling Layla under her arm in that cute way girls do when they dance together. Kurt hunches and scowls more and more with everyone who bumps into him.

Layla dances around me now. We're on the outside of the dance floor. Something slimy brushes against my hand, but it's too dark to really make out anything that isn't right in front of my face. I feel a pinch on my butt. "Hey, now." But my insides are bursting because it's Layla. She cocks her head to the side, moving her shoulders up and down to the poppy guitar rock. She traces her finger along my cheek, and I can't help it: I wrap my hands around her waist. Maybe it's the atmosphere, or maybe she sneaked something to drink while I wasn't looking, but she laughs in my ear.

Then something in my gut turns. I breathe in her hair, and it doesn't smell like anything. It smells clean, like air conditioner. I hold her face, and a grin that is very un-Layla spreads on her face. Her eyes aren't the honey I'm used to. I look around. What if something is possessing her? Behind me, Layla and Kurt finally pull through the jam-packed dance floor.

The Layla in front of me cackles in a way that sounds so wrong coming from her pretty face. The Layla behind me stares, eyes wide. She closes the gap between the three of us so that the two of them stand facing each other in front of me. I grab the other Layla's ponytail and bring it to my nose. Lavender.

"What the—"

Layla touches un-Layla's nose. "Does my nose really do that when I smile?"

The un-Layla starts stretching, her hair shortening and darkening, jaw squaring, shoulders broadening until Marty's form returns. I jump back.

"Surprised?" Marty the shape-shifter asks me.

"Dude, you pinched my ass."

"You've got that whole merman prince thing going for you. What can I say? I'm a social climber." He walks backward down the tight table aisles. "I've got some people I want you to meet."

"Is the seer going to be one of them?" Kurt asks, all business all the time. I'm having fun down here. I can't remember the last time I felt fun. Like reliable Tristan Hart who'd take any dare, who could get any girl. Me. Fun. Before the storm, those two things were supposed to be synonymous.

"One thing at a time," I say, following Marty and letting my friends fall in line.

In a corner where there are not twinkling floating lights, but brass gas lamps fastened on the walls, is a group of guys who look like they should be on the cover of one of my dad's '80s rock records. They have the long tousled hair, the leather, the ripped jeans, and the perpetual look of amused boredom. I feel awkward here, the uninvited kid at the party who just stands there. I have never been that kid until right now, and it sucks.

Marty walks up to a tall blond guy who wears a white undershirt and a black leather vest. They talk to a guy who looks about my age, maybe eighteen. Although that doesn't mean much in a place like this if Kurt is 103. The second guy has brown hair that comes to his shoulders. He wears a Hawaiian shirt and has a predatory slouch. The sunny outfit contrasts with his pale skin, and my senses scream—*vampire*.

"Why does everyone seem so serious?" Layla asks.

Marty shrugs. "You try being immortal. You get to be seventeen and human, and your problems are bad enough. Then when you're seventeen forever, you have bigger things to worry about."

The vampire in the Hawaiian shirt focuses on me. His eyes aren't exactly a spectacular color. I'd think they'd be red or super black, but other than the pale skin and dark circles under his eyes, I'd figure he was just a really white kid who never slept.

He lifts his chin at me and holds out his hand. It's like grabbing something out of the freezer.

"Frederik Stig Nielsen," he says with a slight accent. Not British, but from somewhere over there. "I heard your grandfather liked my asphodels."

I look to Marty with my best *what-the-fuck-is-he-talking-about* face.

Marty pats Frederik on the back. "You found a name you liked! Good for you, buddy."

Frederik shoots a menacing look at Marty. Then again, his pronounced brow makes him look like he's always scowling.

"Oh, yeah, he thought they were awesome." I'm not exactly lying. He did seem interested in them, but what else am I supposed to say to him? *Hey, is there any Type O on tap?*

Frederik points to the tall blond guy watching us with bemusement. His eyes twinkle in the kind of way that musicians' do. "How rude of me. This is Röaan Recklit."

We shake hands. *Good grip, good grip.*

"Sorry," he says, releasing my hand. "I forget my own strength."

"Tristan," Frederik starts, "the boy today at the beach, the disappearing boys around the city. It's not human-related, but it has nothing to do with us either. I don't want the alliance hurt because there is no Sea King until the next full moon. I don't know anything about you, but Marty deems your character worthy. I trust him implicitly." He turns to Marty with a grave face. "You forgot my order of Andes Picante."

"Bro, there was a mangled human body on the boardwalk. We can go back for it, but Tristan's looking for someone right now."

"My teacher, Olivia Pippen."

Marty rolls his eyes when Frederik shrugs. "You know, the seer who can read voices? She has the decade of bereavement at Thorne Hill? Is it too much to ask that you pay attention to my ex-girlfriends?"

"Oh *her*. I saw her dancing a minute ago. She doesn't like me much."

"How come?" *Since you're such a charmer.*

"Because she can't read me."

And hopefully also not a mind reader. "Why?" I feel like I'm two again.

312

"I'm a man of few words."

Right, glad I asked.

I turn to plead with Marty once again. "Do you know where she would've gone?" He holds his hands up, and I know what he's going to say. *I'm neutral.* My heart beats a little faster. I'm fucking this up utterly. "Kurt, let's try—"

"Kurt's gone," Layla says.

"What do you mean, Kurt is *gone?*"

She shrugs. "I mean, he was standing right behind me, and now he's not there anymore. He's gone."

I scan the crowds for him, but it's so dark. Where would he have gone? Why now? I mean, I know I'm a little hard to get along with, since he's all serious merman guy, but come on. I thought we were getting past that.

The Vampirettes have put away their instruments and are walking toward us, shaking hands with some people. They smile with ruby-red lips and fangs that glisten in the gaslight.

"Frederik," one says in her high soprano voice. "You up for some moonbathing?"

Frederik shrugs. "Sure."

Two of the girls jump up and clap their hands. "Röaan, you coming?"

"Nah, I have some scouting for next Friday's show." Röaan turns to me. "I hope everything works out. We're playing next Friday. My band's Low Key. I'll introduce you to some smokin' hot Valkyries. Oh, and"—I brace against his hand, slapping my chest in what *he* probably considers a friendly pat, and I consider a heavy beating—"bring some of those sea princesses I heard were in town."

As he strides back to his table with the confidence of a rock god, two guys stand and give up their seats for him. Must be nice to be so in command.

The Vampirettes look bored. "Well, the moon isn't going to stay at its peak forever. I think those stupid lights gave me a bit of a tan. What do you think?"

"You look great, really icy pale," I say, and she gives me a girlish smile.

Frederik looks past my shoulder and, for a second, arches his eyebrow. I never thought I'd meet someone with even less of an emotional range than Kurt. He exchanges glances with Marty as Kurt walks through the crowd holding on to a girl. From far away they look like friends holding hands. Then you notice how white their fingers are from him squeezing. That and the pallor that replaces her usually blushed cheeks during class. She's in a tight black dress with her hair gathered all on one side. She does her best to keep her cool, but even though I can't seem to smell other supernatural beings, the fear is in her eyes.

Marty leans in close to me to whisper, "You need to take this outside, bro."

"Ms. Pippen, I only want to talk."

Her smile is hard, bitter. Not that I blame her. "Really? You hardly ever talk in my class."

The lead singer of the Vampirettes claps her hands. "The beach?"

Frederik walks past us slowly, casually. There's something soothing about his presence, considering he could drain you dry if he wanted. I'd like to be that calm and collected during any situation. He motions straight ahead, leading the way out "The beach."

Right, a man of few words.

chapter
FORTY-FIVE

think you left Lisbit aching for you, bro," Marty tells Kurt,
walking backward through Luna Park.

"She's not my type," Kurt says, leaving me to wonder what his
type could possibly be.

He holds on to Ms. Pippen's arm as the Vampirettes frolic
through the Coney Island night with faces tilted toward the sliver
of moon. One takes a pink cotton candy from a cart and keeps
walking. They tear puffs in greedy bunches and let the sugar melt
on their tongues.

Marty slings his arm around my shoulder. "Ooo, candied
apples." He stops and pays for one and bites into the hard red shell.
I wonder how he can be so nonchalant all the time considering the
things he knows, the things he must see. Maybe his shifting isn't
just physical. Maybe it applies to his feelings too, because I don't
see how he can walk around eating candy at Luna Park as we take
my English teacher practically hostage. I hope one day I can learn
to fix my feelings like him and Kurt.

"The Vampirettes, they're, like, housebroken, right?"

He takes a smaller bite, making yummy faces that rival the group of little girls not too far from us eating chocolate-covered Oreos. Suddenly I wish we hadn't put him in this situation. "Technically, New York is a safe zone. Once this is all over, and you're Sea King, I'll have to explain it to you. Right now, you have to think about your mission. If you're worried about the vampires, don't be. Frederik doesn't drink human blood. Well, not for, like, two hundred years."

"What about the girls "

"The girls might bite, but they don't kill. Vampire killings are easy to find, because after they feed on human blood they're basically euphoric and are pretty sloppy about cleaning up the bodies."

"Good to know."

We're the last to follow down the ramp and onto the sand. Up ahead the girls pull their polka-dot dresses over their heads and wave them in the air like flags. They dip their toes in the cold water and shriek. Frederik picks a spot where the tide won't hit, sits, and then leans back on his elbows.

I follow his stare at the speckles of stars. Suddenly I wonder, "Aren't you guys supposed to, like, sparkle or something?" And immediately wish I hadn't.

Frederik stands up so quickly that he doesn't disturb the sand. He grabs the front of my shirt and growls—his eyes are black as the night sky along the horizon, and red veins fray against the white of his eyes. His sharp canines are exposed.

"I. Don't. Sparkle."

He lets go of me and becomes regular bored Frederik again, no fangs, no bloodshot eyes. Just a dude sitting on the beach at night.

Marty shakes his head all, *Yeah, I should've warned you about that.*

"Tristan." Kurt calls me. He holds my English teacher farther away from us. I make my way to them, trying to slow my racing heartbeat.

He breaks his grip on her, but says, "I won't go far."

Ms. Pippen screams in frustration. The wind undoes her hair from its neat little tie and blows it all around her. "What? What do you want?"

"You mean you can't *see* the answer to that?"

"Funny. You really are smarter than you look, Tristan. You never talk in my class, so I had no idea what you are."

"Welcome to my pretty exclusive club."

"You know, isn't it enough that I'm punished by having to teach in that school for a human decade? I also have to get dragged out here by your mermaid lackey?"

"It's mer*man*, lady. And what do you mean by punished?"

She pushes her hair away from her face, the moonlight casting a silvery light on her cheekbones.

"My grandfather, the Sea King, gave me a shiny, sharp present. Don't make me use it."

She straightens her back and crosses her arms over her chest. I look away. "You have to tell me what you want first."

"I want you to tell me if there are any oracles in New York City."

"If I don't, are you going to kill me?"

I hadn't thought about that. "I—"

"I don't want to get involved in your politics."

"You're already involved."

"You don't get it." She shakes her head. "You may be half fish, but you're still so human."

"You sit in class making us read aloud and what do you do? You see our futures. You keep those secrets to yourself. What else have you seen that could make a difference?"

I don't know if it's the slight chill in the sea breeze, or if she's scared, but her lips tremble. "That's the irony, right? I can see, but I can't say. That's why I got in trouble. Things were pretty bad for me a few years ago. I had two sisters and a brother to take care of, because our parents got deported back to Romania.

"One day I read a man who was going to win the lotto. I played his numbers. I changed his future, and he walked off the subway tracks. It's against the rules to use your powers for your own personal gain. So they took my sisters from me. Then they put me up at Thorne Hill High School, grading English papers."

"That's tough."

"You're telling me. What's the point, Tristan? What's the point of having a power if I can't even use it for the ones I love? The ones who *count*. The Universe picked the wrong girl for this 'gift,' because me? I don't care about the greater good. I just don't get to make the rules. I didn't ask for this."

"You think I *did*?"

"Which is why you don't have to do it." She holds my hands in hers, a gentle plea. "You don't have to be the next Sea King. What's in it for you? Do you think you'll ever be with Layla? Do you think you won't have to use that shiny pitchfork to do things you'll hate yourself for? You're just a kid."

The truth of her words washes over me and makes my skin itch. What is in it for me? I've never known what I wanted to do with my life. I've only wanted to swim. That's all I've ever been good at. That and, well, girls. She's right. I don't have to be Sea King. I can let one of the other champions win. They're been part of that Sea Court longer than I've been alive. They know things I don't.

Then I think of Nieve. She's going to come for me whether I'm king or not. I can feel it the way I can feel the ebb of the tide right now. I think about the boy on the boardwalk with his leg gnawed off, the bald man who *didn't* have to pull him out of the water. Because I want to. Because if I don't, my world is just going to keep crumbling.

"I need to know, Ms. Pippen. I need to know if I'm wasting my time up here."

She grunts. "Fine, but you're getting a D in my class."

"Make it a C minus? I have to stay on the team."

"You can't be on the team if you're Sea King," she singsongs.

"Just tell me what I have to do. Have I talked long enough for you?"

"It has to be continuous." She snaps open her purse and pulls out a paper with her familiar red markings all over it. "Forget the red pen. Just read me the text."

I read.

> Full fathom five thy father lies;
> Of his bones are coral made;
> Those are pearls that were his eyes:
> Nothing of him that doth fade
> But doth suffer a sea-change
> Into something rich and strange.
> Sea-nymphs hourly ring his knell:
> Ding-dong.
> Hark! now I hear them—Ding-dong, bell.

"You've got to appreciate Shakespeare," she says. I follow her eyes behind me, where she watches my friends

"Today, if you please."

"It's your lucky day, merboy. There is an oracle in New York, but I don't know where it is. I can't see it."

"What do you mean you can't see it?"

She shakes her head. "I mean I can't see it, okay? Either she's blocking me, or your future isn't fixed because you haven't made up your mind yet. Whatever it is, I can't get a clear reading."

"So give me something else to read," I shout. This isn't me. I don't do things like this. I put my hands on her shoulders and squeeze. "I'll read it over again." My mouth is dry. My heart is racing. My temples pulse in that way they do just before I see Nieve. I shut my eyes and let Ms. Pippen go.

Footsteps rush up to us. Ms. Pippen falls backward on the sand. She holds herself with her hands.

"I'm sorry," I tell her.

Ms. Pippen picks herself up and dusts the sand off her dress. "No. Not yet you aren't."

chapter
FORTY-SIX

Should we let her go?" Layla's voice startles me.

I don't know how long I've been sitting on the sand, but long enough that I can't see Ms. Pippen on the beach anymore. I wave dismissively. "She doesn't know where the oracle is. She says it's here in New York, but that's it."

"That's not helpful."

"Tell me about it."

"Come." Layla holds out her hand to me. When I clasp it, it's warm in mine. "Let's take a walk."

It's been so long since Layla and I have really been alone together. I steal short glances at her. It's amazing to me how beautiful she's become in a few weeks. One day she was my best friend, one of the guys. Today she's Layla, the girl who brought me back to life. Technically, I was already alive, but still. The girl who got on a ship in the middle of the night, because she thought I might need her. What she doesn't know is that I always need her.

When I look at her now, I want to tell her that I love her. I know it like I know that I'm part of the sea. She weaves her fingers through mine, something we've done since we were little, but right now it means so much more. I need to know. I need to know how she feels too.

"How's Alex?" I say.

"Who?"

"You know, big orange Alex? The guy who chauffeurs you in the white BMW?"

"You're a moron," she says. "That wasn't Alex. That was my cousin Nick. Also, big and orange. But eww?"

"He picks you up."

"He works at Steele Gym by Thorne Hill Cemetery, so my aunt's been making him. You know, little ole damsel-in-distress me."

I laugh, slightly relieved. "Well, tell her you've already got someone to save you."

"I don't need any saving, Tristan." She hops onto the rocks barefoot and walks along them, arms out for balance. When we were smaller and they looked bigger than they do now, we used to pretend we were climbing cliffs in the middle of the ocean, running away from James Bond villains and saving the world.

"Whatever you say, I promise I'll always be there for you."

"So now you're also Pinocchio in addition to a mermaid?"

"Mer*man*."

"You have to come up with something less fruity."

"How about mer-stud?"

"Mer*bro*."

"I kinda liked merdude.'

I stand right behind her at the end of the rocks. The water splashes cold around us. Lavender and honey mingles with that sharp ocean smell. She leans her back against my chest, and I can feel her heart racing against mine. I trace the length of her arms with my fingertips, surprised at how warm she is despite all the goose bumps on her flesh. I kiss the bare skin of her shoulder, surprised at the heat on my mouth, the heat of her skin. The way my skin prickles everywhere as she lets herself sink against me.

"Layla." I say her name, but I don't have anything to follow. I just want to say it. Layla, Layla, Layla. If I told her I loved her and then did something typically *Tristan*, I'd never forgive myself. So instead I whisper, "Close your eyes."

"Why?"

"Trust me."

"The last time I agreed to that, you and Angelo streaked across my backyard at the same time my dad came home."

"Just do it."

She shuts her eyes.

I pull my shirt over my head and drop it on the rocks, along with my sandals and my shorts on top of my backpack.

"What are you doing?"

"No peeking."

She has her hands over her eyes. Though I wouldn't mind if she peeked. I stand, close my own eyes, and breathe in the salt in the water, and then I feel the change in my veins, my legs. I jump into the water, feeling the numbness of the scales covering my legs until I kick in one motion as if I've been doing it my whole life.

There's a second splash. I swim to her, the scales along my arms glistening in the moonlight. She breathes short and shallow. Her teeth chatter when she says, "You're shiny."

"Yeah, right. Vampires don't glitter, but I do."

"Right? My belief system is totally shattered. I'm going to have to let my mom take me to confession tomorrow."

I splash her a little. "Come, get on my back."

"Said the crocodile to the monkey."

"So let me get on your back, then."

"Fine. Turn around, and I'll get on."

I do, and she wraps herself around my neck, her legs around my waist. "Don't forget to hold your breath." I make us dive a little and flick my fin until we swim out a few feet. I don't want to go out too far, because I don't know the kinds of things that are out there this time of night. I want us to be able to swim back without any problems.

I stop and flip her over so we're face-to-face. She puts her hands on my chest.

"Stop," she says in a whisper I can barely make out over the rustle of the water. "Stop doing this."

"I'm not doing anything." I'm barely touching her, just trying to hold her afloat.

"Yes, you are," she says, still pulling herself closer to me like a rope she's trying to climb.

"I'm not."

"You're doing some *mer*-thing."

"Layla, I don't know what you're talking about."

"Then why do I feel this way?" She looks away sadly.

"Please, look at me." I cradle her cheek in my palm. "What way?"

I could lean in and kiss her if I wanted to. She might kiss me back for real this time. Her hands shake in mine. I press her closer so there's no water between us. She's weightless against me. My skin is hot everywhere we're touching. I can't stand it anymore. I part my lips and lean down at the same time she lifts her face up.

The force of her mouth on mine pushes us back. I've never had to balance myself on one tail before. I push us backward, and we sink into the water. She gasps for breath once and keeps her lips parted against mine. She runs her hands all along my arms, and I trace the soft length of her spine. My gills flare as quickly as my heartbeat. I want to hold this moment, just this, for as long as she'll let me.

Then she pushes me away, holding her last breath in her puffed cheeks. I let her go, and she reaches out for the surface. She slaps the water and lets loose with an angry and frustrated scream. She swims toward the rocks. In her pink lace underwear, she pulls herself out of the water and puts her clothes back on. They cling to her in wet patches. She wrings out her hair at the same time that she walks away from me.

"What did I do wrong? I thought it was pretty stellar."

"You know exactly what you're doing, Tristan Hart." And there it is. She says my whole name the way she does when she's pissed.

"I told you," I say. I feel the stinging pain that comes with shifting back into my legs. I have to paddle before the numbness on my feet goes away. I push against the tide that's pulling. There are still scales on my legs. When I brush them, they crumble into sand. "*I said*, I'm not doing anything."

She grabs my clothes off the rocks and throws them at me. "I don't believe you. You're putting some kind of spell on me or something. I saw how those princesses make people act. Like lunatics. It isn't *funny* to make people feel whatever you want them to. I'm not just one of those girls you pick up and then toss aside after you get bored with them. I'm not—"

There's so much fury in her voice that I'm too stunned to say anything. What can I say, other than to keep denying it? How can I make her see that she kissed me back all on her own? Her eyes gloss over, but I know she's not going to cry. She's too strong to cry.

She turns around and leaves me with my heart still in my throat, my feet sinking deeper and deeper into the sand.

chapter
FORTY-SEVEN

A couple runs toward Layla and me. I've followed her to the boardwalk, where the others are waiting. They weave through the rows of garbage cans, holding sizzling sparklers in each hand.

"We've been looking all over for you guys," Ryan says. The red rawness of his lips and the sheen in his blue eyes hints otherwise. "Angelo and the guys are setting up at my house. My folks have gone to our North Carolina house for their anniversary. Who are *they*?"

Behind us, the Vampirettes, Frederik, and Marty disappear into the Luna Park entrance.

"Just new friends," I say.

Thalia and Layla each grab Kurt by a hand and start walking away from the shops, past the parachute tower and the Cyclones field and toward Sea Breeze.

Ryan walks with heavy feet and his eyes on the ground. He flicks the dead sparkler stick into a passing garbage can and sighs.

"What's wrong?" I ask, because he clearly wants me to. It's not that I don't care, but I've got my own girl problems.

"I just—Do you think I have a chance with her?"

For a moment, I'm tempted to be a real friend and fill him with "go get her, guy" pride. But then I remember that Thalia isn't my cousin. She's a mermaid, and she's eternal. I remember the promise she asked me to make. I didn't exactly say yes, but I didn't say no either. I'd have to be king before I could decide that. Sure, she feels this way now, but what about in a couple of days? Just then Layla glances back at me, and I get that choking feeling again, like my heart jumps up and gets stuck. I know how fast feelings can change.

I go, "Remember the Rebecca incident?"

"Rebecca was different. She was a brat. She thought just because my parents have money that I'd be like her other boyfriends and buy her jewelry and shit. All my money is in a bank account that I can't withdraw from until I start college. Which I may not live to go to if they ever find out I cut class today and threw a party."

"You don't have to prove anything, you know."

"Oh, come on, Tristan." He puts his hands in his pockets and kicks the sidewalk as we walk. "White Bread? Wonder Ryan? I know they're just jokes, but sometimes the guys get out of hand with it."

My insides pang a little with guilt. "They *are* jokes. It's not your fault everyone thinks you're a stuck-up white kid from the *only* gated community in Brooklyn."

"You're white and your parents have nice things."

"Yeah, but I get all the guys dates."

At least that gets a laugh out of him. He shrugs. "I guess. I guess she makes me feel cool. The way she looks at me. Your family has strong genes. The iris colors—"

I can't have Ryan questioning our family heritage too deeply. I pat him on the back a little too hard. "Forget all that. Forget Jerry and Bertie and their shit. Forget Rebecca's bratty ass. I mean, did she even—?"

"She was my—first—do *not* tell the guys. I beg you. I don't even know what god you pray to, but swear on him, please. And do not tell Thalia."

"I won't. Cross my heart. Let's pray on one of the Hindu guys. They don't get enough attention."

The smell of ocean is strong. The waves crash hard. My lungs welcome the sea air, with bits of sand carried in the breeze. But then I get a whiff of a familiar stink—the rotting fish smell of the merrows. I wonder if they're out there waiting for me. Suddenly, I don't think this party is such a good idea.

"I just wish she lived here, you know? Then I'd be sure that we could have something."

I think of Layla and me kissing. We didn't think. We just went for it. Granted she thinks I'm putting a mer-spell on her and is mad at me, but that's because she's scared of what she feels. I deserve it, I know. But I'd rather have her hate me until she comes around than never have kissed her at all.

"Cut the crap, man. Don't tell me you've been holding hands and planning this party all day. Your freaking shirt's inside out. Just have fun together. Be a man. Show her how much you like her. I mean, if you left Angelo alone in your house to set up for a party, you're definitely braver than I thought."

chapter
FORTY-EIGHT

Farther down the street, where the boardwalk comes to a rocky end, are the biggest houses in Sea Breeze. They're so new you can still smell exterior paint drying on the window shutters.

Ryan's front lawn is packed with spiky-haired dudes in white undershirts and spray tans that border on toxic. They're surrounded by girls in micro shorts and bikini bottoms meant to showcase winking belly rings and tramp stamps.

The crowd spills into the living room, where Steve, the school's radio DJ, is set up. A guy with floppy blond hair is jumping on the couch. A pillow comes out from somewhere and hits him right on the head, knocking him on top of a group of girls, who roll him right back onto the carpet.

We follow Ryan through double doors leading to the kitchen. On the smooth marble countertop is a keg with rows and rows of red and blue plastic cups lined up. Angelo runs in chasing one of the princesses, Kai. They push against the glass doors leading to the backyard pool and head out. Kai holds her knees and then shoots her hands in the air as she dives in, dress and all.

"Don't worry. She won't shift here," Kurt says beside me.

"She's the least of my worries," I say. "Do you spot Maddy?"

He shakes his head. "Can't you smell her?"

Then I realize I don't remember what she smells like. Despite my new Mighty Merman senses, I don't think I even noticed.

We step into the backyard. Tiki lights line the bushes. Soft blue lamps surround the pool, which even has a tiny waterfall. It's almost like being back on Toliss. Layla gets called over by a group of lifeguards from the Brighton Beach side. They whisper something in Layla's ear, and she brushes them away with a cute little laugh.

I wonder what they asked her. Whatever it is, she finds my eyes through the crowd. It's not like she's never looked at me before. She's been looking at me for the past sixteen years. But now she *really* looks at me, and I can't hear anything except my heart pulsing in my ears. How can she think this isn't real?

The girls wave us over, sloshing foamy beer down their arms.

"You're Tristan, right?" Brighton Beach girl asks. She has tan lines from wearing her sunglasses on the tower too long.

"Yeah, how'd you know?"

"I remember seeing your picture right after, you know, the storm. In, you know, the papers."

I forgot I was a local celebrity. "What's your name?"

"Cindy."

"This is my cousin Kurt."

Kurt waves at them, tucking his hair behind his ear. His body tenses as he fights the urge to bow. Layla catches it too, because she's smiling at him.

"It's so weird seeing you without your uniform," Cindy says, pointing down at me.

"Actually," I go, "the real uniform is under here." And even as I say it, I want to bite my lip. I can feel Layla's eyes burning holes into the side of my face. Why do I even say things? *Why, Tristan? Why?*

Cindy giggles. "Ohmigod, you're *so funny!*"

"He's hilarious," Layla says flatly. "Aren't you supposed to be looking for something?"

She's jealous. Of course she's jealous. She gives me all this crap about how I make her feel this way, but if I accidentally flirt with someone else, I'm the bad guy.

"Duty calls," I say, leaving the other lifeguards with question-mark faces and Layla trying her best to not smile at me.

Inside, the steady bass of a hip-hop song makes everyone bob their heads without even realizing they're doing it. Up the beige carpeted steps, there's a line for the bathroom. I don't even bother trying to wait. A door is cracked open to my left. The room is all white and light blues, from the walls to the duvet. The wind blows through the balcony window, the temperature having dropped quite a bit since this afternoon. I know Maddy isn't here. I know I need to be looking for her. But I have sand in places sand shouldn't be.

I rummage through my backpack for underwear, but I forgot to pack it. Great. Fine. I don't need underwear. I'm a merman, after all. As I step out of my shorts to take my Speedo off, I catch the light scent of smoke, something sweet like burning flower petals.

The curtains blow open more, and this time someone steps forward from the window. I stumble to get my cargo shorts on and end up slipping on the soft carpet.

"Very smooth," her pretty voice murmurs from where she stands. Gwen's white-blond hair is weighed down with salt water and sand. She puffs rings of purple smoke past her pink lips.

"What the hell, man?" I finish pulling my shorts on, trying to mask the embarrassment creeping its way up my torso. Not that I have anything to be embarrassed about, but still.

"I'm no man, Tristan," she says, tracing the shape of her silhouette. She's in a bikini that looks like it's all made of crochet and pink sequin, like if it moved at all, you could see the little bits that she's hiding. She hooks her thumb on the sheer silver-and-gold wrap thing around her hips. "In case you can't tell yet."

"It's just something to say."

"You seem jumpy. Come, have a smoke."

I don't know why I look at the door, as if someone is going to come and tell me not to do what I'm about to do. I'm not doing anything wrong. I pull my backpack on and follow her through the curtain. Form here we can see everyone in the backyard, on the boardwalk, and on the bit of the beach that's in front of the house.

"You missed the sunset," she says. "It was exceptionally beautiful today."

"Yeah?" I reply, just for something to say.

"It's my favorite time of day."

"The end of it?"

"The beginning of night."

"What are you doing here, Gwen?" I don't know why I keep asking her that. I like having her around, I've decided. She's not like everyone else around me.

"I have nowhere else to go." There's something raw about the way she says it. The automatic light above the balcony goes off. "I spent all day swimming. Went to court for a bit to see if they had news of Elias."

At the mention of his name I look away. Down by the pool a guy picks up a girl and throws her into the water. Her top comes off with the force of it, but she just holds her hands in the air and woo-hoos.

"No news?"

She shakes her head.

"Don't take this the wrong way, but you don't seem so upset."

I tuck a bit of hair behind her ear, and when I do, I see something I would never notice unless I was this close to her. Right over the razor-thin slits where her gills would be is a long scar that runs from the opening of her ear down to her clavicle. It nearly blends into her, so it looks like a thick vein of extra skin. It must've hurt like hell.

It startles both of us. That I would touch her so absentmindedly. That I would even notice.

"That was an accident," she says.

"Someone accidentally tried to cut you open?" I don't know

why, but I'm suddenly angry for her. I don't want to ask if it was Elias, if this is the real reason she doesn't care that he might be missing. That he'd never be around to do this again.

"Would you be able to do it?" she starts. "If you were forced to marry a man and pretend that you cared about his every whim, his every mood, every desire—And if I didn't do as he asked, fixed things to his liking with my magic—"

"Actually I don't think I'd ever be forced to marry a man."

She punches me lightly, but at least it makes her smile.

"Elias swam into our palace with sea-horse loads of gold. Somehow he knew of me. He wanted me. And my father gave me away without even saying good-bye. My lady-in-waiting came in to pack for me and told me where we were going. That's why I'm not at court. I'd be expected to sit around waiting for his return. Dead or alive."

The sharpness of her words is startling. It really is a different world. "I don't get why you have to hide your powers. Everyone knows Thalia can talk to her sea horse."

Gwen forces a laugh. "It's not that I'm hiding. I don't believe we should be forced to reveal all parts of ourselves. After all, there was once a time when we all had magics. But like anything else, when you suppress it long enough, you forget it. If you really wanted to, you could make yourself forget anything."

I don't think that's true. There's nothing that would make me forget my parents or Layla. But I don't say as much. Instead I say, "Show me something."

She tilts her head to the side and looks at me with those gray eyes. She takes a long puff and blows the purple smoke out slowly. Her fingers reach up to the swirling smoke, where they take the shapes of a mermaid and a merman. They swim around each other; they have faces and arms, and lips, which they aren't shy about using. They run their hands against each other so hard that I think they'll go right through the smoke. She twirls her fingers again, and they're pulled apart. Their faces contort, their arms reach for one another. They look up at Gwen with ghoulish faces. And then the smoke goes out, and the only thing that lingers is the smell of burning flowers.

"What the—" I start. "And Elias knows you can do that?" *Knew. Elias knew.*

Something dark passes over her eyes. "Magic isn't *bad*. But it's considered dangerous. The Sea King always worries we can't be trusted with it."

"Can you?" I adjust the weight of my backpack. I can feel the thin hum of the sword. "Be trusted with it?"

She doesn't say anything. I think of how quickly she used it to help Layla win. It's not her fault Elias attacked me, but if she hadn't done it, everything might be different now. We stay in this silence, staring over the railing. Right below us the lifeguard girls and Layla are watching Kurt talk to Thalia. If he would look up, he'd see me and Gwen watching them.

The giggles from below drift up. Cindy is loud-whispering to the other girls. "Ohmigod, he's so totally *hot*. Why are all of his cousins so totally hot?"

Gwen rolls her eyes. We lean closer and hold on to the metal bars. It looks like we're in a little prison.

"Even the girls!" another girl says.

"It's so unfair," a third girl adds. "At least there's finally more eye candy than Tristan."

"I always though Tristan was just a man-slut who thought he was too hot for everyone."

The girls laugh. Layla doesn't say anything in my defense. Do they know that we kissed only minutes ago? Would she even tell them?

"I don't think you're too hot for everyone," Gwen jokes, elbowing me in the side.

"Har-har." I wish I had a bucket of water to dump on them.

Cindy gasps, like she just got hit with the mother lode of ideas. "You should go talk to Kurt, Layla."

"Why?" she says defensively. "It's not like I haven't talked to him *before*."

"Yeah, but you said you think he's hot. So you need to go ask him if he has a girlfriend."

"He doesn't."

"Did you *ask*?"

Layla groans. "No, but he never talks about one."

"Guys never say it unless you ask. It's like they think they can get away with it if you don't ask. So it's technically not lying."

Girl Number Two chimes in, "Yeah, I *hate* when they do that."

"He's not like that," Layla says, and I hate that she comes to Kurt's defense and not mine.

She stands up with protest, taking time to smooth out her tank top. She pulls her ponytail loose and shakes her hair out. The lifeguard girls whistle.

Gwen laughs. "Ugh, I can smell their humanity. It's like a burning tar pit."

I force myself to laugh, because my skin is on fire as Layla walks up to Kurt and Thalia. Thalia says something and points to the house. Layla shrugs and Thalia walks away, handing Kurt her backpack. I bet they're asking where I've gone. Kurt adjusts the bag on his shoulder. Even with his human clothes and surfer-dude hair, his violet eyes stand out. People take turns stealing quick looks at him. He catches himself bowing at Layla when she stands in front of him and smiles at his feet.

She tucks her thumbs in the pockets of her skirt and shifts her entire weight to one side. I've never seen her flirt before. Not really. It's not that she thinks I'm making her like me; it's that she doesn't want to tell me that she wants *him*. Of course, Tristan. How could you be so stupid? I want to puke. I want to jump over this railing and toss him in the water, rip his face off for talking to my girl.

Gwen stands up. "*Boring* I'm getting hungry." She loops her arm through mine and kisses my cheek with her glossy lips. "Cheer up, little merman."

"Huh? I'm not upset."

"Sure you're not." She says this matter-of-factly.

I'm glad she doesn't pry. I decide I like Gwen. She's like the friend who is brutally honest with you even when you want someone to help you nurse your wounds.

"You're a prince, Tristan. You should learn to keep your emotions from your face."

I open the door. She thumbs my cheek where her sticky pink lipstick must have left a trace. Someone bumps into her, sloshing a cup full of beer all over Gwen. Her gray eyes darken like the sky getting ready for a thunderstorm. A thunderstorm directed right at Maddy, who stands in a white David Bowie T-shirt and a long black skirt. Her eyes are drunken headlights as she pats Gwen's hip where the beer sloshed.

Maddy laughs and hiccups. She slurs an apology. Then she sees me. Her eyes fall to where my cheek is pink with lipstick. I wonder how many things could go wrong all at once without me even trying.

"Maddy." When I say her name, her eyes focus.

I hold on to Gwen's hand to appease her, and her eyes go back to their unstormy gray.

"Your cousin?" Maddy says. "The one with the green hair? You know? She said I needed to come see you."

She wobbles where she stands. She pulls her braids off to one side, and when she does so, her necklace gets caught. She pulls too hard and the chain breaks. It slides down her shirt. She cups her hands over it to stop it.

"What is that?" I don't care that I'm yelling.

Maddy shakes her head, but she loses her balance and gropes at the air. The necklace keeps sliding. I hold on to her by the waist. The Venus pearl falls to the wooden floor with a thud.

"You lied to me," I say.

"You cheated on me!"

Thalia ascends the staircase and takes in the sight of us. I don't know who she's more surprised to see, Gwen or Maddy.

"Let go of me!" Maddy pushes me off her, and we both grab for the necklace at the same time. Her fingers clamp around it. I'm flashing back to junior high football when we had a coed team for about a second. I always lost the ball, because I didn't want to hurt the girls. She elbows me in the gut and steps on my feet.

"Maddy, you don't know what you're doing. I need that back."

From outside the house there's a crashing noise, like windows breaking and things falling into the pool. Gwen doesn't miss a beat and grabs hold of Maddy's arm. The three of us run down the carpeted stairs.

"Ryan." Thalia pushes girls out of her way and runs ahead of me.

"What is that *smell*?" Gwen covers her mouth with her free hand.

I can feel the heat of my dagger, like it's burning its way through the backpack. Kids race past us out of the house as we run toward the backyard. The music is still blaring, masking the screams.

In the kitchen the floor is covered with broken glass. Some guy has a phone shaking in his hands as he tries to dial 911 but messes up every time. Outside, anyone who couldn't run away is hiding behind lawn chairs, bushes, and garbage cans.

Gwen lets go of Maddy and rushes to the poolside. Princess Violet is lying with her hand against her chest. There's a shard of glass sticking out from it. The girl's green eyes are full of tears.

Gwen pulls out the glass and helps her stand up. Angelo swims out of the pool. He doesn't notice the bloody cut on his shoulder, or he doesn't care. He just drapes the princess's arm around his neck and helps her inside.

The lights in the house go out, which only leaves the mosquito torches that line the backyard. The darkness is still. The merrows are hiding.

Kurt pulls out a thin bow, and the metal symbols on it catch the firelight and glisten. I fumble with the zipper to my backpack. The blade of my knife glows in the dark. Thalia brandishes two long and thin swords.

"I shouldn't have come here," I say. "I should've known."

Layla looks at me and speaks. But as a scream rips through the scared silence of the backyard, I can't even hear her.

chapter
FORTY-NINE

The merrows seem to come from nowhere and everywhere at once.

One with yellow scales along his arms seems to be more human than fish. Then he bares his rows of shark teeth. He smells the air and lets loose with an angry wail.

"Stay down," I tell Maddy, pushing her as gently as I can behind a patio chair.

In the meantime the yellow merrow has vanished. Kurt wrestles with a hammerhead merrow who looks like nothing but sinewy strength. Angelo runs out brandishing an aluminum baseball bat. I'm ready to run to Angelo's side, but he's caught a red one with a face like something that hasn't surfaced from the depths of the sea in years. Once it's dead, it starts decomposing, but he keeps swinging.

Their rotting flesh and black blood covers the ground, sticky under our bare feet. We stand waiting as the merrows hide in the shadows again, watching us.

Maddy is pulling on my shirt. "What's happening?" She cries when she realizes there's a thin line of blood on her arm. I wipe it off. It isn't hers. It's dripping from above us.

The yellow-scaled merrow wrestles with someone on the balcony. It's so dark I can't see who he's fighting, I can only hear the loud snap of a neck. The wail of triumph. The heave of the body over the merrow's head. He throws the limp body over the balcony but misses the pool by a few inches. The body rolls over once until it lies on the blue tiles, broken. Then again until it falls into the pool with a splash.

Not it. He. Until *he* falls.

"Tristan!" Kurt yells. The hammerhead is on Kurt's back, jaws open to bite.

I run.

I slip on the slick ground.

I keep my blade out and cut cleanly across both the hammerhead's ankles. When I right myself, I see Thalia's thin dagger pierce the creature's neck. The weight of him collapses on top of Kurt, and they topple into the pool.

Maddy screams. A blue merrow sniffs at the air around her.

It smells me.

It goes in for her.

I don't think about the fact that they're yards away, that if I miss by a few centimeters I will probably slice off my ex-girlfriend's face, which might make her like me even less. What I do know is that I can make it. I know it like I know I'm my mother's son. I throw my dagger and it pierces the merrow's spine.

The merrow stumbles once, deteriorating into mush as he does. It's like smelling a fish market and burning sulfur in chemistry class at the same time. It's not the most opportune time to think that I'll never get the smell off me. The black blood splatters over Maddy's clothes.

I walk over and pull my dagger out of what's left of the merrow's back.

Gwen walks out of the shattered doorframe. There are black smudges on her white-blond hair. "The human authorities are on their way. I can hear their sirens."

In the pool, the body of the dead boy floats face down. The water is muddy with merrow chunks and blood. Kurt lies on his back with his bow clutched to his chest. Layla bends down at his side. There's a long gash on her arm. How could I have been so stupid? I get on my knees and hold Maddy's face in my hands. She rubs her cheek against my dirty palm.

"I'm sorry," I say. "I can say it a million times and it won't matter. But this does. I can't explain it now. I don't know if I ever could. But I need that necklace."

She sobs once and shuts her eyes like she's still trying to shut me out.

"Or this is just going to keep happening."

She puts her shut palm over mine and opens it slowly, a flower blooming in the dark. The Venus pearl is in her hand, glowing pink in the blinking light above us. We're both so still that the automatic motion detector light goes out.

When I take it from her, the lights come back on. I pocket it before she changes her mind.

I slink her arm around my shoulder. I press my lips on her cheek and she pulls away.

"You stink," she says.

"Tell me something I don't know."

Behind us, those who notice the quiet come out of their hiding places. There is so much confusion, but it's mostly a lot of screaming poolside. My insides churn when I recognize the clothes. Thalia's small, shaking frame is draped over his still body. The lights of the house come back on. The floor is littered with glass, and the stone ground is stained forever.

None of that matters. I have the pearl in my pocket, but it doesn't matter, because I let this happen. I did nothing, and now Ryan is dead. His gaping blue eyes stare at nothing. Thalia takes his hand and presses it against her wet face. She smooths his hair back. She brings her fist down on his chest. Between all the cries the only one I hear is hers.

"Stay," she says in a whisper so small, I'm not sure she even says it at all.

chapter
FIFTY

Get up," she says in my ear. "Get up right now."

Gwen grabs my hand and pulls on it. I can't move. I can't close my eyes. For what seems like forever, I sit in the shadows of the back-yard watching as the others mourn Ryan's body. I watched it happen. I didn't know it was him. I could've done something. I should've kept my worlds separate like Kurt said. How can I protect everyone I care about? I can't. I have to go through with this. I can't keep losing.

Gwen's hand slaps across my face.

"That hurt."

"It was supposed to."

She stands above me, holding her hand out. I take it and don't let go as we run along the narrow path around the house and into the front yard.

"What are you doing?" She hesitates as I pick out one of the bikes parked out front. I pull out my dagger and cut the chains off.

"Just put your feet on those little metal bars and hold on to me."

"Tristan." She says my name nervously.

"Don't worry, hold on to me. You won't fall."

I can hear the police cars once we've put distance between us and the music. Gwen's arms are cool against my sweaty, stinky skin. She wraps them around my neck without strangling me. I pedal. We wobble at first, but I put all of my leg muscles into it, and we glide fast, past the rows of houses with families clutching each other on their lawns because something terrible has happened in their perfect neighborhood. I pedal with the wind in my face, zooming down the Coney Island summer street.

—

At the entrance to the subway station, the "e" in Coney Island flickers super fast until it just goes off completely. People stare and take pictures like it's the most wondrous thing they've ever witnessed.

A police officer with his back against the wall stands up when he sees me. I hold the bike over my shoulder so maybe he'll think I'm covered in mud. He sniffs the air, and even though I'm not standing directly in front of him, he makes a face like he wants to gag.

"Everyone is looking," Gwen says. I would think she were used to it.

"Well, I'm covered in merrow goo and you're half naked. Of course they're looking."

"Was that a compliment?"

"No." I stop at the MetroCard station and feed it money.

It pops out the yellow MetroCard, and I love that Gwen, with all her smoke-bending magic, stares at it with her eyes wide open and says, "How did you do that?"

I wiggle my dirty fingers near her face and snap them to make her jump back. "Magic."

She purses her lips.

We use the big entrance. Four lines leave from here, and I don't know where to go. I dangle the pearl in front of Gwen. "If I were an oracle, where would I be?"

Her gray eyes follow it. I wonder if I could hypnotize her by doing this long enough. She taps her chin with her index finger, completely oblivious to me. "I don't know about oracles, but if I were a magical object with an owner, I could find her anywhere."

I push the bike to the map on the wall. "We're here." I glance around to where people walk in and out of the train station. Ryan is dead and the world continues like it didn't even happen. I shake my head to focus. "What do I do?"

"Just hold it near but not against. It should guide you to her."

A bald man walks past with his children in hand. "Daddy, that man stinks so bad!" The man gives me a nasty look but smiles at Gwen, the mermaid princess.

"Stand over there, will you?" I ask her.

"Why?" Hands on hips.

"Because if you're standing there smiling, no one will pay attention to me."

"Oh." She leans against the bike, reminding me strangely of the posters on Angelo's bedroom walls.

I feel so stupid holding a pink pearl against a grimy subway map while a mermaid queen in a bikini stands against a bicycle. Nothing happens at first, but just when I'm going to pull away and blame it on Gwen, the chain pulls against my hand. Like a magnet, the pearl runs along the map, past Brooklyn, past the Verazzano Bridge, and I curse at the thought that we might have to go to Staten Island. But it rights itself and shoots straight up to Manhattan, past the Empire State Building and Times Square, right to Turtle Pond in Central Park. "Got it."

"Good, because that man just gave me this." She holds a twenty in her hands.

"I should keep you around more often."

We make it through the doors just as the conductor announces them closing. I grab a seat in the middle by the maps. We're alone.

"May I?" She holds her hand out to me, and I place the pearl in the center of her palm. It's funny how the lines in her palm are so different from mine, thinner and shorter. I don't know what I'm expecting her to do—make it bigger, make it dance. She makes a sweet, pensive sound, then hands it back to me. The train lurches and she falls on top of me. The bike falls to the floor. For a second all I can think about is crochet and sequins.

She pushes herself up and gets comfortable across the three seats with her feet on my lap. She wiggles her toes, which I guess is a mermaid thing. The newness of feet.

"Stop thinking about it," she says.

"How can I stop thinking about it? I see his face when I shut my eyes."

"There's nothing you could've done."

"I hate when people say that. Because it's not true. I could've been faster. I don't expect you to get it."

She regards me coolly. "Just because I've seen a lot of death does not mean I'm immune to it. Tristan. This isn't a game. It's a war of few, but still a war. You have to decide that you're going to come out of it alive or not at all."

"You know, Gwen," I say, "I'm glad that you're on my team."

"I'm not on your team. I'm on *my* team. You just happen to be on it as well."

"I'll be sure to remember that."

chapter
FIFTY-ONE

We get off at Sixty-Third and Lexington Avenue, a train station so far underground that I lose count of the flights of stairs we have to climb before we're actually out.

"It's like trying to ascend the circles of hell," Gwen gasps.

"Wait a minute. Is there a mermaid hell?"

"Yes," she says, "I call it humanity."

I roll my eyes at her. "Shut up. You love humans."

"I do *not*. Using land as an escape from boredom is natural. It's like taking up a lover or going to one of those theme parks."

Taking up a lover? I shake my head. I've already learned that lesson. "Just for the ride?"

The air is grittier in Manhattan. There are more people on the streets than near the small Brooklyn hangouts. We hop onto the bike and head into the park, which is fairly deserted at this time of the night.

"Another map." Gwen points. I hit the brakes, and she falls onto me. "Now you're just doing it on purpose."

She studies it in the soft light of the lamp post. "It's not far. That way."

Something about the way the breeze blows around us and then shifts suddenly to the west tells me she's right.

"This park smells new," she comments.

"That's what happens when you're so old."

"If there were a gentleman here, he'd slay you for speaking to me that way. I'll teach you a thing or two about chivalry yet."

"Didn't they tell you? Chivalry died about the same time as punk rock."

"I think you like to say things that I'm not going to understand on purpose."

"But you're so cute when you're confuzzled."

She smacks the back of my head.

"This isn't right." I stop pedaling, this time slowly so that she doesn't fall off. "No. It's not." I'm no oracle, but the pond is so open, so bare. I can see the water, the ripples of lamp posts and shadows. A tiny movement catches my eye. Between the shadows of buildings that cut right through the night sky, the squirrels scavenging and dogs barking, I don't know how I notice her, but I do.

A tiny woman wrapped about a hundred times in a deep red shawl stands at the top of a small mount. Her face is blocked by shadows and a mess of black hair. She stands and stares, tilting her head to the side as if something about me is amusing. Then she turns and walks right into a passage of trees, so it looks like the darkness swallows her.

The ground is too littered with rocks and broken branches to take the bike. We feel our way clumsily.

"Keep your dagger out," Gwen whispers behind me.

I unzip the familiar pocket of my backpack and feel for my blade. I can feel Gwen's cool fingers reach out for my wrist, then slide down to my hand. Even on a nice summer night like this, my skin prickles.

"Why isn't she saying anything?"

I shrug but then realize she can't see me in the dark. "Maybe she's mysterious. Aren't oracles supposed to be mysterious?"

"Maybe she's not the oracle. Isn't New York famous for crazy humans?"

"If something is funky, you need to leave without me, okay?"

She doesn't respond, because I know she isn't going to listen to me. The downward slope of the path comes as a surprise. I miss the step and slide down on my heels. My flip-flops come off, and I lose them in the dark. Gwen isn't far behind. I land in a puddle that is part of a small pond. Tiny specks of light wriggle and laugh over my head. They're fairies, about the length of my hand. One of them comes close and presses her whole body against the side of my face. I can feel her teeny, tiny mouth kiss me before she pulls away and hides in the hole of a gnarly tree.

"Fairies," Gwen says distastefully.

I go, "Tell me how you really feel."

"I feel ignored," says a raspy voice on the other end of the pond.

The fairies gather around a white boulder beside the oracle. I can see her face, bathed in the soft fairy light. I know why she wraps herself in so many folds of cloth. She is unlike any of the merpeople I've met. Her face is round and wide. The wrinkles on her cheeks are like the grooves on the side of a melting taper. The whole of her eyes are black, and I shut my eyes against the memory of the black blood coming out of the merrows.

"Does something so ugly offend the young prince?"

I try to right myself and put on my best smile, like she's Lourdes the lunch lady and I want some free chocolate milk. "I'm not offended."

The sound of the park fills her silence—the ripple of the pond, the leaves brushing against the push of the wind, fairy wings flitting faster than batting eyelashes in Van Oppen's class, the very distant sound of cars honking. That's it, the cars honking. It's the only thing that reminds me I'm in the city.

"Come closer," she tells me.

I step a foot in the pond. In five steps I'm in front of her.

"You wait till I ask you to sit," she observes.

In truth, it's because I'm afraid I'll crush one of the fairies.

"What will you give me, Tristan Hart?"

I don't think I'll ever get used to people just knowing my name. I feel for the pearl in my pocket. "What will you give me in return?"

She laughs, a raw brittle sound that reminds me of twigs breaking. "Will you tell me I'm beautiful? The other champion told me I was most beautiful.'

"Have there been others?"

"Just one. The golden son of the West."

"Dylan," Gwen offers. She sits with a few of the fairies watching her curiously.

I don't think I should lie to the oracle's face. Wouldn't she know? Instead I say, "What if I can give you something that was taken from you?"

She sits taller. She smooths her hair away from her face and frowns when she sees my hands are empty. "What can anyone take from me? I, who have nothing to give."

"You're an oracle, though. Right?"

She harrumphs. "In truth, I got the dregs of my sissies. The shaft, as you humans call it. But I like you. Not just because you're young and as lovely as the calm of the sea seconds after a storm. Though you are, you are. Would you stay with me so I can look at you prettily? But no, Sea Kings cannot stay. Unlike golds and souls, you aren't meant to stay."

"Stay where?"

"Why, right where you ought to be, of course."

Of course. Maybe she is a crazy New Yorker after all. I reach into my pocket, and she recoils from me, almost falling off her boulder. I hold my dagger with my free hand and wave it so she can see I mean no harm. Then again, waving a dagger isn't the universal symbol for *I come in peace*. "Don't be afraid. It's only this." The marble-sized pearl hangs between us on its long gold chain.

Her eyes fall on it instantly. Her hands reaches out, bony fingers like twigs in a nest waiting to catch it. I pull it away.

"Your mother. Always the troublemaker she was." She smacks her lips like she tastes something sweet and sticky. "Do you know what that is, boy?"

"It's Tristan," I say, annoyed that she's speaking about my mom. Oracle or not. "But you already knew that. What's your name?"

"That's none of your concern."

"Fine. And no, I don't know what it is. I thought it was just a necklace."

"Just a necklace," the oracle says to the fairy closest to her. The fairy laughs, a thin prickly sound that reminds me of pine needles falling in a cluster. "It's the Venus pearl. It's only made when two clams stick together and have one baby pearly."

I go, "That sounds incredibly gross. Plus, I knew that. What's so special about that?"

"It's the only one I've ever seen of its kind. And it's rightfully mine."

"Finders keepers."

She reaches inside her red shawls, and I pray to whatever gods are out there that she's not trying to seduce me.

"Like I told you, I was born last. The youngest of the last generation of sea oracles."

If she's the baby, I'm afraid to see what the others look like.

"I do not have the powers of sight. Not for the past. Not for the present. Not for the future. My eyes are as blind between the veils as a human to the world."

I'm starting to think we're in the wrong place.

"And yet I can interpret the bones of the sea to the querent. That is you." In her frail hand she holds a handful of something. They click against each other like marbles. Maybe they are bones.

"Ask me anything."

"Anything?" *Will I win?* is at the top of my list. Will I die now? Will Layla love me? Will Nieve find me? It all seems sort of trivial when I say it to myself. When my friend is dead because of me. And for what? A piece of ancient Sea Court? An oversized fork that conducts electricity? Will I ever get my life back? Do I even want my life back? What if after the end of all of this, I screw everything up? Can my team win another championship without me? Can I rule an entire race? How many more are going to die because of me?

"Ask me now, Master Tristan, or the time will pass!"

Why is it that when someone wants to tell you the truth about the matter, you'd rather just not know. We want the truth, but what we really want is to be lied to, to pretend things are going to work out when they probably won't. No one wants to hear, *I don't love you. That dress isn't your size. You're pregnant. The paper you worked so hard on is a C- at best. We're better off as friends.* And here she is, asking what I want to know, and all I want to do is put my fingers in my ears and wait and see what happens.

"Tristan," Gwen urges me.

"I want to know if you actually have a piece of the trident."

She smirks and rattles the things cupped in her hands, and they click like die. She lets go, and they fall on the surface of the pond but do not move. They float around each other until they're completely still for her to look at. "Are you sure?"

She'd make a good poker player, good enough to even play with Mr. Santos. But then a dark shadow crosses over her features. The seashells sink to the bottom of the water, and I'm no expert, but I'm pretty sure she's not too happy about it.

She sets her black eyes on me. "Who have you told of this place?"

"N-no one. Why?"

"You have been followed."

As she says it, my dagger heats in my hand. I turn around when I hear Gwen gasping for air. All the light fairies scuttle behind leaves and boulders, so the light is stretched out too far and the shadows grow longer.

I don't need light to see who followed us here. Elias's hand holds her at the neck. Her pale fingers hold his wrist. Her eyes are open like small bursts of lighting.

"Don't you touch her," I say.

"I already am." Elias's voice is a growl. "She's mine to do with as I please."

He steps forth, still dripping water. He's in the same clothes I last saw him in, but the chain mail around his waist looks more rusted, his skin more green than tan.

"This isn't very champion-like."

He still isn't looking at me. The skin around his eyes is breaking apart. The smell of rotting fish is heavy in the air, and this time *I* have to do something. Gwen kicks at the air as he raises her up with one arm.

Behind me, the oracle in her red shroud is waddling away to safety. I don't really blame her. I just wish my body didn't feel so frozen.

"Especially when she'd prefer a champion like me, right?" I say. The effect is instant. His face shoots sideways at me. "At least I don't stink."

He turns back to Gwen slowly.

I keep going, "You didn't really think she'd sit around waiting for you. She needs a real merman, not a fake king who lost to a human girl."

He tosses Gwen to the side, and I fight the impulse to run to her and make sure she's okay, because she isn't moving.

Elias charges at me, all arms and bare chest, a blurred shadow.

"A little *help*, ladies," I mumble. One of the light fairies flies around us. She pulls at his ears and kicks him, which is like getting smacked around by a Barbie doll, really. All I need is for her to stay close enough that I can see him.

I grab his arms, dropping my dagger, and hold them above my head. He has no weapons, just brute strength. With my knee I get him right in the gut. He tenses up and clutches his stomach. He grabs at his throat, his chest, and heaves for air. I roll over him and start punching him in the face.

I've only ever seen guys get into fights at school, in the park, in the middle of the street. I used to wonder what made the guy winning look so vicious. Now, with Elias's face bloody and tender under my fists, I don't feel any pity for him. I think of how he let everyone think he was dead, how he *hurt* Gwen. And in this moment, I swear to myself that I will never hurt a girl again.

Elias stops moving. I can feel his body go limp under me.

I can't breathe.

I roll over.

Fall into the pond. The water is shallow enough that it doesn't cover my face. The cool of the water is the best feeling against my skin. A fairy floats above my face and lands right on my nose on her little toes. Her body is a slick Thumbelina version of a perfect woman, and her hair lights up at the very tips. Huh. So it's her hair that's the light, not her wings. She flies to my chest and lies there, right over my heart, which feels like it's going to tunnel right out.

I notice Gwen standing over me. The little fairy gasps and runs away, taking the light with her. Gwen puts her head on my chest where the fairy just did, like she's listening for my heartbeat or just looking for a pillow. I rake my shaking fingers through her hair.

"Ouch," she says when I hit a tangle.

"Sorry."

"It's okay. You saved me."

I guess I did. She sits up and stares at her ex-fiancé. I wonder what she's thinking. Is she even a little bit sad? Is she going to hate me tomorrow?

The oracle isn't coming out of her hiding spot behind a small boulder.

"It's okay," I call out to her. "He's not getting up anytime soon."

But he does, because the next thing I feel when I sit up is arms bending me in a headlock. Motherf—

And the voice that screeches in my ear doesn't belong to Elias anymore. It's the one I've dreamt of for days. It comes in heaves, a deep scraping thing. Something inside him gasping for air. Then I realize that the gasping sound is coming from me. I can't breathe.

Closer is the only word I can make out.

Then Elias goes stiff. He falls on top of me, and I have to push with everything I have to roll him off my back. He lands sideways with my dagger in his back. Smoke fumes around the golden hilt.

"Any further and you would've scratched me," I say, crawling over to Gwen, who is holding her hands out like she's waiting for rain. Her palms are raw and red, black in places where fire has burned her.

"Did the dagger do that?"

She nods once, wincing in pain. She dips her hands in the pond and shuts her eyes. The water running over her hands glows. When she pulls them out, the skin is starting to grow back, but it isn't healed completely. "It isn't meant to be touched by anyone but your family line."

"Duh, Triton's blade."

"Triton's blade, indeed." The little voice comes out from its hiding place.

"Thanks for the help, lady."

"Don't you get smart with me." She wags a finger in my face. "I haven't lived as long as I have by fighting battles." The oracle is pulling on a small wooden box with gold handles on either side. From here it looks just like a treasure chest I had when I was in my pirate phase. I used to keep baseball cards and food and a plastic sword in it. This one is solid wood. There isn't a lock that I can see.

"This," she says, "opens to my touch." She grazes her fingers along the lid, like tickling the back of a cat. The lid pops open.

Part of me is expecting smoke and sparklers. Something a little more dramatic than this. Except it really is amazing on its own. It's the bottom of the trident scepter. A piece of long, pointed glass that glows when I hold my hand closer to it. I grab the gold handle of the chest, and the lid swings closed. It's much heavier than it looks.

"Solid quartz," she says, "from the depths of the earth."

It's the same feeling I get when I hold the dagger. Like it belongs to me. I can feel a current, something more ancient than my blade, older than the ground we stand on and the trees that surround us. Still, it doesn't look like it could do much damage.

"It has power on its own," says the oracle. "But it is still incomplete."

"I thought you could only read the bones of the sea," I say.

She chuckles. "Your emotions are plain on your face. You must work on that. Some of us play poker on the nights of the quarter moons. You should come. Learn something."

"I think I will."

She runs her fingers on the chest again, and this time it doesn't open. "You won this with your strength. A king must be strong." She holds the Venus pearl toward me. "You won this with your heart."

"But—you've been missing it for years."

She nods and the soft folds of her face upturn into a big smile, until even her eyes are smiling slits. "Some things have so much more power when given willingly."

I hold out my palm and she lets the pearl drop into my hand.

A gagging noise comes from Elias. And this time it's because he's breaking apart. *Poof*, into nothing.

"I think he's been dead for days," Gwen says.

The oracle shakes her head. "And now you have more to worry about than putting pieces back together."

"Yeah, thanks."

"You're welcome to stay here," she says, which emits squeals from the little fairy girls. "But I'd think you'd want to get a move on." She looks up to the sky, and I wonder what she sees.

I unzip my backpack, and the chest hardly fits. I pull the dagger out of Elias's back. It comes away dripping black. I dip it in the shallow pond to clean it.

"Let's go, girls," the oracle says. She takes one last look at Elias's form. "The squirrels can have him. Won't take long for him to dissipate. Our kind, we don't leave many traces behind in this world."

chapter
FIFTY-TWO

After rinsing and repeating about three times, I don't smell like rotting fish anymore.

At least I smell like rotting fish washed in my mom's lavender and honey shampoo. I trade my muddy backpack for a gym bag that has enough room for the treasure box, a change of clothes for the girls, clean shorts for me and Kurt, a bag of trinkets my mom thought might come in handy, a loaf of bread, peanut butter, jelly, beef jerky, and some regular old junk food.

"I think you forgot I'm the one carrying this thing," I tell her, opening the trunk door to the car.

Dad's still in the driver's seat. The sound of the Beach Boys hits me right in the gut, familiar and distant all at once.

"I'm not going. I can't keep saying good-bye to you," my mom says, pulling a sheer scarf around her shoulders. Her red hair falls like flaming waves around her, and the turquoise of her eyes glistens in the light of the street.

"I'll be fine. I've got good company."

Gwen sort of curtseys at my mom. She's wearing one of Mom's long blue dresses.

My mom nods back at her but doesn't say much else. She kisses my forehead. "Don't forget, you have school on Monday."

"I know, I know," I say, taking on her tone: "*I didn't become a human in this country just so you could drop out of high school.*"

She turns on her sandaled heel and marches back upstairs, where she's going to curl up on the couch, pull out one of her fairy-tale books, and wait for my dad to come back home.

———

Dad leans against the Mustang in the Coney Island parking lot. I grab the gym bag and hoist it over my shoulder.

"I don't have to tell you—"

"Be careful, and don't take candy from strange mermaids."

Dad shakes his head. "No, if you break another cell phone, I'm cutting you off."

"I can't—you guys—I'm trying to save our skins and that's the thanks I get."

Dad laughs, a real chuckle like I haven't heard in a long time.

———

Arion's ship bobs in the steady water. Layla stands talking to him. I can see her from here. My stomach tightens in that nervous way before you see the person you've been thinking about for days, the person whose face you see right before you think you're going to die. Because that's what it was like. Before the wave hit, before the merrows attacked each time, before Elias had a death grip around my windpipe, I saw her face.

Kurt stands at the deck, waiting for us. He holds out his hand, and I look at it for a second too long before realizing that he's trying to take my bag.

"Are you angry with me?" His violet eyes scan my face for any lies. His mouth is tight. "For letting—"

"My mom packed some beef jerky and a clean pair of shorts." I give him my best smile, because I know that I need Kurt on my side. I hand him the bag, but first I take out the piece of the trident. I don't want to let it out of my sight. "Where's Thalia?"

"Below deck, sleeping." I don't know if the tension across his forehead is because we both know there's nothing we can do to help Thalia feel any better, or because he notices Gwen standing behind me. They nod at each other without saying a word, and we gather around the ship's captain.

"Lady East," Arion says, bowing to Gwen.

"Not anymore, I think," she says.

Arion looks confused, and I offer, "I'll give you all the riveting details later."

"I see you've acquired the quartz scepter. I've sent word to Toliss. Soon everyone will know you are not to be trifled with."

"Oh, thanks." Really, you shouldn't have.

"Where to, Tristan?" Arion steadies his arms, ready to steer us in any direction.

Layla folds her chin on her hands and stares out at now-dark Coney Island. The rides have probably been turned off for hours.

The only light comes from the sliver of moon that hits the deck and from the oil lamps that are hung around the ship.

"The Florida Keys," I say. It's an amazing feeling, this is. It's different from being captain of the swim team or just a good lifeguard. It's having people look to me for real answers. The sudden shift of the boat takes a second to adjust to.

"The Florida Keys it is."

I hold on to the hilt of the trident.

Layla laughs. "It's like a giant rock candy."

"I wouldn't try to put my mouth on it," I say. I can feel the glow of it down to my bones. We step back, surprised, as it shoots sparks of light.

I look to Arion, who laughs the way he does at my clumsy humanity. "Don't worry, sire," he tells me. "It is always good to have a little more light when heading into such dark seas."

ACKNOWLEDGMENTS

This book would not have been possible without Adrienne Rosado, friend, agent, and were-mongoose. We are the proverbial little-engine-that-could.

My mother, Liliana Vescuso, the most selfless and hardworking woman in the world. Thank you for having the strength to leave your homeland to start a new life in New York City. For giving me everything I ever wanted, even when I didn't always deserve it.

Para mi Mami Aleja, por ser el corazón de nuestra familia y porque siempre ha creído en mí.

Joe Ponytail, Tio Danny, Tio Rob, Ne, Adrianna, Ginelle, Adrian, Gastonsito, and my awesome little brother, Danny. I couldn't ask for a better family and support system.

The wonderful staff at Sourcebooks Fire—the Duo of Awesome, Leah Hultenschmidt and Aubrey Poole; Kristin Zelazko and the production peeps; Tony Sahara for the breathtaking cover; and my publisher, Dominique Raccah.

Mr. David A. Johnson, the best teacher in New York City. You teach more than social studies. You teach us that we can be our very best selves. Yes, the train *is* moving.

To the awesome English department at Martin Van Buren High School (2001–2005) for letting me express myself, even if it meant painting on the department walls.

Meg Kearney, a lover of words and writers. Thank you for all the writing opportunities you've given so many of us over the years. You are a goddess to the writing community.

Ann Angel for reading my very first manuscript and showing me what to look for when self-editing.

Sarah Jane Jaramillo for the beautiful photography portraits.

Kelly, TS, Hannah, Steph—who were my cheerleaders, outline readers, and playlist givers.

And to the real *Röaan Recklit* for every nugget of inspiration I've taken from you. But especially for knowing I could do this, even though I always threatened to quit.

Write on, like,

Zoraida

ABOUT THE AUTHOR

Zoraida Córdova was born in Guayaquil, Ecuador, where she learned to speak English by watching Disney's *The Little Mermaid* and Michael Jackson's *Moonwalker* on repeat. Her favorite things are sparkly, like merdudes, Christmas, and New York City at night. She is currently working on feeding your next mermaid fixation.

You know you want to visit her at www.zoraidawrites.com.